CW00687763

MIXTAPE SERIES TRACK 2
FOUNDED ON TEMPTATION
KAT SINGLETON

Founded on Temptation

Printed in the United States of America.
This is a work of fiction. The names, characters, and incidents portrayed in this novel are either products of the author's imagination or used fictitiously.

ISBN: 979-8-9851486-6-4

Cover Design and Formatting Images by Ashlee O'Brien with Ashes & Vellichor
Edited by Victoria Ellis of Cruel Ink Editing & Design
Formatted by Victoria Ellis of Cruel Ink Editing & Design

DEDICATION

To those who are vulnerable enough to let their guard down and fall deeply and passionately in love.

"I AM EITHER AS GUARDED AS A
PRISON CELL OR OPEN AS A WOUND.
ALWAYS ONE EXTREME OR THE
OTHER. YOU'LL EITHER KNOW
NOTHING AT ALL ABOUT ME OR,
EVERYTHING THERE IS TO KNOW."

- BEAU TAPLIN

RILEY

I've died and gone to heaven. At least, this is how *I* picture heaven. I'm forty-thousand feet in the air with a full spread of fancy appetizers to devour and there's not a single screaming baby or coughing passenger in sight. Never in my mortal life did I imagine having this much leg room on a flight. But, this isn't just any flight. I'm on Nash Pierce's private jet. Award winning, pop mega-star Nash Pierce.

Stuff like this doesn't happen to me. I'm just a normal girl from a tiny shit-hole town in Ohio. Growing up, I lived in a middle class family. While I didn't want for anything—aside from maybe ten minutes alone in the bathroom before my brothers were banging down the door—this private jet is a far cry from my upbringing.

I'm not sure if the heaven I envisioned was even this luxurious. Hell, I didn't think my ass would even see a first-class seat on a *commercial* flight in my lifetime.

But alas, my best friend Nora is banging a popstar, allowing me to reap the benefits.

Months ago, she became a backup dancer on Nash's tour. Amid touring, the two of them had gotten *really* close. When Nash contacted me asking if I'd be able to fly to Colorado to surprise Nora, I couldn't say no. Even if it meant pissing off my boss to do so.

The cabin shakes as the wheels of the small plane bounce on the runway, signifying the end of my paradise.

"We've landed. Thank you for flying with us today," the pilot says over the intercom.

I'm too busy shoving the plush blanket I was handed before takeoff into my purse to notice the tall figure standing next to me. He clears his throat, causing me to jump. When I look up, I find an extremely attractive pilot looking from me to my purse with a mischievous grin.

Shit. I've been busted.

"Enjoy the blanket, Mrs. Adams?" he asks.

"*Miss*," I correct, kicking my purse with my foot in an attempt to hide the evidence.

"Delightful." His arm extends toward me, a silent offering. "I'm Jake."

I place my hand in his, allowing him to pull me off the plush leather seat.

"I take it the flight was satisfactory?" he asks, his hand squeezing mine ever so slightly before letting go.

I snort, regretting it the second the horrid sound leaves my mouth. "Uh yeah. You could say that. How do you fly coach again after something like this?"

"You don't." He says, giving me a wink. "You've never flown private before? I'll give you a little tour. Would you like to see my cockpit?"

My brain registers this as, "*Want to see my cock?*" which fuck, I need to see a therapist if that's the first thing my mind goes to.

My eyes scan over his stark white uniform. I'm sure he does have a nice cock… pit.

Picking my purse up off the floor, while still trying to hide my theft, I look at him with a smile on my face. "I would *love* to."

His hand is warm on my back as he leads me down the narrow aisle, stopping in front of the entry to the cockpit. He ushers me into the small space, gesturing for me to take a seat in front of a large control panel.

I *definitely* shouldn't be allowed to be this close to so many important buttons. I accidentally spilled my spiked fruit punch all over the DJ's laptop at my junior prom. Since then, I've steered clear of important flashing buttons.

Staring down at the panel in front of me, I'm positive I shouldn't be touching anything, which is *exactly* why I go ahead and run my hand across it, swiping every button.

"Woah, there," Jake says from behind me, his breath tickling the back of my neck. He leans down, the brim of his hat bumping against the side of my face.

"I want to wear this." Not waiting for his permission, I slide the hat off his head. We maintain eye contact as I pull the hat on. Moving the blonde hair off my shoulders, I look up at him, smiling.

"How do I look?"

"Hottest pilot I've ever laid eyes on." His gaze is intense, making my own cheeks flush.

"Better be," I state, turning to face forward again. My orange nail traces the lines of the oddly shaped steering wheel.

"Captain?" a voice says from the opening.

The two of us turn to find one of the stewardesses standing in the doorway.

"Mr. Pierce is here for..." she nods her head in my direction.

He sighs, "Right. Thanks, Lydia."

She disappears once again, leaving Jake and me alone.

"I better get out there," I mutter, brushing my hand against Jake's. "Moody popstar waiting on me and all..."

He laughs, backing up until he's out of the small room and standing in the aisle. "You're probably right. What a shame."

Following him out, I walk toward the exit, basking in the warmth on my face as I step off the plane. "I'm keeping the hat."

The two of us make our way down the stairs, me with the stolen blanket and Jake with my suitcase.

Stepping onto the tarmac, I don't see Nash yet, but common sense tells me he's probably in the massive black SUV parked not too far away from us.

"Will you be flying with us again, Miss Adams?" Jake asks, his arm rubbing up against mine.

"I sure hope so."

"Me too. Maybe I could take you out after?"

I'm about to answer him when I see one of the SUV doors opening. Nash steps out, a pair of sunglasses perched on his face. He seems deep in a conversation with someone still inside.

"Miss Adams?" Jake catches my attention. Looking up at him, I give him a nod. He seems like just the kind of fun I need. He can show me around that cockpit a little more.

He's talking about the places he can take me when we stop in front of Nash.

I've got to hand it to my best friend, she's done *very* well for herself. Nash is hot. Smoking hot.

"Nash! Have you met my friend Jake? He let me wear his hat." I nod toward Jake while also pointing to my hat.

An agitated voice carries from across the hood of the SUV. "Of course he's met him, he signs his paycheck."

Who the hell is this guy?

My eyes sweep over to the man with an attitude. "And you are?"

Nash steps closer to me, throwing the guy on the other side a nasty look. "His name is Sebastian. Someone whose paycheck is also signed by me."

The guy—*Sebastian apparently*—shakes his head. He fiddles with something on the hood.

Hot damn, who pissed in his cheerios this morning?

Trying not to glare, I change the subject, telling Nash he's ruined me from flying coach ever again. Screw stale pretzels in a tiny bag. I want the full snack spread flying private gets you.

Nash goes to take my suitcase from Jake, who I've suddenly realized is all tensed up. "So your flight was good, I presume?" Nash asks.

I try to hide my smile. Looking at Jake, I say, "Real good. It was full service."

A cough comes from Sebastian at the same time Jake excuses himself, quickly grabbing the hat off my head before scurrying away.

Shit. Does that mean our date is off?

"Was it something I said?" I question under my breath, watching Jake retreat away for a moment before turning to face Nash.

I take a step closer to Nash, inspecting him. He looks incredibly uncomfortable, glancing at Sebastian, then back to me. "Can I help you?" Nash narrows his eyes at me.

Pulling off his sunglasses, I give him a good once-over. "Just had to get a good look at the famous popstar who's fucking my best friend."

I hand him back his sunglasses, leaving him and Sebastian both standing there clueless. Finding my way to the back of the SUV, I open my door and slide into the backseat.

They exchange a few words, giving me the opportunity to really get a look at Sebastian. I'm left wondering if every person who works for Nash has to be attractive, as if it's a requirement.

Sebastian has an All-American type look to him. His dark hair is cut short on the sides of his head, bringing more attention to his sharp jaw and strong chin. The clothes he wears mold perfectly to his body, showcasing defined muscles.

A mouthy asshole who is also *extremely* good-looking?

Just my type.

SEBASTIAN

GOING OUT IN PUBLIC WITH NASH IS ALWAYS A RISK. THE lengths people will go to get a candid photo of him is insane. So when he insisted on coming with us to pick up Nora's best friend from the airport, I was less than thrilled. Never mind that Monica and Tyson, the ball-busters on his management team, already had him booked for most of the day doing other things. The last thing I need right now is a lecture from people that don't pay me, but there's no arguing with Nash when he's made up his mind.

Not too long ago Nash talked me and Matt, his personal security team, into letting him go to a music festival with his now-girlfriend, Nora. By the end of the night, half the world knew about the outing. Rabid paparazzi swarmed us as we fought our way back to the car, and we had fans tailing us nearly the whole way back to the venue. Matt eventually had to speed through a red light to lose them.

Nash's team chewed me out for *being careless* and allowing that situation to happen. Good thing I don't answer to them. Not really. Matt and I answer to Nash. And when he gets a dumbass idea, there's not much we can do other than follow along and get ready for damage control.

Luckily, this airport is small and discrete, so this trip ended up much better than the last one.

At least as far as Nash is concerned.

My grip is tight on the steering wheel as I try my hardest not to look at the girl in my backseat. She'd probably think I was creepy if she knew how much time I've spent looking in my rearview mirror.

That or I'm a very safe driver.

I'm not normally like this. Being a bodyguard for Nash for the last three years has consumed me socially. My life is so heavily entwined with Nash's whereabouts that I never have time to think about women. I have rules for the women I *do* sleep with—one night, no strings attached. We're always on the move, bouncing from city to city, so it's just easier this way. I never have to worry about the complications that come with a relationship or the temptations that new women bring.

Except in this moment.

Somehow, a stunning, witty, *incredibly* flirty woman has been dropped right in front of me, testing my willpower.

We haven't been in the car for ten minutes when Riley asks for the fourth time if we're stopping for food. Nash continues to ask her what she wants, but she keeps shrugging, telling us to pick. He groans, muttering something nearly inaudible under his breath.

Women.

"You know what?" Riley leans forward, resting her elbows between our seats. "I'm feeling a burger."

"Is your seatbelt on?" I ask, keeping my eyes on the road.

Riley tsks, sitting back in her seat. "Trying to keep me safe already? I'm into it."

This time she catches me looking up at the mirror, giving me a playful wink.

Lord help me.

We pass several restaurants before finding a burger joint with a drive-through. With Nash in tow, dining *in* is not an option.

Riley insists on ordering for herself, discovering the child-lock is on, she climbs on the armrest and leans over my lap, clearly not having any idea on what personal space means. Her head hangs out the window like a damn dog. Her back arches, accentuating her round hips. A lacy black thong just barely peaks out of her jeans, inches from my face.

How am I supposed to act professional around an ass like that?

"Can I get the number two with no onions please?" She looks back at me with a grin before returning to the box. "Oh, and do you guys do a Nash Pierce discount? Maybe like a free sha—" I put my hand over her mouth and quickly pull her back into the vehicle.

"What the hell, Riley?" I snap.

She retreats back to her seat. "What? It doesn't hurt to ask..."

Reaching across Nash, I open the glove compartment, revealing a curly bright red wig. He looks down at it, eyes widening before protesting.

"No way."

"Boss, we've been compromised. I need you to get in disguise." I fight back a smile.

Riley curiously fills the gap over the armrest again. "Oh my god, yes. Nash, it's the only way." She laughs between words. "It's a matter of life and death!"

Nash juts his finger out at me. "You're fired." He looks at Riley. "And you're on a coach red-eye back to LA before that thing comes anywhere near my head."

"Oh, the horror!" Riley screams, pretending to faint as she falls back into her seat.

The glove box clicks as I snap it shut, smiling to myself. Matt bought the wig awhile back, actually thinking Nash would cooperate and wear the thing when in public. To this day, I don't think I've ever used it for anything other than messing with Nash.

By the time we get back to the tour buses, the sun has already descended. While Riley and Nora had their reunion, I went to gather the rest of the crew so we could head out to the mountains where Nash had rented a cabin for us.

The plan *was* to get away for a night, to unwind and forget about the stresses of being on tour in the remote wilderness of the Rocky Mountains. We'd have a few beers, relax, and fall asleep in good company. But that was before I met Riley.

Now, I'm not sure how much relaxing or *sleeping* I'll actually be doing.

SEBASTIAN

"WANT TO GO CHECK OUT OUR ROOM?"

We're not in the lodge for thirty seconds before Nash takes Nora upstairs, leaving his brother, Aiden, and a couple of backup dancers alone with me and Riley.

Aiden and one of the backup dancers, Ziggy, volunteer to whip up some food in the expansive kitchen while I check out the rest of the lodge.

Working for Nash has its perks—this is far from your quaint little ski chalet. The entrance and living space ceilings are vaulted, covering two entire floors. Gordon Ramsay would be jealous of the kitchen, which may in fact be larger than my childhood home. And to top it off, a marble fireplace spans nearly an entire wall in the living room.

By the time I check out my room and circle back to the kitchen, there's already an array of different foods lined up on the large island in the middle. Of course Riley, who apparently has a black-hole for a stomach, is sitting nearby on one of the stools. As she notices me, she dips her finger into some sort of dip and slides her index finger into her mouth. She stares at me as she slowly pulls her cheeks in, dramatically moaning. "Wow Aiden, this is delicious."

Watching her do this makes my dick come to attention in my pants. The way her cheeks pull in perfectly, just the way they would if she'd wrap that mouth around me, has me unable to look away.

Aiden throws a dish towel over his shoulder, looking her up and down with a sly smile. "Happy to cook for you anytime, babe."

Aiden's a huge flirt. He can't help himself. Growing up with a famous brother and ideal genetics probably made it impossible not to be, but it doesn't annoy me any less.

The fucker must know he's irritating me too, because his smile expands when he sees me glaring at him.

"Do *you* know how to cook?" Riley asks, moving next to me.

I give her a shrug, nodding over at Aiden. "Probably better than him."

"Are you going to cook for me sometime?"

My teeth bite into my bottom lip as I try not to smile. This woman has no filter—she just spews whatever random thought floats into that beautiful head of hers.

"Probably not," I answer truthfully. I can't even think of the last time I cooked for a woman, if ever. I'm not usually around the next morning to even think about making them a meal.

My life has been built around physical relationships—some good, some bad. It's all I've ever known. It's all I *want* to know.

"What a shame," she says, taking a step closer to me. "You could make me breakfast in bed after you have *breakfast in bed.*" She reaches out to tap my pec playfully, but I catch her wrist tightly in my grasp.

She looks at me inquisitively.

Bending down, I bring my face close to hers. "I don't need it to be morning to have my favorite meal." My eyes flick down to my hand, her pulse thumping wildly against my fingers.

"Out of my kitchen!" Aiden demands, snapping his dish towel in the air.

Riley pulls her arm out of my grasp, taking a few steps away from me.

Ziggy whistles as he looks up from chopping vegetables. "Hot damn. I could cut this sexual tension with my knife."

"I don't think you need a knife," Riley says, fanning herself. "It would easily cut with a plastic spoon."

Ziggy chuckles, looking over at Aiden in solidarity. "It appears everyone's getting laid here but us."

"I need your hormones out of my kitchen," Aiden says, waving his own knife at the two of us. "Shoo, shoo!"

Riley looks at me, hooking a thumb over her shoulder. "We're being kicked out."

"Seems like it." Brushing past her, I make my way to the living room.

We sit opposite one another on the worn leather couch. Riley pulls her legs up to her chest, making herself comfortable—her chin resting on her knees. "So..." she starts, "I need to know more about Nash's big, strong bodyguard."

The corner of my lip pulls up. "Did you get to know Nash's pilot too?"

"Nash's *hot* pilot?"

Air escapes from between my lips. "I guess if you're into pretentious frat guys that wear turtlenecks and buy you jewelry on the second date."

She hides her smile behind her knees. "Aw, are you jealous?"

I shake my head, reaching for one of the throw pillows to give my hands something to do. "I don't get jealous."

"Maybe you haven't met a girl worth being jealous over."

"Maybe that girl doesn't exist."

"I think you're avoiding my earlier question, Sebastian. Surely you've got a story."

Not one I share with people I just met.

Or anyone, for that matter. No one wants to hear about my absent mother or my drug-addict father. About the doped out women that would frequent our house. I have zero intentions of telling her that the only reason I know how to cook is because I had to fend for myself, or how when she reached out to tap my chest earlier I got flashbacks of a sharp, unwanted nail raking over me in that exact place many years ago.

I give her an exaggerated grin. "No story. I'm just a normal guy."

Which is fairly true. For the most part, I've buried my past. Playing the part of a carefree, easy-going guy isn't difficult for me, because that's who I am now. I've spent most of my adult life making sure all the shit in my past stays exactly there—in the past. It's why I love traveling the world with Nash, never able to spend enough time with someone to really get to know them. It's why I have rules. And now, it's why I'm questioning how someone so far from usual—someone who might break all my rules—has me *wanting* to get to know them.

"What about you? Besides eating, of course."

"Oh, me? I'm just a *normal girl*." She mocks. "And I *love* a good story. I'm going to figure yours out, Sebastian."

Reaching out, I grab one of her legs, forcefully pulling her across the couch toward me.

Her knees brush against my thigh as I lean closer. "You're trouble, Riley. You know that?"

She looks me up and down, unaffected by my sudden movement. "And why is that?"

"Because my story isn't something I plan on sharing. Typically, the prying would turn me off, and yet…"

She leans a fraction of an inch closer to me, hanging on to my every word. "And yet?"

I trace a finger over the exposed part of her chest, feeling her heartbeat against my fingertip. "And yet I'm still thinking of all the ways I could fuck you on this very couch."

As if on cue, a loud moan rings out from above us. The

sound makes Riley jump. She scoots back to her side of the couch, looking up in the direction the sound came from.

There's a loud bang, followed by another long, drawn-out moan.

Riley puts her hand over her mouth, laughing. "Showing her the room my ass," she says sarcastically.

"Oh, he's showing her something alright," I joke.

I look around the room for something I can use to drown out the sound of my boss having sex, landing on the TV remote.

"I'm never going to let her forget about this." Riley giggles, biting her thumbnail as I crank the volume up.

"Dinner is ready!" Aiden steps out of the kitchen and freezes in place, quickly glancing over to me and Riley before realizing what was going on above us.

Looking up, he yells into the ceiling, "Nash! For once, can you *not* make music?"

Riley and I both start laughing as Aiden heads back into the kitchen with his hands over his ears.

"Well, when you know what you want…" I mutter, looking directly at Riley.

She holds my stare for a moment before getting off the couch and heading toward the stairs, exaggerating her movements so her hips swing as she walks.

As she climbs the stairs, she looks back at me over her shoulder and says, "For future reference, I like music, too."

RILEY

Everyone else has gone to bed, leaving Sebastian and me alone. Light from the fireplace dances on his face, his demeanor going from playful to serious. The back of my neck tingles in anticipation—all of the flirting and teasing building up to this moment.

"Do you feel it?" he asks softly, running his thumb over his bottom lip.

"Feel what?"

"The tension. The want. The *need.*" His voice is husky, laced with desire.

I gulp, only able to nod in response. I've had one-night stands plenty of times before. But this feels different. This feels like it'll change things. As if it'll change the precedent for all one-night stands to come.

The fire crackles next to us, the only sound in the room aside from our heavy breaths. We're holed up in the mountains, the rest of the world asleep. It feels like we're the only two people in the world, which only adds to the exhilaration.

He reaches across the couch, his fingertips brushing the top of my foot, over my shin, and up to my knee.

There's thick fabric between his skin and mine, but his touch still has goosebumps rising on my skin. He maintains eye contact, watching my every move as he directs his hand further and further north.

Once he reaches my hip, he slides his hand underneath my sweatshirt. His touch is warm against my stomach. It's the first time I've felt his skin intimately against mine, and I want *more.*

"This is your chance to stop this, Riley." His words contradict his touch, because as he utters that sentence, his fingers are pushing deeper into my skin.

"What If I don't want to stop it?" I whisper, reaching out to touch him.

His head snaps back, his fingers wrapping tightly around my wrist. "I do the touching."

My hand lays limply in his grasp. "But..."

"That's the rule for tonight. And that's all this is, one night... typically I don't—"

"Typically you don't what?"

"Typically, I don't do random hookups. It's just…easier that way." His voice trails off.

I think his words through, trying to process his admission. Typically, men are the complete opposite—selfish—forgetting all about my needs.

But not with *him.*

"Why?" I ask.

The hand not buried in my sweatshirt reaches up to caress my cheek. "I don't want to get into details. Just let me do the touching, okay?"

A brief flash of vulnerability in his brown gaze leaves as quickly as it came. Every curious fiber in my body wants to know why, but now isn't the time.

The twitch of his finger against my skin pulls me back to the present.

Sebastian leans in closer, close enough to rub the bridge of his nose against my exposed neck. "The things I want to do to you, Riley," he whispers.

"Show me," I respond, pulling away briefly so I find his

eyes once again. I drag my sweatshirt up and over my head, letting it fall over the side of the couch.

His gaze burns into my bare skin. His tongue peeks through his slightly parted lips as he examines every exposed inch of me.

I'm not wearing anything sexy by any means. My simple black t-shirt bra isn't meant to seduce, but you'd never know it by the hungry look in his eyes.

My abs clench when he licks his lips hungrily. "Oh, we're going to have so much fun tonight."

He leans closer, caging me in with his toned arms and pushing me deeper into the cushions. One of his hands finds my hip the moment I finally feel his lips on me. He's unpredictable, not starting with my mouth. No. He's a tease. Instead, he brings his warm lips across my shoulder. He kisses the crook of my neck, biting at the tender skin.

I can't help but let out a small moan, relishing in the way his tongue dances over my skin, taking away the sting from the bite.

"From the second I saw you talking to that annoying pilot, I knew I wanted to taste you." He works his way up my throat, nipping at my earlobe. "Seeing you smile at him, wearing his stupid hat…it made me want to take him out."

"It did?" I breathe, tentatively letting my hands find his back. I don't dare try to wander any further, instead letting my hands fist the fabric of his shirt.

He pauses. "What is it about you?" he asks curiously, his lips now almost touching mine. It would be easy for me to lift up and catch his lips in mine. But the anticipation of tasting him has me waiting, the buildup turning me on.

"I had an ex once compare me to sugar. Sweet and addictive, but terrible for him."

Sebastian smirks, "Sugar, huh? We'll see about that..."

It seems like an eternity before his lips graze mine—the sensation lighting my whole body on fire. Timidly, I trace the seam of his lips with my tongue. He opens up slowly, allowing my tongue to find his. Our mouths work together slowly, neither one of us in any hurry.

I'm consumed with the taste of him and how his strong body presses against me, pinning me in place. I desperately want to pull his shirt off, feel his skin against mine, but I don't. The pace is agonizing, but I can't risk losing his touch.

Tonight, I'm going to take whatever he gives me.

My hips buck against his thigh, trying to find friction.

"Eager, are we?" His hand reaches behind me, quickly unsnapping the clasp of my bra. Slowly and deliberately, he pushes the straps down my arms until my breasts are exposed to him.

His eyes trail every inch of my skin, leaving not even one inch of me undiscovered. Finally, they fall onto the peaks of my nipples. Leaning down, he blows on one of them, sending lightning all the way to my core.

"So fucking sexy," he rasps, letting his tongue brush against it ever so slightly.

"Seb—" I moan, getting cut off when he fully takes it in his mouth.

My hands desperately want to trace over every single slope and plane of his body. I want to explore him just like his mouth explores me. Fighting the urge, I get lost in the feeling of his warm tongue circling my nipple.

I didn't know I could be so turned on by somebody playing with my nipples, but holy shit, when he pulls off my pants, he's going to find me soaked.

The warmth of the fire sends a heat wave throughout my body as Sebastian alternates from one nipple to the other. The air is cold against the wet skin left in his wake. One of his hands travels up my stomach until he's palming my other breast. My back arches instinctively, my toes curling when he clamps down on my nipple.

The loudest moan escapes my lips, vocalizing what my mind is screaming.

Feeling brave, I let my hand drift into the waistband of his pants. Doing so makes him stop his assault on my nipples. He pulls away, a hesitant look on his face.

"I said no touching." He clicks his tongue, reaching between us to find my wrist.

"I want to feel you," I pant, desperately missing the feeling of his mouth on mine.

He looks at me for a moment, an unreadable look on his face. It disappears as fast as it came, a taunting smirk appearing instead.

"How about instead, you touch yourself?" His fingers wrap even tighter around me, slowly guiding my hand to my waistband.

"But," I whisper, confused, but turned on as all hell.

"I don't think I stuttered," he replies confidently. "If you can't listen and not touch me, then you're going to touch yourself. Show me what you want me to do."

Holy fuck, who is this guy?

Never in my life have I been this horny. I'm panting with need, wanting this man's touch on me once again. I want to touch him. Badly. But I'd be lying if his demands didn't only fuel my desire.

"Riley..." Sebastian says impatiently. "Are you going to touch yourself for me?"

All I can do is nod, suddenly shy. That's all he needs. Keeping one hand locked on my wrist, he uses the other to tug on my pants. He pulls hard, able to get them down my thighs in one swift motion. Lifting my legs, I allow him to pull them the rest of the way off me.

I'm now completely naked while Sebastian has every scrap of his clothing still on.

With my pants discarded, he goes back to his mission, holding my gaze as he guides my hand closer to my center.

My fingers find the wetness between my legs.

"Can you feel how wet you are for me?" he asks huskily.

I can't find words, too lost in fascination to form a coherent thought. I never imagined I could be so turned on by touching myself for someone.

"Now I'm going to let go, and you're going to touch yourself, you aren't going to touch me. Understood?"

"Understood," I breathe, not wanting to do anything that might end this euphoria.

I know damn well I'm about to have the best sex of my life, and I will not risk it.

He must believe me, because each one of his fingers slowly pulls away from my wrist. My middle finger inches inside me while he leans close to me once again. "Good girl," he mutters against my lips before enveloping my mouth in his.

Only this time, he works quickly, his tongue diving deeper into my mouth.

My finger picks up speed inside me to match the intensity of his kiss. One of his hands cradles my head while the other massages my hardened nipples. His head follows his hand, and he takes my breast into his mouth. There are too many sensations going on at once.

Don't you dare come too soon.

I'm hoping those words stay in my head. I don't want him to know how close to the edge he already has me.

"I want you," I beg, squirming underneath him.

He doesn't answer at first, moving his lips from my chest down to my ribcage. Biting and sucking my tan skin, he makes his way closer and closer to where I work myself. Sebastian stops when his eyes are directly in front of my hand. I pause briefly, waiting to see what he'll do next.

"Don't stop on my account. I want to watch you make yourself feel good. Show me how you like it."

This man is going to make me come from my own hand paired with his words.

A small creaking noise startles me, saving me from an early orgasm. "What was that?" I gasp.

The last thing I need is for someone to catch me like this—spread eagle on an ugly plaid couch while a fully clothed Sebastian stares at me like I'm dessert.

"Doesn't fucking matter," he states. "Everyone knew this was going to happen, anyway." He grabs my wrist once again, this time taking the finger that was just inside me into his mouth. His eyes rolls back in his head as he tastes me. "Wanted to see how you tasted before I did this." Without warning, his mouth presses against my wetness.

"Oh holy *shit,"* I moan, completely overcome with pleasure.

His tongue is magic against me. He moves my hand away, preferring to work alone, and I let it fall limply to my side in obedience.

The pressure intensifies as he circles his tongue around me, grasping my thighs firmly with both hands. My whole body is trembling as he brings me closer and closer to release. I clench the cushions of the couch as the ecstasy peaks, forcing a moan from my lips. My whole body erupts into a mind-blowing orgasm as I buck my hips back and forth against his face. His hand leaves my thigh and covers my mouth in an effort to quiet my moans as I ride the waves of my release.

I haven't even seen his dick and he's already given me the best orgasm of my life.

Even better than the ones from my vibrating purple friend.

"How'd that feel?" he asks from between my legs, sitting back on his knees.

Trying to catch my breath, all I can muster is a measly thumbs up.

"Where did you learn to do *that* with your tongue?" I pant.

He laughs under his breath. "I'm not going to answer that."

Good answer Sebastian, good answer.

SEBASTIAN

My first thought when I saw Riley was that it had been a long time since I'd seen someone carry themselves with such confidence—and I'm best friends with a pop star. She walked along that tiny airport tarmac like it was her own personal runway. Like she had just gotten off *her* private jet, and we were all there waiting for her arrival.

My second thought was anger. Then annoyance. Then maybe even jealousy. For the first time in my life, I wanted something without explanation. It wasn't love at first sight, not a chance, but I definitely didn't want her flirting with the pilot anymore. The moment her gaze collided with mine and I heard that sassy tone of her voice, I didn't want her flirting with anyone but me.

And now, I have her. At least for tonight...it's the rules after all.

The fire behind her creates a soft glow against her skin. She takes a shaky breath in, watching me as I slowly stand up. My body towers over the couch, my shadow covering her lower half.

She comes up to rest on her elbows. Her eyes widen when she takes in the bulge in my pants. "What are you doing?" she asks.

My fingers fiddle with the drawstring of my pants. I focus

on her, hooking my thumbs in the waistband and pulling them down until I've freed myself.

Her mouth falls open slightly as she takes in my length. My fingers wrap tightly around the base, pumping up and down slowly. "Tell me you want it," I instruct.

She bites her lip, smiling at me. "Oh, I want it."

The way her eyes beg for me makes my dick pulsate in my hand.

Using my other hand, I brush against her outer-thigh. She relaxes into my touch. I trace up her thigh, over the curve of her delicious hips, and over to her soft arm. When I get to her arm, I pull on it gently, looking down at her. "Keep this here," I demand, moving her hand to grasp the edge of the small end-table next to the couch. I do the same with her other hand until they both cling to the table behind her head.

"Those stay there."

She squirms underneath me, her chest rubbing against mine. "You're bossy," she jokes.

"Maybe. But don't let that stop you from telling me exactly what you want."

"This. I want this. Fuck me, Sebastian. Right freaking now before I spontaneously combust wondering if *that*," she looks down at my dick, "will even fit inside me."

I can't help but laugh.

Of course she can make jokes sound sexy.

"Let's find out," I offer. Stepping away for a moment, I rifle through my pockets before finding my wallet. Riley licks her lips as she watches me pull out a condom and roll it down my shaft.

"Are you sure you want this?" I ask, one of my knees resting on top of the couch cushion.

She lets out a long sigh, pinning me with a look while her hands stay over her head. "For fuck's sake, Sebastian. Yes, I want this. You have me all fucking hot and bothered, my arms clutching this cheap piece of wood just *waiting* for you to get inside me."

Moving closer to her so that her thighs rest on my hips, I run my length along her slit. Her eyes flutter as I tease her folds and push my way in.

"Yes," she pants, moving her hips to meet mine.

The way her hands are placed over her head forces her tits into the air. As I push myself even deeper, I take one of her pink nipples into my mouth.

"Fuck, you're wet." Her head tips back in pleasure, her hips finding a rhythm against mine.

She moans—loudly. Loud enough that if someone is still awake in this house, there's no doubt they'll hear her. Shit, even asleep and with doors closed, there's a chance they'll still hear her. This time, I don't muffle her—the screams make me pump harder, wanting more.

I reach to take both breasts into my hands, pinching her nipples as I move in and out of her. Her head snaps forward, her brown eyes fixed on my own. Our bodies find the perfect tempo together. She feels perfect wrapped around me, showing me exactly how she likes it.

Her hands clamp down tighter on the table. "Sebastian," she moans.

Needing to feel more of her, I pull out and hurriedly flip her over until her back is exposed to me. "Oh," she exclaims, shifting her weight forward and arching her back.

"I didn't think it could get much better than you sprawled out on this couch for me," I say quietly, squeezing her ass. I bend down, biting one of the dimples on her lower back. "But it turns out, your ass in the air is even sexier."

"Hey," she pants, pushing back towards me until her asscheeks are rubbing against my dick. "Who said you could stop?"

Her wetness slides over me, up and down in a tantalizing

motion. I let her have her fun for a moment before I take back control. My palm runs down the length of her spine, stopping when I reach her tangled hair. I let my fingers wrap in it gently.

My other hand grasps the spot where her abdomen meets her hip. I hold on, inching myself into her once again. Her body relaxes with her moan.

"Fuck. Why do you have to feel so good?"

I laugh, picking up speed. "I'm wondering the same thing about you, trouble."

Her arms brace against the armrest as I thrust into her.

Releasing her hair and wrapping my arm around her chest, I guide the top of her body off the couch, pulling her up until her back is flush against my chest. I sit back on my heels, our bodies molded together perfectly. Following directions, she rests both of her hands on the tops of her thighs.

The new position has me seated even deeper inside her. It also gives her leverage enough to pump up and down on me. I kiss the back of her neck before turning her head to find the side of her mouth. Our tongues meet, my mouth swallowing every one of her moans.

"I'm going to come," she says against my mouth.

Her admission has me close. I squeeze her tightly and take back control, right on the edge of release. Her whole body shakes as her climax releases all over me. I force my mouth tightly onto hers, trying to stifle the sounds of our mutual pleasure. She spasms around me as I pump into her a few more times, finding my own release.

My entire body tenses as I come, getting lost in the feeling of our joined bodies. My fingers dig into her skin as I pulsate inside her. The two of us ride out our orgasms, the fire now feeling incredibly hot against my body.

Her body melts against mine. "Well fuck, Sebastian," she mutters, staring out in front of her. "How the hell am I supposed to get off with my purple pal when I've had this?"

I laugh against the back of her neck, her words catching me off guard. "Sounds like a personal problem," I tease.

She sighs, lifting her hips until I'm sliding out of her. Turning slowly, she angles her body so she's facing in my direction. Her eyes track over my face. "Why did you have to be hot *and* mind-blowing in bed? I mean *really*, how is that fair?"

I shake my head, pulling the condom off. Reaching over her shoulder, I grab a tissue from the box sitting on top of the end-table. I roll the condom up in it, trying to think of an answer. "Life's not fair. Other guys and your little purple friend are just going to have to get over it."

"Yeah, well, I'm sure I can find a new friend. One that has turbo mode or something."

"You sure know how to stroke a guy's ego."

She falls back onto the couch, her hand coming up to wipe her forehead. "I rarely fuel the fire of a guy with big dick energy, but I'm making an exception. You can have *all* the energy because that was amazing. Paul isn't going to cut it anymore," she says sadly.

"You named your dildo Paul?"

She looks at me as if that's the dumbest question ever. "Of course not. Paul is the IT guy who lives in my apartment building who I hook up with occasionally."

"You're fucking a guy named *Paul?*" I say in disbelief. "I can't say I'm shocked he's giving you boring, vanilla sex."

She chews on her nail, mulling over something. "I thought I liked vanilla."

"Thought?"

"*Thought*," she repeats. "Turns out I like more of a variety, who knew?"

"I haven't even got started."

Her eyes light up. "Oh really?"

I nod. "Really."

"Show me."

"We could just go to sleep," I offer. I hadn't known her long when I accepted my attraction to her. Maybe it was seeing that dumb hat perched on her head as she flirted with the pilot. Maybe it was when I got a peek at her black thong. No matter what it was, I knew that if she continued her flirting, and let it lead to us sleeping together, I wasn't going to say no. I'm just wondering if this is something we should continue all night or if it would be better for us to go our separate ways now.

She shakes her head, standing up to gather her clothes. "I'm going to pick all of this up and take our stuff to the bedroom."

"*Our?*"

"Yes, ours. You're going to meet me in my room and we're going to see how many more orgasms you can get out of me. Who needs sleep? Let's do it again and again. If we've only got one night, we might as well not waste it."

She leaves me standing in the middle of the large living room, watching her naked figure retreat up the stairs.

I'm left with two options. The wise choice—go to bed and forget her—or the choice I *want*—to take her up on her offer.

It doesn't take me long to decide. She's barely made it halfway up the stairs when I follower her, not thinking about what this will mean in the morning.

MY HAND SLIDES ACROSS THE SOFT FLANNEL SHEET, REACHING out to find the other side of the bed cold. I can't say I'm surprised that Sebastian isn't here to greet me this morning. He made it clear last night that he doesn't do mornings.

The sun peeks up over the mountains and through the panoramic windows in my room as I massage my neck. It's entirely too early to be awake, but the entire room is already filled with light. It's too sunny in here to go back to sleep.

My whole body aches as I stretch my arms above my head. I'm sore in places I've never been before. Sebastian had me contorted into positions I didn't even know existed.

I think I might have pulled my vagina.

Last night was hands down the best sex of my life—by a landslide. The kind that gives you a hangover afterwards. The kind you could get addicted to. He's the worst kind of combination. He's electrifying. He's got an outgoing personality *and* he's great in bed. All of this paired with his mysterious vibe makes me very, very intrigued.

Luckily, I'm no stranger to hangovers and it's tough to get addicted to something that only happens once. I'm not going to get all doe-eyed for him just because the guy knows how to fuck.

Nope, not me.

I'm trying to work out a kink in my back when a furious

tapping starts at my door. "Riley?" Nora says from the other side of the door. "Are you awake?"

I groan, kind of wishing I was still asleep. "Yes, I'm awake. Not like I could've slept through your assault on the door anyway."

As soon as Nora opens the door and I get a glimpse of her, I know that something is wrong. We've been best friends for as long as I can remember—I can read her like an open book.

She sniffles, making her way across the room until she climbs into bed. Her hair is in a bun perched on the top of her head, bobbing as she crawls her way toward me. My arm lifts, allowing her to burrow in beside me.

"What's wrong?" I ask.

Her body starts to shake before she gets any words out. "Nash told me he loved me," she sobs, her voice muffled against my armpit.

I take a deep breath in, trying to collect my thoughts. Usually, this would be a good thing. Nora is currently living out her dream job of being a backup dancer on a popular world tour. It's what she's wanted to do for years. And now the popstar has fallen for her. The problem is, the job offer came at a price. Nora was only hired to get close to Nash, make him fall in love if she could, and then break his heart. Apparently, his management team is ruthless, and wanted to use his heartbreak as inspiration for another platinum album.

"Oh," is all I can say at first. I'm trying to find the words to comfort her, to make her feel better about her decision.

It sounds fucked up—real fucked up. Which is why she wasn't going to take it at first. She's one of the best humans I know, and it weighed heavily on her conscience. After talking it through, the two of us had decided she should follow her dreams—that there was no way *the* Nash Pierce would ever look twice at her. We thought it was a win. But somehow, he did look at her—a lot more than twice. He fell for her.

And she fell for him, too.

"I have to tell him, Riley." Her lips quiver as she cries even harder.

I stroke the top of her head, trying to move the giant bun out of my way. "Yeah, you do. Tell him before somebody else does. He needs to hear it from you."

"He'll never forgive me," she sobs.

I nod. "Maybe. But he deserves to know. He's a good guy, Nora. Better than we thought. Maybe the two of you will still figure it out."

She sighs, finally removing her face from my armpit. If it was anyone else, I would've been a little self-conscious of the proximity she had to it. "I wrote him a note in his journal, but I'm going to tell him tonight. After the show."

Making eye contact with her, I ask, "You don't think you should maybe tell him sooner? Like this morning?"

"I want to, but he's got this whole agenda planned for today. I don't want to ruin it." Her voice is sure, tears no longer spilling from her eyes. "I'll tell him after."

"You know I love you no matter what, right?" I ask.

Nora nods, wiping at her cheek with her shoulder. "I'm not sure *I* even love me, knowing what I've done. He loves me, Riley. And I love him. I should be shouting it from the rooftops, not dreading it."

"You made a mistake, but if you guys love each other, I know you can make it work."

A shaky breath leaves her body. "I hope so. I really hope so." She stares down at our entwined hands for a minute. Finally, she looks back up and says, "Take my mind off this. Tell me *everything* that happened with Sebastian."

I feign innocence. "I have *no* idea what you're talking about."

"Riley, we literally caught you both naked in the hallway last night."

It was more like early morning, but I think I played it off pretty smoothly.

“I think you have me confused with someone else.”

She catapults toward me, grabbing my hair and moving it from my neck. "Is that so? Care to admit why you have marks all over your neck then?"

My hand comes up to slap my neck, my eyes going wide. I'm up and out of bed in an instant, making a mad dash to the en-suite bathroom. As soon as I get in front of the mirror, I discover she isn't lying.

There are hickeys all over my neck. Some are darker than others, but there's no mistaking what they are. Proof of last night is scattered all over my body.

I didn't know people in their twenties even gave hickeys anymore.

But apparently, Sebastian does.

"I'm guessing you two had fun?" Nora shouts from the bedroom.

"Well," I say to myself in the mirror, inspecting the marks, "these are going to be fun to hide at work on Monday."

"You okay in here?" Nora says, her voice getting closer until she comes into view in the doorway.

"I look like I've been attacked," I mutter, rubbing my neck.

Nora laughs. "You look like you’ve had some pretty good sex."

I scoff. "I refuse to believe any woman has ever used the term 'pretty good' when referring to sex with Sebastian. That man has a side to him I would've never guessed."

Nora raises her eyebrows. "Do tell."

Deciding that today will *definitely* be a hoodie day, I stop worrying about my reflection, knowing it will be mostly hidden underneath the baggy fabric.

"I don't think it was any kind of secret that Sebastian and I had an instant sexual attraction."

"Slight understatement. The two of you acted like you wanted to rip each other's clothes off all night last night."

I wave dismissively. "Yeah, like I said, neither one of us

was trying to keep it a secret. He's hot. I'm hot. Why the hell not?"

She laughs. "Mhm."

"He's just so cocky and sure of himself. I kind of expected him to be selfish in bed. A guy that asks you to ride him all night without worrying if you came or not."

Nora's nose scrunches. "Okay, I don't need *every* detail."

"But he's the complete opposite. Once it was the two of us—he was quieter, more deliberate with his words and actions. It seemed so different from his personality. In the bedroom he's bossy, but also fucking attentive. I came so many times. I thought that was only possible in romance books."

Nora shakes her head at me. "Sebastian? Deliberate and attentive...no way."

"You better believe it, Nora Boo. The man is totally different in bed."

"I would've never guessed," she says quietly, walking back into the bedroom.

I follow her out, stopping when I take in the appearance of the room. The comforter and countless throw pillows litter the floor. A curtain has been ripped down and lies over a reading chair. There's a picture hanging lopsided above a small dresser, and one of the lamps is tipped over on the ground.

"Must've been one wild night," she teases, walking over to align the picture.

"You can say that again. I think I'm going to be sore for weeks."

A commotion downstairs catches our attention. "Where is Nash anyway?" I ask when it occurs to me she's not with him, a shock since he planned this whole getaway for her in the first place.

"He had to take a phone call with Monica and some other people. He told me to grab some coffee while I wait, but instead I found you."

I pull on a pair of underwear and leggings, not bothering to change out of the shirt I threw on sometime early this morning when I was cold and had to pee. The lack of sleep catches up with me as I try to stifle a yawn. "Well, I could definitely go for a coffee."

SEBASTIAN

THE HOT COFFEE BURNS MY TONGUE AS I SUCK DOWN WHAT I believe is my fourth cup today. Riley and I were up most of the night, meaning I got little to no sleep. Not that I regret using every last second of the night to worship her body—making damn sure she remembers me. But I do wish the coffee served backstage at craft services was a little stronger. I've had two cups in the last thirty minutes alone and I'm still struggling.

Once everyone got up and moving this morning, we had to head back to the venue. Nash has his hometown show today, which really tends to bring out the crazies. Old elementary-school girlfriends, past one-night-flings, and guys that *used to be best friends with him* are among the hometown crowd Matt and I have to fend off during the various press and fan obligations before and after the show. There's usually not much downtime.

Which means I've seen little of Riley today. I did see her briefly this morning, and got a good laugh out of her trying to hide her neck and chest from everyone. I almost forgot my one-night rule when I caught a glimpse of one of the marks I inflicted peeking out from her hoodie. The sight made me want to inspect every single bit of evidence left by our night together.

But that would only complicate things. I'm not convinced

that more than one night with Riley would even be healthy. Her personality rivals my own, we'd probably eat each other alive if we ever had to actually have a conversation.

"Everything go smoothly last night?" Matt asks me, returning from filling his own cup of coffee. Craft services is tucked into a small corner of the backstage area. There's a table lined with all sorts of food that local restaurants donated.

The opener for Nash is currently on stage, which means he's busy getting ready for his set. Typically, providing security for Nash is a 24-hour job, but there's enough security provided by the venue that we don't have to worry about him during the show. This is about the only time we have off on tour.

"Sebastian?" Matt asks, looking at me over the brim of his styrofoam cup.

"Oh, yeah, sorry, it went really well. No complications at all."

At least as far as Nash is concerned.

Matt nods, picking up a discarded magazine from the table and flipping through it.

Matt has been with Nash longer than I have. He's head of the security team and acts like Nash's dad, even though he's not actually old enough to be. He takes his job very seriously, barely ever joking around, too focused on the job at hand.

Often, he gives me lectures about how I need to take this job more seriously. Most of the time, I ignore him. This job is the one thing I have in my life that I'm proud of—I take it *very* seriously. But I'm closer to Nash, and I recognize a darkness in him that I see in myself. I do my best to make him laugh, make him hate his life a little less—I know it helps me enjoy life a little more, too.

Growing up, I couldn't always make people laugh. My jokester attitude only fueled my dad's rage. I tried not to care what he said to me. His insults rolled off my back easily—most of the time. It's hard to take too much to heart when he's an alcoholic ex-con who refuses to sober up and get his life together. His vengeful hands were a lot harder to avoid, though. The small scars on my body from the beer bottles and cigarettes tell the story of a past that I've tried to forget.

I refuse to let that man dull my outlook on life. Even with the shit hand I'd been dealt, I still believe the best in people. And unlike my father, I want to help spread positivity. So it's been my mission for years to be the guy people could count on for laughs, to brighten their day when it's dark.

I hadn't realized I was zoning out until I hear Matt saying my name with a raised voice.

"Are you with it tonight, man?" he questions, setting his coffee down next to him.

I raise my coffee, taking a large drink. "Working on it."

"It's Nash's hometown show, we're going to have to be with it for the meet-and-greet. Remember the last one? Where some girl from his middle school came in a wedding dress and hired an ordained minister?"

I try not to laugh—knowing Matt isn't trying to be funny—when a stunned Monica runs up.

"We've got a problem," she says slowly.

I've never seen fear in her eyes—I didn't know Monica even had emotions. But the look on her face is unmistakable.

Matt and I both jump to attention. "Is Nash okay?" he asks, as we head towards the dressing rooms.

"Stop!" she shouts behind us, making us both turn around. "I need to tell you something," she looks around as she moves closer, "something I don't want others hearing."

Furrowing my eyebrows, I look over at Matt, but his face tells me he's just as confused.

Monica leans in. "Listen. Nash and Nora broke up. It wasn't good, and now he's spiraling. Hard. I can explain more later, but for now we've got to make sure he doesn't do anything stupid."

Shaking my head, I respond, "What? They were so happy this morning. What happened?"

"Sebastian, we don't have time for this." Her voice is more annoyed now.

"If you want our help, you better make time." I demand.

Her bony shoulders lift as she sighs, her face slowly gaining its usual composure.

"We did something we believed would be in his best interest, and then his stupid ex came along and ruined everything."

"Explain. Now." I emphasize the words.

"We need to get to Nash." Matt interjects.

"Walk with me." Monica motions for us to follow, her stilettos clicking along the concrete as she walks.

"I didn't know what else to do," she continues, "the label didn't like his last album. People weren't connecting with it. It didn't feel genuine like his previous one. We just wanted to help get him back on track. We hired someone to..." she pauses, looking for the right words, "make him feel again. We thought a backup dancer would be perfect."

"Nora," I breathe, feeling my heart picking up pace in my chest. Dread overtakes me. I've seen first-hand what a broken heart does to Nash—to my best friend.

The crowd lets out a deafening roar, interrupting our conversion. Monica's eyes grow wide. There's only one thing that would cause the crowd to react like that.

Matt and I jog the rest of the way to the side of the stage just in time to see Nash, cup in hand, finish rising up on a lift from beneath it.

A tiny misstep as he speaks tells me he's already been drinking heavily.

"This isn't how I planned it," Monica says from behind us, slightly out of breath.

"What did you think was going to happen?" I demand angrily, speaking before Matt has a chance to.

"He wasn't supposed to know it was us. That slimy ex of his just showed up and fucked everything up." She's yelling now, trying to speak over the noise from the crowd. "I don't know how much he's had to drink, but it's not good."

"I'd be fucking drinking, too, if I learned that the girl I was falling for was a manipulative liar. Add in the fact that the people who are supposed to be in his corner had their hands in the deceit. What the fuck, Monica?" She tenses at my words.

Nash addresses the audience, taking a drink as he pauses. He's doing a good job of pretending to be okay until he looks over to Nora. I know the devastation on his face. I've seen it before. And I know we're only a few drinks away from him losing control.

Throughout the time I've been with Nash, I've seen him at highs and I've seen him at lows. Watching him right now, I can already tell, this is going to be his lowest low.

I watch, useless from the sidelines as his world falls apart over the course of his set. With each song that passes, he dives deeper and deeper into his drink.

Anxiety grips me as I realize the next song is *Preach*. The song was originally written when his now-ex had cheated on him. It's an extremely personal and vulnerable song. It's also the song where he and Nora have an intimate dance together.

Nora takes her usual spot behind him, but instead of starting the song, he begins speaking to the audience. My stomach turns as he recalls the origin of the song and the heartache that followed.

"Turns out, I had *no* fucking clue what heartbreak was then. No fucking clue," Nash says looking back at Nora. "Now I do. And it fucking *sucks*."

Monica steps up next to me. "Should someone stop him?"

I'm too focused on Nash to realize Tyson, his publicist, has joined our small crowd of worried spectators. "This is going to be a PR nightmare," he complains.

The beat starts to play, pulling everyone's focus back to the stage. My eyes are locked on Nora as she performs. She seemed so innocent, so good for Nash. I'd never seen him so happy.

How was I so wrong about her?

Even now as they dance on stage, she looks sad, regretful, apologetic—probably just an attempt to save face from the fallout.

Monica looks over at Tyson with disgust. "What did you expect? He's a loose cannon and we just *destroyed* him. We shouldn't have expected anything different. What we did was…"

I cut her off, "Was heartless as fuck."

She winces, and the smallest bit of remorse flashes across her face.

"I know." Monica doesn't give any other excuses. All she does is stare out onto the stage, biting a painted fingernail while watching Nash carefully. Silence follows for a moment as we all hold our breaths, waiting for *Preach* to end.

"So we're just going to let him come apart in front of all of these people?" Tyson breaks the silence, putting his cell phone to his ear.

"I don't know, okay?" Monica snaps. "I don't know what to do. I don't know what's best for him."

Shaking my head angrily, I say, "Oh, now you don't know? You should've thought about that before your *good intentions* caused this." I point toward Nash and Nora as the song concludes.

I'm about to continue berating Monica and Tyson when both Riley and Aiden find us.

"Hey, everything okay? Is he always this…negative?" Aiden scratches his head, looking out toward the stage.

"Not typically," Monica answers first, "it's complicated. He had some news broken to him before the show, he's taking it hard."

Aiden looks confused. "What news?"

Before any of us can respond, Riley whispers, "Oh no."

Her brown eyes widen as they find mine. The expression on her face says everything.

"You knew," I breathe, studying her reaction.

"Knew *what?*" Aiden insists next to me, his eyes bouncing between all of us.

"Aiden look—" Monica begins trying to usher him away from the group.

"I want answers," he says, letting her lead him away. Tyson and Matt also leave the group, both of them taking a perch closer to the stage. They talk closely, sending weary looks toward Nash.

I'm left alone with Riley. She looks up at me apologetically.

"You knew," I repeat solemnly.

She bites her lip, looking away from me. Her head finally giving a slight nod.

My teeth clench together, biting back the vicious things I want to say to her. I've only known her for a day, but I thought I had a better read on her. I sure as hell thought I knew Nora better.

Fuck. Nora. Sweet, funny, compassionate Nora was here for all the wrong reasons.

I never would've known.

And then there's Riley.

An enigma. The first girl I've met that's piqued my interest from the moment I saw her. The first girl that somehow managed to stay on my mind beyond just one night. And the second girl to betray me today.

"It wasn't my place to say anything…" she says, having to raise her voice over the crowd.

I laugh. "It wasn't your place? Fuck, Riley. How could you spend time with both of them, seeing the way he looks at her, knowing she was going to ruin him?"

"She's my best friend. It isn't that easy."

I let out a fake laugh. "It seems easy to me. As a matter-of-fact, it seems pretty damn simple for anyone with a conscience."

My blood is boiling, my heart pumping faster as I take everything in. Nash was happy. For once, Matt and I weren't having to pull a drunken, defeated shell of a man out of some bar every night. For the first time since I'd started working for Nash, he was sober more than he was drunk or high. But now, as he falls apart in front of thousands of screaming fans, I know things are about to get a lot worse.

Nora, the girl I thought could save Nash, ended up being the one to ruin him.

And the woman standing in front of me could've prevented it.

"We didn't think he'd even look at her. We never would have…"

"Well, he did," I cut her off. "She had every opportunity to come clean. *You* could've encouraged that." I press my finger against her chest. "Was last night just another cover?"

"Sorry, I'm a little drunk," Nash slurs on stage while he fiddles with his guitar.

"I need to go," I tell her, barely able to look at her as I walk away.

She grabs my arm. "Sebastian, wait."

I look down, inspecting her hand on my bicep for a moment. There's a small, unfamiliar part of me that doesn't mind the touch—that craves it despite everything. Normally it'd be terrifying, but right now it's infuriating. The same hands that were begging to touch me last night have no place being anywhere near me now.

Prying her hand off, I take a step back. "Don't touch me."

"It wasn't a cover, Sebastian. Not at all."

"Don't talk to me. I'm not interested in anything you have to say at this point."

"I thought we could at least talk about it," she pauses, "what about last night?"

I smile. "Last night meant *nothing*. We fucked. That's it. Another meaningless lay."

"You don't mean it." She sounds hurt. As if *she's* the one who should feel hurt right now.

"You don't know a fucking thing about me. But I know enough about you. Enough to know I'm out of here. I don't do schemers or liars and you just so happen to be both."

She starts to open her mouth but I turn around and walk away.

Nash needs me right now and I have nothing left to say to her.

MY FIRST PRIVATE JET EXPERIENCE WAS MUCH MORE FUN THAN what will likely be my last. The blankets didn't feel as soft, I barely touched the food, and the hired pilot wasn't as fun. It's hard to enjoy such frivolous things when the events of last night keep playing in my mind.

I guess I should be grateful that Nash still paid to fly me home. If the situation was reversed, I'm not sure I'd do the same. Even so, it's difficult to feel gratitude when your best friend's heart has been ripped out of her chest.

Leaving Nora this morning was one of the hardest things I've ever had to do. She spent the entire night crying against me in my hotel room. Nothing I said could calm her sobbing—she loves Nash, and he's gone. What she felt for him was real. Even the small amount of time I spent with Sebastian was real. We may not have met them under the most innocent of circumstances, but that doesn't mean we intended for any of this to happen.

Knowing she's being kept on tour for publicity, drowning in guilt as they travel city to city, only adds to my pain. She's been through so much in her life as it is, but I've always been there for her when it mattered. Until now.

When Nora first left for the tour, I remember thinking our apartment seemed incredibly empty. We'd moved out to LA together, so we were always spending time with one another.

Now, when I step into the dark apartment, it feels even lonelier than the day she left.

My keys make a loud clunk as I toss them onto the counter. I have a million things I need to do to get ready for work tomorrow, but all I want to do is curl up in bed with a cheesy movie.

For some reason, I keep thinking about the last words Sebastian said to me. All I wanted was a chance to explain myself, for him to understand why I did what I did. Just like he would obviously do anything for Nash, I would do anything for Nora. I expected nothing more than a night, but it's also difficult to focus on anything knowing he likely hates me.

Lost in my thoughts, I start a load of laundry, making sure I can wear my one good bra to work tomorrow. I manage a couple more menial tasks before the weight of the last twenty-four hours forces me into bed. I fall asleep shortly after my head hits the pillow.

It seems like I only slept for five minutes when my blaring alarm wakes me up. I reach out to grab my phone and silence the noise, but instead, I accidentally knock it into the small crack between my nightstand and bed.

I groan, hitting my pillow in frustration. If my entire life wasn't on that phone, I might just leave it down there.

"I hate mornings," I mumble, sitting up to peer into the small crack. I shove my arm between the two pieces of furniture, the tip of my finger barely able to touch my phone. I inch my way to the device until I finally get a good grasp on it. Not wanting to hear the alarm for a second longer, I smash all the buttons before even lifting the phone from the crack.

"Siri," I hold the device close to my mouth, "can you try not being so fucking annoying?"

Unfortunately, anything other than ear-piercing probably

wouldn't have woke me up. I'm basically running on one decent night's sleep in the last three nights, and I'm still emotionally drained from the trip. On top of that, my job as a glorified errand girl requires me to be extremely punctual so I can deliver just the right temperature of coffee to my douche boss at nine every morning. If there isn't a piping hot americano sitting on his desk before his first meeting, I won't hear the end of it for the rest of the week.

I get my ass into gear, getting ready for the day. Pulling outfit after outfit out of my closet, I try to find *something* that will hide the fading hickeys on my neck. This would be a lot easier if I lived somewhere with colder weather. That way I could get away with wearing a turtleneck. Unfortunately, I live in LA. If I showed up to work with a turtleneck, I'd get more looks than the hickeys would. Back in high school I had two outfits I used for this exact purpose, but that was before I grew these hips.

Finally, I settle on a blouse that manages to cover my chest and part of my neck. Using concealer, I attempt to cover the rest of my neck while frantically finishing my morning routine.

I'm hustling to my car as fast as possible when our crazy neighbor, Billy, yells at me from the sidewalk. "Riley, can we talk for a minute?"

My heels click against the concrete as I blow past him. "I can't today, Billy. Sorry!"

"It's Bill," he grumbles, waving a newspaper in the air. "Did you see that UFO last night?"

Shaking my head, I pause, turning to face him completely. "I did not, but I've really got to run."

"I know I saw one last night. Right over there," he points the newspaper over my shoulder.

I don't have the heart, or time, to tell him that he's pointing in the exact direction of LAX and what he probably saw was a plane, not a UFO.

"Crazy! Maybe The Guardians of the Galaxy are coming to save us all."

"Those movies are trash!" he yells.

He's ranting to himself about the movies as I slip into my car, terrified of the LA traffic I'm bound to face.

The last thing I need on this Monday morning is to piss my boss off. I've had a shit couple of days, so I'm really praying the next few go as smoothly as possible.

My prayers fall on deaf ears. Apparently, I've pissed off the universe because there's *two* separate accidents along my morning commute.

It's twenty minutes past nine when I finally park. Scalding hot coffee drips down my wrist as I race to make the overflowing elevator. The courteous thing to do would be to wait for the next elevator, but not today. Today, I say *screw courteous* as I shove myself into the packed elevator like a sardine. Some woman with a short bob cut talks away on her phone, giving me a dirty look as she elbows the coffee in my hand. I give her one right back, sticking my tongue out at her for good measure.

She continues to stare me down as I step off the elevator.

The office of Modern Millennium is bustling this morning. I've been working at this magazine since Nora and I moved out to LA. You would think after years of busting my ass here I'd have a position higher than an assistant, but *surprise*, I'm still a glorified coffee runner.

One of my coworkers greets me from her small cubicle, but all I can do is give her a faint smile, too busy running to my boss's office to stop and chit-chat.

Holden McAllister is the kind of boss romance books are written about. He's rich, charming, and hot as hell, but he's also a total asshole. I've worked here for three years and he still barely knows my name. His good looks do nothing to thaw his icy demeanor.

As soon as I step through the open door, his gray eyes pin me in my place.

He's standing at his desk, looking through a manila folder of documents. "You're late," he says coldly, his eyes flicking to me and away again.

I scurry to his desk, placing his coffee in the same spot I do every day.

"Sorry, there was a lot of traffic," I say calmly, as if I'm talking to a caged bear and not a grown man. Typically, if someone is a dick to me, I'll have a snarky remark to throw right back at them, but not with Holden. Holden makes me feel like I'm a little kid all over again, and not in a good way.

I'm constantly trying to impress him, thinking *maybe* one of these days he will promote me to something other than an errand-girl.

My dream is to be a writer here at the magazine. I want to have my very own column about a small-town girl trying to make it in LA. I know I'd be able to put a unique perspective on it. Right now, when you pick up a magazine and read about the latest happenings in this city, you're reading it from the perspective of someone who's grown up in this world.

My ideas would be fresh, unique, and I *know* it would make a difference for the people like me, people who come here with big dreams and no idea what to do with them.

But for the time-being, I'm the least qualified person to give advice given I can't figure out how to upgrade my position from coffee-fetcher to writer here.

"First, you're late. And now you're not even listening." Holden's harsh tone breaks me out of my thoughts, he's now a couple of steps closer to me.

"I'm listening."

"I don't like to repeat myself..." he pauses, as if he's trying to remember my name.

"Riley," I say.

His chestnut eyebrows pull together. "I know your name. The pause was to see if you could come up with a better excuse than traffic."

My mouth hangs open. I don't answer him quick enough because before I can give a response, he's talking once again.

"We live in one of the busiest cities in the world— it's a given that traffic anywhere in LA will be shit. You should plan accordingly." Undoing the button of his suit jacket, he comes around to the front of his desk, sitting on the edge.

The new position puts him way too close to me. I back up instantly, almost tipping a cup of pens over in the process.

"What do you need help with today?" I ask, trying to nonchalantly change the subject. He doesn't have the patience to listen to all the reasons I was late, and I don't have the energy to defend myself. The last thing I want to do is give Holden a reason to be even more of a dick than usual.

Holden slaps a list down on the desk, close enough for me to get a look at it. I see seven items neatly ordered in his chicken-scratch handwriting. He reviews his expectations for the day. Four of the seven items include me fetching various items for him. *Shocker.*

His phone rings, allowing me to slowly sneak away, list in hand. I make it to the door when he says my name.

"Riley?"

I turn around to face him, noticing he's put the caller on hold.

"Forget something?" I ask, waving the list in the air wondering if I'll have to add something to it.

He shakes his head, a scowl on his face. "Do a better job of hiding your hickeys next time. You're an adult, act like it."

Fuck, fuckity, fuck.

WATCHING SOMEONE YOU CARE ABOUT FALL APART IS ONE OF the hardest things in the world.

Becoming their glorified babysitter with front-row seats to their misery? That's just torture.

"There goes my shoes," I sigh, trying to shake vomit from them.

"Sorry," Nash slurs.

"Don't worry about it, Boss."

He almost runs straight into the bathroom wall as I try to steer him to the toilet. My wet shoes squeak against the bathroom floor.

Nash makes gagging noises as I rush to try and get him in front of the toilet for this one.

Over the course of a few weeks, he's plummeted into a deep downward spiral. We've gone from city to city picking up the pieces from his benders, each one worse than the last. Tonight, we had the distinct pleasure of dragging his unconscious body from a VIP booth while cameras captured every moment.

We were supposed to be on the road heading to his next tour venue, but Nash had to stop and get *one* drink. Neither Matt nor I were dumb enough to believe him, but he's the boss.

By keeping Nora on the tour, his team is slowly killing

him. Every time he has to perform with her, he does more to forget—pushing his body closer and closer to its substance limit. Luckily, the American leg of the tour is close to coming to a close. Monica informed us that Nora won't be traveling overseas with us. Good riddance.

The sound of Nash's retching fills the lavish hotel bathroom. I sit on the floor next to the toilet, watching him empty his stomach over and over again.

Matt and I have been taking turns staying with Nash after his nights out in an attempt to protect him from himself. Tonight is my turn, so I get the comforts of puke covered shoes, a hard tile floor, and the sounds of vomit hitting toilet water.

I quickly work at removing my shoes, tossing them into the large jacuzzi bathtub behind me before I lean against it. My legs stretch out in front of me, one foot crossed over the other.

"How are you hanging in there, bud?" I ask, playing with the leather strap of my watch.

"Fuck off," he groans, spitting something into the toilet.

"You know," I offer, "you could avoid this whole feeling like shit thing if you just didn't down vodka like it was water *every single night*."

Reaching behind me, I pull a stark white towel off the hook it's on. I toss it toward Nash, watching it land on his lap. He mumbles a thanks, using it to wipe around his mouth.

Nash flushes the toilet. "I'd rather feel like this than feel the empty pit in my stomach. I can't be around her sober. She has me all sorts of fucked up, I still love her despite it all, and this is the best way I know how to forget her."

Standing back up, I busy myself by fixing him a glass of water. This is the most Nash has opened up to me so far and I want to be an outlet for him. "Do you think it'll be better when she's off the tour?"

He sighs, snatching the glass from me as soon as I hand it to him. I wait as he gulps all of it down.

"Honestly? No. I'm scared that having her gone will hurt even worse." When he looks at me, his eyes are bloodshot. All I want to do is scream at the girl who willingly made him this way.

I still can't figure out why someone would ever do something so cruel.

Taking the glass from him, I fill it up again, trying to hydrate him as much as possible.

"I, for one, am glad she'll be gone. I think some separation from her is exactly what you need."

He looks at me sadly. "Why do you think that?"

"It isn't healthy for you to constantly be around her. Screw everyone forcing you to pretend you're still dating for *good publicity*. You need a clean break."

"I don't know what I need. Sometimes, I still think it's her."

I let out a defeated sigh. "How can you still love her after something like that?"

He leans back, his head falling into the wall. "Have you ever been in love, Bash?" Nash uses the nickname he gave me only weeks after I first met him.

Running a hand over my mouth, I shake my head. "Can't say I have, boss. Can't say I want to either," I answer truthfully. In theory, being in love sounds exactly like something I'd want. Companionship, somebody to make the nights less lonely. Things I never had growing up. Things I wanted desperately. But it's because of my upbringing that I know the realities of life. I know that love is far more complicated than people make it out to be. I know that it's hard for me to believe that love conquers all when it couldn't even stop my father from doing the things he did.

Nash looks at me, puzzled. His tired eyes roam over me. He takes his time before he speaks again. "One day you'll understand. Just because somebody hurts you doesn't mean you love them any less."

"That's messed up."

The corner of his mouth twitches upward. "Never said love wasn't the most fucked up thing in the world, it's probably why we're all so addicted to it."

The color has started to return to his face and his words no longer slur together, evidence that the cocktail of liquor and drugs has started to leave his system.

"What ever happened with you and Riley?"

The question surprises me. He was there when Nora caught us naked in the hallway, but we'd never actually talked about it. I'd like to tell him I haven't even thought about her since the hometown concert, that the night in the cabin was just another unmemorable fling. But that would be a lie. The truth is, I have thought about her. I've racked my brain trying to figure out how she could seem so genuine while keeping such a devastating secret. I've stayed up at night trying to figure out how someone so cold could feel so warm. Most of all, I've beat myself up. Because even as I watch Nash come undone before my eyes, I can't bring myself to forget her—to hate her.

But in his current state, Nash doesn't need to know the truth.

"What about her? You know me, I can't be tied down." I give him a cocky, fake smile.

"Man, I really thought she might be the one to tame the beast."

"Nah. Turns out she's just as bad as Nora. And, no offense but," I motion toward him, "I'll pass."

He lets out a small laugh. It might be the first genuine laugh I've heard in days.

"Really? This doesn't look fun to you?"

We both smile for a moment. If nothing else, the thought that he may not go to sleep sad tonight is worth the ruined shoes.

"Are you ready for tomorrow?" Changing the subject, I

extend my hand out to help him up. He's wobbly on his feet when he stands. Pulling his arm over my shoulder, I assist him in making it to the oversized bed in the middle of the hotel room.

He falls face down into a pile of throw pillows. His feet hang limply off the side of the bed. I don't know how it could possibly be comfortable, but he's going to be sleeping in a bed and not on the bathroom floor for the first time in a long time, so it's a win in my book.

I'm in the process of pulling the boots off his feet, thinking he forgot about my question, when he answers. "Yes. No. I don't know. I hate interviews, and having to pretend everything is perfect between us just sounds miserable."

Tomorrow Nash and Nora are set to go on a popular talk show to promote the tour—and of course to talk about their relationship. Or at least the relationship they're pretending to still have for the public. The show was booked when things were still perfect between the two of them, and his team wants to maintain that illusion for good publicity.

"You know you can tell them you won't do it, right?"

"I know, but..." his words drift off as he gets lost in thought.

"I'm here for whatever you need." I set his shoes at the foot of the bed, retreating the small distance to the bedroom's doorway.

He turns to his side to face me. "Fuck yeah you are. You have to be. It's your job."

I smile, shaking my head. "You know what I mean." He's right, technically he's my boss. But over the years, we've developed a strong friendship. He's the closest thing I have to a brother—I'd do anything for the guy. But seeing him like this reminds me why I don't do relationships.

As I reach the door to his room I turn around and find him already snoring.

"Good night, Nash."

A ZOMBIE HAS RETURNED IN PLACE OF MY BEST FRIEND AND I don't know how to fix it. Nora returned early from the tour, but she hasn't been herself since she got here. For someone who can never shut their mouth, I can't seem to find the words to comfort her.

For weeks I've tried to convince her to go to our favorite restaurant. I got on my hands and knees to beg, even offering to pay—still no. And that's if she responds at all. Most of the conversing we do is between her sobs or after groaning at me to leave her alone to wallow.

But enough is enough. I'm through with letting her drown in her own sea of remorse. I'm over it with an uppercase 'O'. It's time for her to get out of the same ratty old t-shirt she's had on for weeks, and get some freaking pants on, at least for a day.

That's why I'm staging an intervention. One that involves a shower—for her—some food that is not warmed up by the microwave, drinks with way too much alcohol, and a night club. All in that specific order.

The sound of my heels against the concrete echoes off the walls as I near my apartment.

It was a busy day at work and we could *both* stand to let loose a little.

For some reason, Holden has been nicer to me recently.

He even cracked a joke a few days ago. It was an awful one and it barely made any sense to me, but still—I'll take it.

There's a new intern in the building, and she seems to be his newest target. For once in my career, I didn't have to step foot into a coffee shop last week. *Nope.* I got to sit my ass in a desk chair and file paperwork all day.

It was glorious.

Even though I'm no longer at the bottom of the totem pole at work, I've still been kept incredibly busy. We're hosting a gala soon, and all of the celebrities that have graced our cover in the last year are supposed to attend. I've been training the new intern, but I'm desperate to prove my worth to Holden and the rest of the company so I'm working overtime on a few small tasks for the event.

Which means—I'm a *little* stressed. It doesn't help that every time I walk in my apartment I'm met by my emotionally-draining best friend. I'm starting to get concerned with the amount of *Golden Girls* reruns she's watched. I keep expecting to come home and find her playing Bunco with women three times her age.

"Honey, I'm home!" I sing-song, barging into the apartment.

Things begin to slip out of my hands as I attempt to balance a bottle of wine in one hand and a premade charcuterie board that cost half my paycheck in the other. The door makes a loud *thump* against the thin drywall—the same area that's already been patched twice from similar enthusiastic entrances.

Deciding to worry about that tomorrow, I continue my trek into the apartment to find Nora nowhere in sight. I sigh, setting everything from my hands onto the counter.

"*What a wasted entrance,*" I mumble, making my way to her bedroom.

I have to dodge old popcorn bags and laundry as I make my way to her bed. The only indication that she's even in the bed is the top of her ponytail peeking out from underneath the covers.

Using a pen I find on her desk, I beat the metal base of her lamp like a drum. "Wake up, sunshine!"

Nora startles, her head flying off her pillow. "What the *hell,* Riley," she yells.

I beat the metal a few more times before letting the pen fall to the ground. Shrugging, I walk up to the bed, pulling the blankets off her. "Well, you missed my grand entrance, so this was the next best thing."

Nora nestles deeper into the bed, pulling her knees against her chest in the fetal position. "Go away," she mutters, burrowing deeper into the covers.

"Not happening," I sing, hiking a leg up so I can crawl onto the mattress. As soon as I'm on the bed, I go to stand, jumping up and down to jostle her body.

I know she's annoyed the moment her red-rimmed eyes find me. Her glare does nothing to deter me. I continue to jump up and down, watching her body flop around underneath me.

"I'm breaking you out of your post-breakup slump. We're going to drown ourselves in margaritas and then shake our asses!"

"I'm not leaving the bed today," she announces, crossing her arms over her chest.

I tsk, jumping up and down some more to keep her attention. "You are *absolutely* getting out of bed. I've given you plenty of time as the mayor of woe-is-me-ville. It's time to pull on our big girl panties and move on with our lives!"

"I don't deserve to be happy."

I stop jumping, mulling her words over. "It's time to give yourself a break. Are you just going to wallow for the rest of your life?"

"Maybe. Or at least until it's clear that Nash isn't falling apart. Have you seen the news? He's a mess right now."

My knees fall to the bed. I crawl across it until I'm grabbing both her phone and laptop from the open space next to her.

She sits up. "What are you doing?"

Dodging her outstretched arm, I thumb through her phone.

"*Riley,*" she repeats.

Holding her technology out of reach, I look at her. "I'm solving a problem."

She raises her eyebrows. "How so?"

"I'm making sure you can't see anything of his anymore. It isn't healthy. This is the first step of your intervention."

"Interventions are for people with problems," she counters.

A laugh escapes my lips before I can rein it in. "Nora, darling, I love you. I really do. But the fact that you can't see the problem here *is* the problem. You've got to move on, and you're starting by taking a shower. You smell."

Lifting her arm, she takes a sniff. "I don't smell."

Rolling my eyes, I climb off the bed and playfully swat at her foot. "You definitely smell," I grunt.

Once I've pulled her halfway off the bed, she stops putting up a fight. It might be because I'm dangerously close to pulling her completely off the bed. A few more good tugs and she'd be face planting onto the floor.

"Okay, I'll get up if you stop pulling!" she shouts, her fingers still gripping the comforter tightly.

I pause, but keep a hold of her ankle. "You promise?" I ask suspiciously.

"Yes, I promise. Just stop pulling before I fall off the bed."

"Fine," I say, letting go. I walk toward her bathroom to turn on the shower. As soon as it's on, I make my way back to the kitchen. I pull out the new body soap and lotion I bought for her.

When I walk back to her bedroom, I find the hideous t-shirt she's been wearing for weeks discarded in her laundry basket. "Oh my god, you're relentless," she says under her breath. "I promise you I'm going to get in the shower, you don't have to watch me undress."

Ignoring her comment, I hand her the bag of items. "Take these and use them," I instruct.

She looks inside the bag and then looks up at me confused. "Why did you get me new soap and lotion? I know you think I've been in hibernation, but I still have my own stuff."

"Yeah well, in one of your emotional breakdowns you admitted that Nash loved the smell of your soap, so we're changing it."

"But I like smelling like roses. He liked it."

"Hence the reason we're changing it. Go shower. I'm going to pop open a bottle of wine and find a good pre-game playlist. We're going out on the town Nora, even if I have to drag you out of this building to do so."

"Fine," she huffs, clutching the bag to her chest and heading toward the bathroom.

As soon as I hear her shut the bathroom door, I'm walking to my bedroom. It doesn't take me long to change out of my work clothes and change into something suitable for the club.

I haven't been laid since the night with Sebastian, and I'm ready to end this recent dry spell. I'd encourage Nora to do the same, but I'm fairly confident she isn't ready for that. Which is cool. She can lock it up for five years for all I care, I just need her to not smell like a dumpster if she dances next to me.

I've eaten over half the olives on the charcuterie board when she finally comes out of her room. And I'll be damned —she's *dressed*.

I mock rubbing at my eyes, blinking dramatically over and over again. "Am I seeing things?" I joke. "Is my best friend bathed *and* dressed up?"

She looks down at her minidress, embarrassed. "Shut up. Where's the champagne?"

My ass flies off the barstool. I grab the champagne glass, thrusting it toward her, nearly spilling the bubbly all over the both of us.

"I thought this moment would never come," I marvel before taking a sip from my own champagne glass.

Closing the distance to the small island, she sits down on the other barstool. "I'm only doing this because I know if I don't you won't leave me alone about it."

I down the rest of my drink before shrugging. "You're probably right."

"I'm probably going to regret this tomorrow," she states before folding a piece of cheese into her mouth.

"You're also probably right." A mischievous grin spreads across my face. "At least, I hope so. The nights we regret are always the most fun."

RILEY

THE INTERVENTION WAS A HUGE SUCCESS—FOR A MOMENT. Nora was finally starting to act like herself again. We laughed, we danced, we drank an unfortunate amount of alcohol, and eventually we passed out with our shoes still on. It was amazing.

But I suppose all good things must eventually come to an end.

Just as I think we're in the clear, Nash goes and performs a song on live TV about Nora. And it's a *doozy.* I wasn't even the one in the relationship and I still felt like crying.

So, I've lost my best friend again.

Between working doubles to prepare for the gala and Nora locked away in her room, I almost never see her anymore. Nora and her sister Lennon are really my only girlfriends, and with Lennon out gallivanting around the world and Nora hibernating in guilt, I have no one to talk to.

Which is very unfortunate because I'm dying to tell somebody about Holden. About the prolonged stares. The casual jokes he slides into conversation every now and then. I wish I had a girlfriend to obsess over and dissect every single thing my asshole boss has been saying to me. But I don't.

And tonight, I'm getting a much needed break. There's a slight lull in between tour stops right now, so my good friend Ziggy is in town. I texted him an S.O.S as soon as I walked out to drink my morning coffee and heard Nash's new breakup song playing from Nora's room on repeat.

I'm trying to work an eyelash curler, getting real close to taking out an eyeball when Ziggy knocks. I walk to the door, opening it and throwing my body at him for a hug.

"My hero," I say against his chest.

"Damn girl, didn't know you missed me so much." His arms are tight around my shoulders as he hugs me back.

Laughing, I pull away, hitting him in the stomach. "Yeah well, I need back up. We need Nora to stop listening to that damn song of his. She's torturing herself."

Ziggy nods, fully aware of the song I'm talking about. Ziggy is a dancer on Nash's tour. He and Nora became close during auditions for the tour. After rehearsals started for the tour, he started hanging out with Nora and I more. Even while they were on tour, he and I kept in touch.

Ziggy is the best kind of person to be around. He's always got a smile on his face and would do anything for anyone. He doesn't even realize that he's a huge flirt, and he's got the best style of any guy I know.

If he wasn't already like a brother to me, I would be first in line to go on a date with him.

He barrels into the living room as if he owns the place. Bee-lining straight for her bedroom, he gives no warning before tossing her door open.

"Hey, Nora, it's time for us to move on from the sulking Elle Woods to the *I'm going to Harvard to kick some ass* Elle Woods!"

I follow closely behind Ziggy, trying not to laugh at Nora's shocked face.

"Ziggy, what are you doing here?" she asks in surprise.

"And how do you know *Legally Blonde*?" I chime in.

Ziggy looks over his shoulder, rolling his eyes. "I grew up with four sisters. Plus, it's pop culture. Who *doesn't* know that movie?"

I nod. "Touché."

Grabbing the corners, Ziggy pulls on the comforter until Nora is fully uncovered.

"Ziggy!" she yelps, rushing to cover herself. "What if I hadn't been wearing clothes?"

I roll my eyes, never in my life have I seen her go to bed without wearing clothes. Me on the other hand, I always sleep naked.

I'm more comfortable that way.

"You forget that we toured together for months. We lived on a tiny little bus together. We've done ice baths and dress rehearsals together. I've basically seen it all, babe. And while you're smoking hot, you're fully in the friend zone for me." He winks, clapping his hands before trying to pull her up from the fetal position.

Unlike how she acts with me, she doesn't put up a fight. She lets him pull her up without any arguments.

"I don't know if I should be offended," she laughs.

What the fuck, she's laughing with him? I haven't been able to elicit anything more than a grunt—or a sob—from her over the last few days.

"Don't be offended," he says, letting go of her hands and taking a seat next to her. "So what are we doing tonight?"

"Well, *I* have to finish getting ready for this event. I'm going to try and not throw up from nerves in the process."

Nora's eyes widen. "Oh my god, how did I forget?"

I shrug. "You've had a lot on your mind, I get it."

She shakes her head, burying her face in her palms. "No, I've been a shit friend. You've been planning this gala for *months* and I forgot. I was supposed to help you with hair and makeup, but I've been too busy feeling sorry for myself."

"Don't worry about it," I say dismissively. "You're nursing a broken heart. You get a shitty friend hall-pass."

"Well, you look gorgeous," she offers, taking in my appearance. I'm glad she doesn't notice the small smudges of mascara I had to cover with eyeshadow because of my whole eyelash curler incident. Or that my lips have had three different shades of lipstick on them, my mind too indecisive to settle on just one.

"Thank you! Now I just have to squeeze all of this," I point toward my body, "into my dress."

"Don't worry, you'll look great," Ziggy reassures, quickly grabbing Nora's phone before she can grab it from the bed.

My eyes narrow, zoned in on Ziggy. "I never said I wouldn't. I know I'll look hot as fuck." Flipping my hair over my shoulder, I head back to my room to finish getting ready.

Walking to my closet, I stare at the emerald green satin dress I've been dying to wear since the moment I spotted it in the store window.

I almost had a heart attack when I saw the price, but the saleswoman talked me into trying it on. It *was* on sale after all.

The moment the fabric touched my body, I knew I would sell my left tit to own it. To wear it. And that's basically what I did. I handed over my credit card, holding my breath and wondering if it would even go through.

Now, running a hand over the silky fabric, I regret nothing. I'm ready to wear this masterpiece out into the wild. I'm hoping it'll help me find a suitable bachelor tonight. This gala should have a plethora of sexy men in suits gallivanting around—it'll be a playground for single women like me.

I handle the dress delicately as I finish unzipping the garment bag and pull the dress the rest of the way out. Carefully, I slip it onto my body. The shiny, emerald fabric falls to the ground. A slit goes all the way up to the top of my leg, dangerously close to showing off my thong.

The bodice is tight around my chest, pulling my breasts up. I finger the thin straps that cut slightly into my shoulders, admiring the plunging neckline that doesn't leave much to the imagination when it comes to my cleavage. At my waist, the fabric switches from being tight on my body to falling loosely to the floor. When I move, my leg peeks out from the pool of fabric, making the dress *so* much sexier.

I stare at myself in the full-length mirror, pleased with my decision to say yes to the dress.

I'd do me.

I straightened my blonde hair to perfection, the mid-length locks pinned away from my face with two stylish clips. I'm not one to typically wear a lot of makeup, valuing extra sleep over getting up early to apply a full face. But tonight, I went all out. A combination of smoky browns and shimmery golds outline my brown eyes. There's one-thousand layers of mascara on my thick eyelashes, making them extra dramatic. My lips are lined in a dark brown and filled in with a darkly hued nude.

After I'm satisfied with my appearance, I grab the heels I picked out to match the dress. Leaving my closet, I walk to my bed and take a seat, sliding my foot into each heel. The nude straps of the heels buckle around my ankle delicately. When I stand, I'm now a few inches taller. I grab the clutch I picked out from my dresser, opening it to make sure I put the items I need in it.

Finally ready, I switch the light off in my room and meet Nora and Ziggy in our small kitchen.

Ziggy turns around when the sound of my heels sound against the floors. He whistles. "Damn girl."

"Stunning," Nora says after coming around the island to wrap her arms around me. "My best friend is smoking. Don't have *too* much fun without me."

I snort. "Your best friend has been doing damage control for *you* and your breakup for the last few weeks. Tonight, I'm letting loose. Fingers crossed the gala runs smoothly and I can stop with all the work and play a little, too."

"Well, don't have too much fun without one of these," Ziggy says, reaching into his back pocket and pulling out a condom. "I'm not quite ready for the responsibility of being a cool uncle."

I swat the gold-foil package away from me as soon as he holds it between us. "Thanks for worrying about me, Zig, but I'm a responsible lady and I'm always prepared. And flavored condoms, *really?*" I question, eyeing it.

Shaking his head, he places the condom back in his wallet. "Don't hate. This is all some random gas station had available while on tour. Gotta be safe, ladies."

"I hope the two of you have a blast. I'm going to head out. Holden wants us there early to go over a few things."

We say our goodbyes and then I'm off.

As I step into the elevator, I attract the stare of a group of guys, the price of this dress already proving worth it.

Now all I have to do is make sure it's laying on the floor tonight next to a guy's tux.

SEBASTIAN

THE BOW TIE AROUND MY NECK SEEMS INCREDIBLY TOO TIGHT. My fingers wrap around the fabric, pulling down on it to try and get it a hair looser.

"Stop messing with it," Monica says from the limo seat next to mine.

"Stop telling me what to do," I toss back.

Monica purses her lips, looking away from me and back out the window.

"Why do we have to go to this to begin with?" Nash asks from across the limo. He pulls a flask from the inside of his suit-jacket, taking a long drink. Once he's done, he offers it to his brother, Aiden, who turns it down.

Monica crosses her legs. "Because you committed to attending six months ago. The magazine did a huge feature on you this year and you're getting honored tonight. You're supposed to give a speech." She reaches into her purse, pulling out a neatly folded piece of paper.

"We've prepared one for you," she says confidently, handing it over to Nash.

He takes it out without saying anything, his eyes scanning over the words.

Aiden on the other hand, doesn't stay quiet. "So it's not enough to control who he dates? You've got to dictate what he says as well?"

Monica rolls her eyes at him and focuses back on Nash.

Aiden's eyes narrow on her angrily. "I told him he should've fired you after what you did."

She sighs, playing with the chain of her necklace. "You've mentioned. Frequently."

He smiles, the gesture not quite meeting his eyes. "Good. As long as we're all clear here."

Nash sits up straight, handing the piece of paper back to Monica. "Play nice, you two."

Aiden laughs. "I'll play nice when you get rid of the bitch that put a price on your heart."

Matt and I shoot each other awkward glances as this plays out in front of us.

"Bitch? Really? You couldn't come up with anything better than *bitch?* C'mon, Aiden. If you're going to throw insults like a big boy, at least make them creative."

I try to hide my laugh behind a cough. Monica has taken constant ridicule in the aftermath of Nash and Nora's breakup, but she rarely fires back.

None of us are really sure why she's still here. After Nash told her she was fired, she agreed to leave. Her only request was that she had a chance to talk to him in private first. Matt and I waited outside her office for hours as the two of them hashed things out. Somehow, she'd managed to convince him to keep her on, despite everything. When we asked Nash, he was cryptic but confident. She was to stay, no questions asked.

And that was that. We haven't tried to pry any further since then. Truthfully, he hasn't really been clear-headed enough since then to even have a conversation like that.

No matter how much I care about him as a friend, he's still my boss. It's not up to me who he employs. If it were, she'd be ruined.

So I've gone back to barely tolerating her. It's not like Monica and I were close before everything happened anyway.

Aiden, on the other hand, hasn't been afraid of letting

everyone know *exactly* how he feels. He's visiting Nash for the weekend, and I think we've spent more time in the crossfire between Monica and Aiden than we've spent being there for Nash.

"Nothing to say back to that?" she taunts, pushing her shoulders back and looking at him triumphantly.

"Oh, plenty of things come to mind," Aiden says, leaning forward so he's getting closer. "But you aren't even worth another breath of mine."

"Enough," Nash demands, slapping his leather seat. "The two of you are giving me a fucking headache."

"We're about to pull up," Matt announces, looking out the window.

Monica maintains eye contact with Aiden for a few moments. I have to hand it to her, she doesn't let his continuous insults deter her. Sometimes I swear she isn't human, and that normal emotions don't apply to her. Finally, she looks away from him and glances down at her phone. "Are you ready for the red carpet, Nash?"

He groans, pulling at the collar of his shirt. "Why did no one tell me there was a carpet?"

"We did," Monica responds. "You don't have to do interviews. In fact, I suggest, you *don't* do any interviews. You just have to stop and smile for a few photos."

I turn to Matt. "What's the play for us?"

"There should be enough security at the event that we don't have to hover over Nash. We'll just stay close as he does the photo ops on the way to the doors. Once inside, it'll be a bit more lax. It was hard to come by tickets for this gala, and the magazine has assured me that security is tight."

I nod, trying to loosen the bow tie one last time before we exit the car. At events like this there's typically a lot more security than normal. A-list events can elicit the crazies, so whoever is hosting the event typically hires top-tier security agencies. For every event like this, we have to send the agency a list of known stalkers for Nash. People we know that are freakishly obsessed with him. We send their names as well as photos so security can keep an eye out.

"After the carpet the two of you should have some fun tonight. Let loose." Nash gestures between Matt and me.

Monica doesn't seem to be too fond of this idea. She starts to shake her head, opening her mouth to speak but Nash beats her to it.

"You don't have to say it, Monica. I know they won't, it was just an offer." He looks between Matt and I. "I know you guys are too busy babysitting me to have any fun."

Aiden grabs the flask from his brother's hand, taking a long drink. "I'll be busy taking shots with an actress. Hey, is that girl from the new superhero movies going to be here? She's hot as *fuck*. I heard she does all her own stunts. I'd love to see how that converts to the bedroom."

"Are you even old enough to be drinking?" Monica says bitterly.

Aiden responds by taking another drink from the flask. As soon as he's done, he winks at her, wiping his mouth with the back of his hand. "Trying to control me too, Monica?"

Luckily, we're all spared from another argument as the limo comes to a stop. The partition that separates us from the driver lowers slightly.

"We're up in line," the driver announces.

Monica runs a hand down the red, beaded fabric of her dress. "Ready?"

Matt crawls out of the limo first, and I follow directly behind. Rows of screaming press and eager fans line the red carpet, making it impossible to hear. For a brief moment all eyes are on me, giving me a taste of the limelight Nash grew up in. It's blinding, exposing me to endless judging eyes—something I'll never get used to.

The moment passes as quickly as it came, everyone turning to focus on Nash as he exits the vehicle. Cameras illuminate his face, revealing a forced smile. It's a smile I've seen one too many times in the aftermath of his breakup. I know firsthand the pressure of putting on a facade, pretending to be okay when inside everything is crumbling to pieces. But I've never had to do it in front of so many people.

The crowd noise is mostly jumbled, but out of it I catch a few comments aimed at Nash.

"Nash, how are you after the break-up?"

"Nash, what happened to Nora?"

"Nash, is it true Nora was paid to go out with you?"

Fuck this.

Lunging for Nash, I grab his arm and pull him past the rest of the photographers and press waiting ahead. I leave Matt and the rest of our entourage behind as I quickly usher Nash to the doors of the venue. My ears are ringing as I pull the door closed behind us.

"Thanks." Nash looks over at me with a smile—a real one.

He doesn't need to say anything else. Leaning against the door I let out a sigh, and take in the moment. For the first, and probably last time this evening, it's quiet.

RILEY

That's it. I'm convinced that I'm meant to attend fancy galas like this for the rest of my life.

This is the most fun I've had in a while, and technically I'm *working.* When I arrived, Holden had me complete a few things before giving me the rest of the night off. I'm not sure where this new Holden came from, but I'll take it. Part of me feels bad, wondering if the new intern is now taking the brunt of his grumpiness. But, I've paid my dues, so I don't feel *that* bad.

I'm standing at a buffet table lined with hors d'oeuvres when Holden walks up.

"You did good, Riley," he tells me, taking a sip from his whiskey tumbler.

I'm a few drinks deep, and against my best judgement reply with, "Is that a compliment Mr. McAllister?"

I pop an olive into my mouth, slowly chewing while he mulls my words over.

"It's possible. So don't forget it, I don't give them often."

I nod. "Oh trust me, I know."

"Is this the part where you tell me I've made an ass of myself to you?" He quirks an eyebrow, his fingers still wrapped tightly around the glass as he takes a step closer to me.

Abort mission, you cannot flirt with your boss. Right?

I'm seconds away from crossing the line of appropriate

conversation with my boss when I nearly drop my plate of food.

Because walking through the door is a man I would recognize anywhere.

Sebastian.

In a room surrounded by some of the best looking people in the world, he fits right in. His all-American look is even sexier clothed in black-tie attire. There's no denying he's attractive in everyday wear, but put the man in a suit and he's dripping with sex.

He walks in behind Nash, and for anyone else he'd probably fade into the background. But not for me. I don't see how anyone could look anywhere but at him. It doesn't help that I've seen every bare inch of that man. That his body has taken me to places I didn't know existed.

"Everything okay?" Holden asks, leaning close to grab my attention.

Nodding my head up and down, I try to focus back on him, but it's no use.

I knew Nash was originally supposed to attend. He had been featured in our magazine earlier this year. But after the fallout with Nora, his team had contacted us saying he could no longer attend. Apparently they had a change of heart.

Now I'm panicking. Sebastian and I didn't exactly part ways amicably. Not to mention, I have no idea how Nash will react to seeing me.

"Are you sure?" Holden persists, grabbing my shoulder.

Before answering, I decide to take *one* more peek across the ballroom at Nash's group. My eyes slowly wander in that direction. I regret it as soon as I do, because my gaze collides with Sebastian's.

He watches me carefully. If he's shocked to see me, he doesn't make it clear. Nash says something to him, but when Sebastian doesn't react, Nash follows his gaze directly to me. Only he *does* show surprise when he spots me.

Nash smiles, rapidly closing the distance between us.

No no no.

Holden has continued our conversation on his own and is in the middle of saying something to me when I interrupt him.

"Holden, I don't have time to explain but I need you to do me a favor."

"You ignore me and then ask me for a favor?"

I grab ahold of his hand, forcing it onto the small of my waist.

"What are you—"

"I'll explain later, but right now I need you to pretend to be my boyfriend to help make somebody jealous."

He looks at me in shock. "That is highly inappropriate. I'm your boss."

I roll my eyes, annoyed. "I just need you to pretend for two minutes. I'll do whatever you want at work. Work late, get your coffee, grab your dry cleaning, just *please* pretend to be my boyfriend."

I anxiously look toward the group heading our way. Nash is gunning straight for me, the rest of the group including Sebastian in tow.

"Yeah, you'll be explaining later," he says, playing along by pulling me closer into him.

"Riley!" Nash announces, stopping in front of Holden and I. He rakes his eyes between the two of us. "I wasn't expecting to see you here."

"Babe," Holden says from the corner of his mouth. "You didn't tell me you knew Nash Pierce." He pulls me deeply into his side, looking down at me, a forced and confused smile on his face.

"She didn't?" Nash asks curiously. A moment later, he's holding his hand out in front of Holden. "I'm Nash. Just Nash."

Holden shakes it. "Holden McAllister. Chief of Staff here at Modern Millennium. Pleasure to finally meet you."

Holden is all business as Nash introduces his whole entourage. When he gets to Sebastian, I look down at my feet, for the first time in my life I'm nervous in somebody's presence.

Even though I'm not looking at him, I can feel his hot stare on me.

"So, you two?" Nash questions. When I look up at him, he's looking at me mischievously. I'm wondering if he can see through my lie.

Holden looks down at me, appearing to suddenly remember he's my fake boyfriend. He leans down, giving me a soft kiss on my cheek. "Yes, us two. We're together. How do you know my girlfriend?"

Sebastian makes a deep noise in his throat, catching my attention. When I manage to make eye contact with him, it feels like he can read my every single thought. He watches us carefully, probably picking apart every single interaction between Holden and me.

"Let's just say, your girlfriend is friends with someone I used to be close to. We go back a little. Right, Riley?"

"She hadn't mentioned," Holden says honestly. I shrug, my mouth suddenly incredibly dry.

"You didn't?" Sebastian asks from Nash's side. He stares me down, waiting for me to answer. I wasn't expecting him to speak. I was hoping Nash led the whole conversation—or even better, that this whole conversation never happened.

My eyes go to Monica, then Aiden and finally, Matt. I'm hoping one of them will intervene. I'm desperate for this whole entire meeting to be over with.

"Can't say she did, man," Holden answers for me. His fingers are tight against my waist.

"I know damn well she can speak for herself, *man*."

Holden looks from me to Sebastian, clearly shocked. "I'm sorry, I didn't catch your name."

"Doesn't matter. I had your girlfriend moaning it not too long ago."

Monica looks horrified. Matt looks embarrassed. Aiden looks amused. I can't tell what Nash is thinking. And Sebastian, he looks damn proud of himself. I want to knock the smirk right off his face.

"You have no right," I seethe, grabbing Holden by the arm. I start to pull him in the opposite direction. Looking over my shoulder, I refuse to look Sebastian in the eye. "It was good to see you, Nash. Enjoy the event."

I keep pulling all six-plus feet of Holden until we're on the opposite end of the ballroom. The enormous space has been separated into several different areas for the event.

Finally, we stop in a corner far out of sight from Nash and his group.

"Rileyyyy," Holden drags out my name slowly. "It seems you've got some explaining to do." He runs a hand through his hair, looking at me expectantly. I groan, fidgeting with the skirt of my dress awkwardly.

"That wasn't supposed to happen," I admit, taking a deep breath.

"Elaborate," he chides.

A waiter walks by us with a tray full of champagne glasses. I greedily grab one off the tray, almost knocking down the other carefully placed glasses in my haste.

I chug the champagne until my glass is empty. As soon as it's all gone, I hold the glass in front of me. "Damn, that's some good champagne," I mutter.

"You're avoiding the conversation," Holden points out, grinning.

"What, me? *Never.*"

He raises his eyebrows, waving his hand in the air as if to say 'get to it'.

"Okay fine. My best friend dated Nash Pierce and I slept with his bodyguard. And then my best friend broke Nash's heart and I kind of knew about it. It may have made things awkward for Sebastian and me. Not that we were going to be anything more than a hook up *anyway*, but yeah. It's not a big deal." I stop talking, aware that I've begun to ramble a little too much.

Holden runs his fingers through his hair. "Not a big deal?"

I try to shrug nonchalantly, slightly freaking out on the inside.

Sebastian is here. In this ballroom—and definitely seemed a little jealous. Of course, that was the entire reason for pretending to date Holden, but I didn't think it'd actually *work.*

It could just be my mind playing tricks on me. I'm still furious at the way Sebastian dismissively spoke to me during the hometown concert. I didn't expect to marry the guy, but to say I was just another *meaningless lay* really struck a chord. If I was able to make him second guess that statement, even just a little, that'd make my evening a whole lot better.

I shouldn't even care. I shouldn't even be thinking about him right now. But damn, does he know his way around a woman's body. And he looks sinfully hot in a suit. And that combination is lethal for a woman who hasn't been laid since the last time we were together.

"Can we just pretend this never happened?" I plead, nervously chewing my lip in embarrassment.

He thinks my words through. I'm preparing for him to say something smart-ass, or worse, he brings up how inappropriate it was for me to have him pretend to be my boyfriend. He's my boss after all. Surprising me, he says, "You got it. As long as this won't cause any drama tonight."

I fervently shake my head. "Oh, it won't, I'm staying as far away from that group as possible," I state, meaning every word.

He laughs, looking over his shoulder. "I should probably get back to it."

"Yeah, of course." I nod, waving as he walks away.

As soon as he's gone, I let out a sigh of relief. I'm happy to be alone, allowing me the time to regain my composure. I'm not easily distracted, but Sebastian's bluntness to someone *he* thought was my boyfriend has thrown me off.

Thankfully, this is a huge event, and there's a good chance I won't see them again tonight.

I decide to head to the ladies room, needing to freshen up, AKA, get my shit together. The first bathroom I try has at least ten security guards waiting outside of it. There's a line forming to enter. Judging by the amount of security detail waiting outside, the bathroom is jam-packed with celebrities.

I wander around the venue, dodging different groups of people before finally finding a small two-stall bathroom tucked away in a secluded corner. To my surprise, it's empty.

Stopping at the bathroom counter, I open my clutch and begin to reapply my lipstick. I'm swiping it across my bottom lip when the door swings open. Looking up over my shoulder through the mirror, I almost drop the lipstick when I see who's looking back at me.

"Sebastian," I say in shock.

He doesn't answer me, all he does is watch me in the mirror. His gaze is intense. Being the object of his attention has me feeling like prey.

"What are you doing here?" I get out, still looking at him through the reflection in the mirror.

"I'm asking myself the same question, trouble."

My heart bangs in my chest at the mention of the nickname he coined from our night together. There's silence after his admission. We watch each other through the glass mirror.

The longer we sit in silence, the more I remember how big of an ass he was earlier.

"That comment you made to Holden was unnecessary," I

say, finally turning around to face him. Even though his presence is addicting, I still have some of my wits about me.

"Did I hurt the feelings of your uppity boyfriend?" he drawls, taking a slight step closer to me.

"Oh, fuck off," I say annoyed. "Holden isn't uppity. You're just being a dick for no reason."

"For *no* reason," he mocks.

"Yeah. There's no need. Not everyone needs to know we slept together once."

Ignoring my comment, he takes another step closer to me. I try to retreat, but my back bumps into the marble bathroom counter.

"My reason for being a dick," he starts, ignoring my latest comment, "is that no matter how much I know I should stay away from you, seeing you tonight—with another man—has me fucked up."

My mouth parts.

He stalks closer. Not a single part of our bodies touch, but the look on his face makes it feel like he's exposing the most intimate parts of me.

"I saw his arm wrapped around you and I remembered when it was *my* hands all over you."

His arms brace against the counter, caging me in. The marble digs into my skin as I press back into it. My mind is telling me to avoid his touch, while my body is begging for it.

"I've had to watch my boss, my *best friend,* go through hell. I shouldn't want to be anywhere near you, but yet..." his words fall away.

"But yet?" I breathe, staring at his bow tie, too nervous to look him in the eye.

"Yet all I can think about is how bad I want to fuck up that lipstick you just meticulously applied."

When I look at his face, I find his eyes hungrily looking at my lips. The attention has me rubbing them together anxiously.

"All I can think about is how you can't make up your mind," I throw back at him. I shift my weight, maneuvering in a way that exposes all of my leg. He looks down at it, and I know exactly what I'm doing to him. I'm doing it on purpose. It's fascinating to watch him lose control of himself.

"I shouldn't want you," he admits. He slides his hand across the counter, making it seem like he's going to touch me, but he stops before his skin touches mine.

"The drama between our friends doesn't involve us." My words are true, it *shouldn't* involve us. At least I think. It's difficult to think straight with him this close.

"But doesn't it?" he asks carefully. "What does it matter to you now? You have a boyfriend..."

"Boyfriend," I repeat. I'd forgotten about the charade I'd roped Holden into earlier.

"Even if I did want you, I'm not touching you if you have a boyfriend, Riley."

I probably should tell him that I was lying, that I was thrown off-kilter by his sudden appearance and wanted to find a way to stick it to him. But this jealous version of Sebastian is hot. I'm freaking into it.

His eyes take me in. He's not bashful about checking me out. Taking his time, his eyes fall to the plunging neckline of my dress, to where my cleavage is on full display. Then he moves on to the leg that juts out of the fabric.

"If you didn't have a boyfriend, I'd push that tiny strip of fabric that's holding your dress up down your shoulder," his voice is full of lust. "I'd slip my hand underneath the fabric, pulling it down until I'm met with the sight of your tits." His hooded eyes slip to the point on my body he's discussing before he looks at me again. There's so much want in his eyes. "Then I'd repeat the action on the other side, until that dress of yours is only being held up by those glorious hips."

I can feel the erratic beat of my pulse thumping in my

neck. My fingernails scrape against the counter as I try to better steady myself.

"If you didn't have a boyfriend, I'd take my time worshipping those tits the way they deserve. I'd bite and suck, mark them up, let everyone know that I was there. That they're mine."

My breath hitches in my chest.

"Want to know what I'd do next, trouble?" He lowers his head so our mouths are only a fraction apart. One slight movement and I'd be tasting him once again.

I swallow, not able to find words. All I can do is nod.

"If you didn't have a boyfriend, I'd pick you up and set you on this counter. Then I'd drop to my knees in front of you. I'd take this leg right here," his eyes flick to my exposed leg, "and I'd run my lips against the inner part of your ankle. And then I'd take my time making my way all the way up your leg. I'd make sure to run my mouth over every *single* erogenous zone you have there, making you pant my name before I even make it to that sweet little pussy of yours."

My thighs clench together, incredibly turned on by his words.

The man hasn't even touched me and I'm dripping wet with desire.

"Then, I'd remove the pathetic scrap of fabric you're covering yourself with," he moves to the side of my head, his lips brushing against my ear, "and let you ride the fuck out of my face."

He watches me closely, waiting for my next move. I want so badly for him to take me right now on this counter. But to have him, I have to admit to my lie—something I don't want to do. I can either admit to him that I was only using Holden to make him jealous or I can keep up the charade, and miss the opportunity to have my body worshipped by this man again.

What little control I have left vanishes when he licks his lips.

My hands come up to grab his face. "I don't have a boyfriend, now stay true to your word and kiss me, you asshole."

He doesn't hesitate, his lips eagerly crashing against mine.

SEBASTIAN

I KNEW SHE DIDN'T HAVE A FUCKING BOYFRIEND. I SAW through her lie the moment it spewed from her mouth. The way he touched her made it pretty evident that he had no idea how to treat her body the way it deserved.

Even so, I don't like being ignored and I certainly don't like being jealous. Not over someone I shouldn't even be involved with.

I'm mostly over the fact she knew Nora was planning on hurting Nash. She protected her best friend, I can't say I wouldn't have done the same.

What has me hesitant is the fact that Nash is still reeling from the damage Nora caused. I shouldn't be involved with anyone from her life. I should be keeping my distance, staying loyal to my boss and friend. I don't want to put my job at risk by getting involved with her.

Yet the moment I saw her walk away from her imposter boyfriend, I had to follow her. I had to talk to her, to see her, to be the object of her attention.

I wanted to feel her come apart underneath my touch once again. I was desperate to hear her back talk. She's the furthest thing from timid and it turns me on.

Those lips of hers are laced with sin as they mold against mine.

She kisses me angrily, to which I return with my own fury.

Furious with myself for giving in.

For wanting her this desperately.

For *needing* to feel her unravel underneath my touch again, one night wasn't enough.

I grip her waist, pulling her across the counter until she's pressed up against me. Her long fingernails dig into my scalp as she takes what she wants from me.

"This means nothing," she pants. When she pulls away, her lipstick is smeared, her lips already red and swollen.

And we've barely even began.

"Thought that was pretty evident, trouble," I tell her, stepping away. I head to the door, flipping the lock to ensure no one interrupts this.

"Yeah, well, I'm still pissed you made me out to be some girl with a crush after last time."

I smirk, stopping in front of her once again. "Were you not?"

She rolls her eyes, clearly annoyed with me. I fucking love it when she rolls her eyes. I'm fucked up.

"You're too cocky."

"Thought I had the right to be after my cock had you screaming all night long." I run a finger over her exposed knee-cap. She shivers, making me smile.

"Just because you gave me a handful of orgasms doesn't mean I'm suddenly going to fall in love with you. You're not the kind of guy a woman falls in love with, Sebastian. You're the type of guy that shows a woman what she will *never* have with the man she ends up settling down with."

"Well as long as we're on the same page there."

"One day a girl might tie you down, make you stifle your fuck-boy tendencies."

"Doubtful. I'll treat her like I love her for a moment and then I'll be gone."

"I don't want you to treat me like you love me, I want you to fuck me like you hate me."

"Is that so, trouble?"

She nods, biting her lip. "Now stay true to your word and get to work."

"You're going to have to tell me what you want, in detail." Reaching up, I begin to untie my bow tie. My fingers work quickly, alleviating the pressure from my neck. Each end falls loosely down on my shoulders. I unbutton the first two buttons of my shirt.

"Why do I have to tell you when you can show me?" She leans back, knowing exactly what she's doing by sticking those luscious tits out. I can see the peaks of her nipples through the thin fabric of her dress.

"What's the fun in that?"

I'm anticipating her telling me exactly what she wants. All she has to do is say the words. But I should've known better. She's ready to play this game as much as I am.

"Well, Sebastian, if you're not going to stick to your word, then I'm just going to have to do it myself."

She defiantly holds my gaze as she reaches up, both of her pointer fingers slide underneath the straps of her dress. Ever so slowly, she begins to push the top of her dress down until each one of her nipples are exposed. She isn't bashful as she begins to play with her tits. Her hand pushes them toward the center of her body before letting them fall, the bounce of them making my dick stir.

"Since you won't, I'm going to have to tease myself by playing with these." She twists her nipples gently.

"And once I'm ready…" her hand rubs slowly down her body. Down her sternum, over her stomach before stopping at the point where the fabric gathers around her waist. "I'll have to move on to this."

Her thighs slide against the counter as she pushes them open, the slit of her dress allowing a full view of the wet spot on her panties.

She begins to slip her fingers into the lace fabric, forcing me to surrender to her. My knees hit the floor, eyes now level with the sweetest part of her. Looking up, I find a perfect grin on her face.

"I knew that'd do the trick," she says proudly.

"You're going to pay for that," I sigh, weaving my fingers into the fabric of her thong. Before she can get another word in, I pull the fabric until it snaps in two.

"You're a dick," she says, watching as I throw the ripped pair of underwear to the side.

"What did you call me?" I taunt, picking her foot up and resting her heel against my chest. The position has me perfectly eye-level with her core.

"I called you a dick. That was my sexiest thong. You've got a lot of work to do to make up for that."

"Riley," I respond, caressing the inside of her ankle. "Stop talking."

Making good on my promise, I begin to make my way up her leg. Beginning with the sensitive spot behind her knee, I leisurely take my time making it up to the spot where she wants me most.

Her fiery lips go from spouting insults to moans when I get to her inner thigh. My tongue works against the smooth skin, until finally I'm to the spot I've been dying to taste again.

I run my finger down her slit, making her hips buck in response.

"You're wet for me, trouble," I state. Making eye contact with her, I stick my finger in my mouth and suck.

She groans, her head falling back against the mirror. "Why does that have to be so sexy?"

"Why do you have to taste so good?" I counter, before plunging my tongue into her slit.

She clamps her legs together against my ears as I pull her clit into my mouth over and over again. My tongue and lips work together in a passionate rhythm against her. Her hips begin to quiver as I bring her to the brink of a release, pulling away just before she comes.

I can't hide the smile on my face when I look up at her, cheeks flushed and eyes begging for me to continue. "I said you were going to pay for that stunt earlier."

"Sebastian, you're going to fuck me until I come or I'm going to walk out of this bathroom and never speak to you again."

"Fuck, I love it when you're bossy," I say before ravishing her lips with mine.

Our tongues and teeth collide as I snake my hand back underneath the dress. I'm met with wetness, *so much wetness*. It has me hard as a rock. My thumb massages her clit while my middle finger enters her, curving up slightly.

She tugs on the buckle of my belt, cussing when it gets stuck in a loop. Riley must be as ready as I am judging by how quickly her fingers get busy undoing the button of my pants and unzipping my fly. She's about to reach into my briefs when I gently push her hand away.

"I won't touch you anywhere but there," she says quietly.

I watch her for a moment, before my needs overtake my judgement.

"Okay."

She runs a long fingernail across the skin above my waistband, teasing me just as I did to her. She sinks her hand into my underwear and wraps her small fingers around my shaft. For a moment, I lose myself in the bliss as she begins to pump up and down slowly.

"Is that what you like?" she asks, gasping when I coax another finger in her.

"Is this what *you* like?" I return, analyzing her every move to discern what she likes.

Her breath tickles my neck as she moans. "It kills me to say it, but I don't know if there's anything you could do that I *wouldn't* like."

As soon as she speeds up, I move my hips backwards, freeing myself from her grasp.

Her bottom lip juts out in a pout. "What do you think you're doing?"

"Well, trouble, I'm about to remind you what a proper fucking feels like." I pull out my wallet, ripping open a condom and sheathing myself in it quickly.

I bend down, picking up my forgotten bow tie from the ground. She watches me curiously.

"What are you doing?"

"Hands out," I demand.

She obeys, sticking them out in front of her. I use one hand to fix them into the correct position. As soon as she's wrist to wrist, I take my bow tie and secure it around them. I lift her arms over my head, her wrists coming to rest at the back of my neck.

"Will you fuck me now?" She shifts her weight, spreading her legs wide open.

Pulling her across the counter until she's on the very edge, I lean in close. "Gladly."

My hands slide underneath the dress to find the curve of her hips. I ease myself into her slowly. I'd forgotten how perfect she fits around me.

I try to move as much of the fabric of her dress away as I can. The piece I thought she looked so sexy in an hour ago is now frustrating me by covering part of her skin.

With her wrists bound and wrapped around my neck, there's no way for Riley to brace herself. She has to lean into me, allowing me full control as I push deeper and deeper.

Her heels dig deep into my thighs as I pick up speed.

"It feels too good," she pants. "I'm going to come." Her head falls backward, exposing the fragrant perfume on her neck.

Bending down, I run my lips and tongue over her flesh. "Go ahead," I say, my lips moving over her skin. "But know you're going to have to come again. I'm not done with you yet, trouble."

Her orgasm must be building. She begins to lift her hips, dictating the rhythm she wants. I match her speed, able to tell the moment she reaches her climax. Her moan bounces off the walls as her hips buck and she pulsates around me.

When her head falls limply against my chest, I slow down and then pull out.

Her head pops up, "What? You didn't…" I interrupt her by pulling her off the counter so she's standing.

Due to the heels, she's only a few inches shorter than me. I lean in, trapping her mouth in a kiss while reaching behind my head. In one fell-swoop, I pull the end of the bow tie until it frees her wrists. Before she can do something she's not supposed to, I grab her hips and spin her around.

"Hands on the counter, trouble." My hand runs along her spine, gently pushing on her back until she's bent over the cold marble, her ass jutting out at me. Pulling the bottom of her dress up, I trace a finger down the seam of her asscheeks.

In the mirror I can see her breasts spilling out onto the counter. The backs of her thighs are bright red from bouncing against the cold marble. She jerks when my finger reaches her wetness. Playing with the evidence of her arousal, I trace my finger up and down.

"Sebastian." Her voice is strained—needy. She pushes her hips backward, attempting to rub against me.

I tsk. "Eager for more, trouble?"

Her grip on the counter tightens. "Yes," she breathes, her cheek flat against the counter.

I run the tip of my dick along the same path my finger just traveled. This elicits a moan from her. I continue to tease her, sliding only the tip of my length in her for a moment before entering her completely.

I'm not slow as I bring myself in and out of her. To my surprise, she meets every pump with eagerness. She pushes against me, making sure I get as deep as possible. I grip her hips tightly to control the pace as I pick up speed. With each stroke she lets out a short moan as I breathlessly do the same.

She pushes against the counter, straightening her arms and arching her back, looking at me through the mirror. Her nipples graze the counter, tits swinging back and forth. I look up from her chest, making eye contact with her for a moment before her eyes roll back in her head.

"I'm going to come again," she moans, her body going lax underneath me.

"Prove it," I tell her, dangerously close to my own.

Bending over, my chest presses against her back as I continue to thrust into her. I reach all the way around her, palming her breasts in my right hand and bracing myself with my other hand on the counter. The arm wrapped around her squeezes tightly as I begin to empty myself.

We stay fixed in that position while we ride out our orgasms, our panting beginning to fog the mirror in front of us.

Straightening my torso, I back away from her. I glance at the watch on my wrist, realizing I've been in the bathroom for a suspicious amount of time. From the corner of my eye, I can tell she's watching me. I avoid her gaze as I pull the condom off and throw it in the nearby trash can, subtle regret starting to creep in as the euphoria fades.

I don't know what I expected to happen, but somehow that wasn't it. I just finished telling my best friend that Riley was as bad as his ex, and then went and fucked her behind his back. I'm supposed to be the one protecting him. I'm supposed to be loyal.

But deep down, I know I'd do it again, which makes me feel even worse.

As I button my shirt back up, I look on the floor for my bow tie. When I reach down to grab it, she beats me to it, holding it down with the tip of her heel.

"So you're just going to fuck me and not look at me after?" There's anger laced in each one of her words. She puts more weight on it, turning the tip of her heel to hold the bow tie to the ground.

I sigh, looking up at her. "What do you want me to say?"

A laugh escapes her lips. "I don't need you to *say* anything. But it would be nice to be looked at after someone goes balls to the wall inside you."

My eyebrows raise, taken aback by the phrase *balls to the wall*. This woman really has no filter.

RILEY

SEBASTIAN LOOKS AT ME—HIS EXPRESSION UNREADABLE. HE opens his mouth like he's going to say something, but then decides against it.

I huff, stepping away from his bow tie. He snatches it from the ground, quickly extending to his full height and looping it around his neck. His fingers fumble with his bow tie for a while until I finally sigh, stepping closer to him.

"Let me do it." I grab each side, my fingers going through the motions by memory.

I finish the final motion, pulling the last knot through and straightening it in front of his neck.

"That was quick," he says quietly, his eyes focused on me.

I look up at him with a small smile. "When you grow up with brothers, you learn these things."

He nods, grabbing ahold of my arm before I can back away from him. "Riley," he begins, taking a deep breath before continuing. "From the moment I saw you flirting with the dumb pilot, I knew I wanted you. I didn't try to hide it."

I watch him carefully, wondering where he's going with this. The hairs at the top of his head are slightly disheveled. The gel he had put in there was no match for what just happened between us.

"I still won't try and hide it. I'm insanely attracted to you. What just happened, sex with you is…"

I smirk. "The best you've ever had?"

He shakes his head. "It's intoxicating. It's different. But it's also something we shouldn't keep doing. Us getting together just makes things," he pauses, "complicated. And I don't do complicated. Fuck, I hardly do *simple*."

I nod in understanding. "I don't want anything from you, Sebastian. Well, other than maybe your face between my thighs, but I get it. Really, I do."

"How are you so…chill," he asks, looking at me as if I'm an anomaly.

I fix my dress in the mirror, sliding each one of my arms back into the straps, my boobs no longer hanging out for the world to see. When I take in my appearance, I'm not sure how it isn't going to be evident to anybody with eyes that I just had some of the best orgasms of my life. I try to make it less obvious by combing my hair with my fingers and reapplying the lipstick.

Sebastian is silent as he also fixes his appearance.

Once we're both ready to get back to the party, we stand awkwardly in front of one another. It's funny how moments ago he had me splayed out on the counter like a damn meal, but now, communicating is what we find awkward.

"So nothing is bothering you after…" his words trail off as he sticks his hands in his pockets.

I shrug, unlocking the door and pulling it open. I look at him over my shoulder. "I'm not bothered. You're the one who has to remember I'm not wearing any panties for the rest of the night." I don't wait for his response, I walk away, leaving him with that thought to return to the gala.

Not wearing any panties isn't as sexy as it sounded two hours ago. Everything is rubbing together awkwardly and I'm pretty sure the evidence of how good he made me feel is still running down my thighs even hours later.

This would be a whole lot hotter if I was at least able to tease him. There's a huge possibility that with just one quick slip, the most intimate part of me will be on full display to everyone at this event.

I know I said I don't want anything from him, but I'm still annoyed when he refuses to look my way for the rest of the night. Even when I stood across the stage from him as Nash gave his speech—nothing. If on the off chance he does glance in my general vicinity, he seems to stare right through me.

I hate to admit it, but I don't like it.

Sebastian went and ruined my brand new pair of sexy underwear, forced me to walk around with a thigh-high slit and nothing to shield my vajayjay, and won't even glance in my direction to catch a potential wardrobe malfunction.

What a douche.

A hot, sexy, fucking-fantastic-lay douche.

But, now that I'm not reeling from multiple orgasms, I'm coming to terms with the fact that Sebastian is right…we shouldn't get involved with one another.

For starters, things are very messy between the two people we love. Getting too involved with one another could go south, real quick. I don't think Nora would be angry if she found out Sebastian and I hooked up again, but I don't think it would help her get over Nash either. Plus, he's only in LA when Nash is, or when he's not working—which is basically never.

I cross my legs delicately for the twentieth time in the past ten minutes, trying to find a position that doesn't allow too much of a breeze up my dress. Holden is sitting next to me and it's difficult to switch legs without giving him a little peepshow.

"What are you doing?" he asks, his lips strained in a smile as he claps politely for the person on stage.

"I'm adjusting."

"Your fidgeting is making me anxious," he flicks eyes to me, giving me a look that makes me think he knows *exactly* why I can't hold still.

"Don't look at me like that," I chide. "It's like you've never had sex in a bathroom before."

Holden chokes on air, his coughs getting louder and louder the more time goes by. His face starts to turn beet red. I begin to slap his back, wondering if I even remember how to give the Heimlich from when I learned it back in high school.

Wandering eyes start to look at us curiously, watching as Holden basically coughs up a lung. I wave, trying to give my most nonchalant smile. "Nothing to see here. I think he choked on his own spit or something."

A woman at the table next to us gives us a dirty look. I think I remember her starring in some trashy TV show recently, I just can't put my finger on which one.

Finally, Holden regains his composure. He gives a silent apology to the people around us by lifting his hand, mouthing a *sorry*.

I'd be dead if looks could kill. "What the hell, Riley?" he says under his breath. He reaches out, grabbing his cup and taking a small sip of water.

I shrug innocently. "In my defense, I didn't think I'd make you hack up a lung by pointing out the obvious. What if I was just joking?"

"You just admitted that you had sexual relations with someone at a work function. I could fire you for that." He pauses before adding, "And I don't think you were joking."

I swat at the air dismissively. "I don't believe you. It's not like I make much money anyway."

He shakes his head. "You're fired—for misconduct."

"Have fun training the new intern yourself," I sing. Picking up my champagne glass, I stare at him over the brim of the glass, waiting for his response.

For a second, his eyes find the intern who stands at a table not too far from us. It isn't long before he's looking at me again.

"Fine. You're hired again. But for the love of god Riley, don't go talking about your sex life with your boss. It's inappropriate. And I've already caught you at work with hickeys once before."

"Where does it say in the handbook one can't have hickeys? Plus, you told me I was off for the rest of the night and I could enjoy my time. So I enjoyed."

He grunts loudly. "You're ridiculous."

I lean back in my chair smiling. "I get that a lot."

Finally, I get a smile out of him. It's small—minuscule really. But I just got my boss, a former asshole, to smile. It's good for him to loosen up a bit.

I look away from a smiling Holden, not bothering to hide the reflexive grin I'm wearing. That lingering smile stays until my eyes collide with Sebastian, and I find a pissed off look on his face.

He's not avoiding eye contact now, only diverting his attention to glare at Holden for a moment before looking back at me.

"Is there a story to be told here?" Holden asks. When I turn to look at him again, I find him staring right back at Sebastian.

"Maybe a chapter," I mutter, shifting in my chair once again so Sebastian is no longer in my peripheral vision.

Just like a man to ignore you for hours, but become interested the moment you talk to another guy.

Men. They're unbelievably predictable.

I take a large gulp of the champagne in front of me, finishing off my glass. Setting it back on the table, I face Holden. "If you weren't an asshole to me for years, I'd think you were pretty cool."

"Yeah, well, if you weren't my employee, and clearly involved with someone else, I'd ask you on a date."

His words completely catch me off guard. This is Holden McAllister we're talking about. The same man that would chastise me for being two minutes late with his coffee. Earlier in the night *it did* seem like he was flirting, but I'd honestly forgotten about it after Sebastian found me in the bathroom.

Holden shifts uncomfortably in his chair, running a hand through his hair. "Wow. That was very unprofessional of me. Forget I said anything…"

Call it a weird premonition, a sixth sense if you will, but as Holden backtracks, I feel two eyes staring a hole into my back. My shoulder blades warm, and I'm confident that if I were to turn around, I'd find Sebastian looking right at me.

Knowing what I'm doing is wrong, but not caring anyway, I lean in closer to Holden. "What if I don't want to forget about it?"

Holden's eyes widen. They scan over my face, as if he's trying to figure out if I'm being honest or not.

He runs his hands down the front of his pants. "Riley, I'm your boss. I shouldn't have said that."

I give him a reassuring smile. "Don't worry, boss. I'll forget you ever mentioned anything." I wink, "unless you ever tell me I shouldn't."

The dimmed lights brighten, a subtle cue that the evening is winding down. There's nothing else planned for the gala. The perimeter of the room is lined with tables holding small gift bags, filled mostly with extravagant items from our sponsors. I'm definitely going to steal one on my way out.

Scooting my chair against the floor, I get up, grabbing my clutch from the table. I look down, making sure my dress is adjusted accordingly. Laying a hand on Holden's shoulder, I try to ease the tension written all over his face.

"Seriously, Holden. I've erased your comment from my memory. Stop acting weird, you were just starting to become my favorite boss."

His eyebrows raise. "I'm pretty much your only boss."

"Same difference," I say with a playful eye roll.

Holden stands up, holding up a finger to someone saying his name not too far from us. He turns toward me, his hand resting on a safe place on my back. Leaning closer, his lips fall very close to my ear.

"Have good night, Riley. Don't give the time of day to a guy who only sees you when another man looks at you." Shocking me, he leaves a soft kiss on my cheek.

I'm left spinning, wondering what the fuck is happening as he walks away. My boss just kissed me on my cheek and I *think* flirted with me. All while the guy I just fucked in the bathroom a few hours ago throws dirty looks my way as if it's his job.

I smile to myself.

This dress was *so* worth it.

SEBASTIAN

As soon as Riley leaves me alone in the bathroom, reality begins to sink in. I start to feel guilty for what transpired between us. And then I start to feel guilty about not *really* feeling guilty—at least not enough to apologize for it, or to keep me from wanting to do it again.

It wasn't just her looks that had me interested the moment I met her, it was her 'fuck it' attitude and her blunt personality. She doesn't back down or worship me just because I'm best friends with a popstar. But the thing that has me coming back for more when I know I shouldn't? The way it feels when we're intimate. The push and pull that is being with her.

She stands up to me just enough to keep things interesting. In the bedroom, she takes what she wants while also making me feel like I'm the one setting the pace.

I check my appearance in the mirror, fixing a few stray hairs at the top of my head. I get flashbacks from a moment ago when she looked at me through this mirror, her gaze not wavering as I plowed into her from behind.

My hand swipes over my face, trying to rid myself of the memory before I'm hard all over again. I try desperately to *not* think of her walking around with only a small barrier between that sweet spot between her thighs and the rest of the world.

Exiting the bathroom, I meander around the gala until I find the group I arrived with sitting around a table. Nash looks bored to death as he stares at the ice cubes in his empty drink. Matt looks impartial as his eyes roam the room, always on duty even when he's technically not supposed to be. Aiden looks at Monica with disdain as she has a conversation with someone I don't recognize.

Dodging a few waiters with drinks, I take the empty seat next to Nash. As soon as I sit down he looks at me, his eyes bloodshot. Rubbing his lips together, it takes a moment for a smirk to grace his face.

Leaning forward, his index fingers tap the collar of my shirt. "You've got some lipstick right there," he slurs.

I try to play it cool, acting indifferent while I try to figure out how the hell I didn't notice such a monumental mistake. I pull at my collar, trying to see what he's pointing to, but I can't find it.

When I look at him to say just that, he's wearing a cocky smile. "Got you."

Rolling my eyes, I nudge his shoulder. "What was that for?"

"*That* was for playing it off as if you didn't just get together with Riley."

My jaw slackens, my mind preparing to plead my case to him.

A waiter hands him another drink. He takes it happily, thanking them before taking a generous gulp. "Don't worry about it," he says. "I'm apparently not strong enough to let go of my vices either."

"She's not my—" I'm cut off by him speaking.

"Look, Bash. I'm not going to tell you who you can or can't sleep with. I'm not that guy. *But* I will tell you not to lie to my face about it. I've had enough liars in my inner circle to last a lifetime."

"It won't happen again."

He shrugs, shaking the ice around in his cup. "I've said that before."

Turning around, he says something to his brother I can't quite catch. He makes it obvious that he's over the conversation, so I let it end. I don't know what else to tell him.

Maybe she is my vice. Maybe she isn't. No matter what, I know better than to continue this thing with her. There will come a point where she'll ask for more from me, something I'm not willing to give. Women always ask for more, and no matter how different Riley *seems*, eventually she'll do the same.

"What the fuck, Monica?" Aiden yells, snapping me out of my thoughts. He scoots his chair away from the table, rubbing at his shin.

"You're fine," she hisses, her eyes darting to the people around us, probably making sure our table isn't making a scene.

He looks over to Nash. "The bitch just kicked me."

"Well, maybe if you hadn't called me a *lying, scheming, robotic bitch* then I wouldn't have felt compelled to shut you up."

"Jesus Christ," Nash mutters next to me, rubbing the bridge of his nose. "The two of you have got to stop."

"I've tried to play nice with him, Nash. But if he can't let it go then maybe it'd be best if we found you a new manager," Monica says, her voice withdrawn.

"I've said no," he states, his hand hitting the table loudly. His eyes find Aiden. "Whatever grudge you're holding onto, let go of it. She betrayed *me*, not you. If I've forgiven her, so should you."

"The only reason you don't care is because you're too drunk and out of your mind to really think about what she did to you. You aren't thinking straight." His last words are said under his breath.

Nash's posture turns rigid. He points his finger at Aiden. "How I handle this is none of your concern. Get over it."

It looks like Aiden is going to respond, but before he gets the chance someone with the gala is stopping at Monica's chair. They say something in her ear. Her eyes focus on Nash. She nods, standing up and coming around the table to Nash.

"It's almost time for your speech," she tells him, completely ignoring Aiden.

All of us get up when Nash does except Aiden, who stays behind at the table.

Thank god.

When Nash crosses the stage to give his speech, you wouldn't be able to tell how much liquor he's had tonight. He nails his speech. I couldn't exactly tell you everything he said, because I spent the entirety of it doing everything humanly possible to avoid Riley's stare.

I'm trying to forget about what transpired between us earlier. Or *pretend* to forget. But how can I? The exhilarating look in her eyes when I tied her wrists together is something no man would ever be able to forget.

We make our way back to the table amid a standing ovation from the audience. Once sitting, I continue to fight the urge to look at Riley. I can't help but notice the clean-cut man sitting next to her—Holden, I think. When they'd pretended to be dating earlier, I'd called the bluff instantly. Now that I'm watching him more closely, I'm wondering if he wasn't exactly pretending.

His eyes stay on her a little longer than necessary. I follow his gaze.

Did she just wink at him?

He leans in close to her as she continues talking. He's way too focused to not be interested, and she definitely winked at him. Surely she doesn't see anything in this preppy daddy's boy. He could never satisfy her the way I can.

No. She isn't mine. I don't want her.

I clench my fists in frustration. Jealousy isn't something I'm used to feeling, and I don't like it. She just had my cock inside of her hours ago. Seeing her flirt with another man when I know there's next to nothing covering her has me thinking irrationally.

I'm talking myself out of walking over there when, to my relief, she stands up to leave. My relief is brief as Holden gets up to join her.

I watch them carefully, waiting for them to go their separate ways. A gnawing feeling begins in my gut when I watch him place a hand on the small of her back.

The same place my hand was pressed on her in the bathroom. The very place I pushed on to bend her over that counter.

He leans in close whispering something in her ear before laying a kiss on her cheek.

What. The. Fuck.

More importantly, why do I care?

Annoyed with myself, I stalk away before I do anything I'll regret. This is exactly why I have—or, had—rules. I've only slept with this girl twice and she's already living in my head rent free with my dick on a leash.

Maybe if the guy she's flirting with wasn't the complete opposite of me, I wouldn't feel so territorial.

He clearly comes from money. I bet his parents actually loved him, telling him he could be whatever he wanted to be when he grew up.

My dad was too busy throwing things at me to think about my future.

The first time I wore a suit, it was one that was purchased by Nash's team.

I still fumble with a bow tie because until I got this job, I barely even knew bow ties existed. I sure as hell wasn't having to tie them.

Yet this guy—*Holden*—probably knew how to tie one at the fragile age of five.

When I was five, I was learning how to absorb punches so they wouldn't hurt as bad.

Lost in my own thoughts, I don't realize where I'm walking until I take a step outside. The fresh air feels good, even if it's warmer out here than in the building. The best part is that Riley is no longer in view.

My phone vibrates in my pocket. I pick it up, seeing a text from Matt that Nash is ready to leave.

Good. I'm more than ready to get the hell out of here.

The sooner I can put some distance between myself and Riley, and the weird pull she has on me, the sooner I can forget this night ever happened.

RILEY

I'M KIND OF DATING MY BOSS.

It's *very* casual. Like way casual. The two of us are just toying with the idea of being a thing.

But after the gala, things started to heat up for us. It's been nice. Holden is nice. Something I never imagined myself saying.

He's refreshing. He's upfront about his feelings and what he wants. He doesn't send any kind of mixed signals or play any games.

He's basically the complete opposite of Sebastian.

It's been a while since I've even seen Sebastian, but it hasn't been easy to forget him. As I get ready for my date with Holden, I stand in front of my bathroom counter, unable to push away the vivid memory of Sebastian bending me over the counter at the gala. I swipe lipstick across my lips and I'm reminded of a similar shade smeared all around his mouth from our make out.

A knock at the door snaps me back to reality. I shake my head to get rid of my guilty pleasures. Holden deserves my full attention, and he's going to get it.

Opening my apartment door, I find him standing there with a bouquet of flowers. They're gorgeous, with pastel hues wrapped in pretty pink paper.

"Well hello," I laugh, taking a whiff of the sweet scent.

"Good evening, Riley," he says. His expensive shoes scratch against the concrete as he steps closer to me, leaning down to give me a kiss on my forehead.

"You got me flowers," I state, taking the flowers and stepping further into my apartment to find a vase.

The space is quieter than it usually is as Nora and her sister are taking a girls weekend. They invited me to go, but I declined because I was actually really looking forward to this date with Holden.

"I got you flowers," he repeats, casually glancing down at his phone before looking back at me.

I find a vase tucked away in a cupboard and fill it with water, preparing the flowers to go in it. Once they sit nicely on the island, I grab my purse. "You ready?"

"Been looking forward to it all day."

Rolling my eyes, I lock the apartment as he waits for me in the hallway.

"You had meetings all day," I remind him, thinking of his busy work day.

He had meetings with various people all day long. He probably didn't even have time to think about anything but work. It's hard for him to get out of work mode. Holden is the definition of being married to his job. The man is extremely by the book. The week after the gala, he pulled me into his office, informing me of his interest in me. Once I told him I was also interested, he told the HR department before even taking me on a first date.

"Having meetings doesn't mean I wasn't looking forward to tonight," he says, his hand holding the elevator door for me.

"You're something else," I tease. "I don't know how you went from getting pissed at me for being late with your coffee to buying me flowers and taking me on a date."

He wears a devilish smile. "You can't blame anyone for how they act before their first cup of coffee."

I shake my head, stepping into the back of his car. Something I've learned while dating Holden is that he barely drives anywhere, leaving it all to his driver.

Holden slides in next to me, nonchalantly putting his arm over my shoulder as the car pulls away from the curb.

"Where are we going tonight?" I ask.

"We're going back to my place."

I try to hide my shock. "A couple dates in and you're already taking me to your place?"

He bites his lip to hide his smile. "I was wondering what kind of reaction you'd have to that." He shakes his head. "Don't worry, I'm a gentleman. I've hired our own private chef for the evening."

"In that case, you can definitely take me back to your place." I give him a sly wink.

His finger lazily runs across my shoulder. "Dang, if I knew a private chef would've done the trick I would've hired him on our first date."

"Oh but I *loved* going to that motivational speaker conference with you."

He swats at my shoulder playfully. "I don't think you'll ever let me live that down. They said it was a bestselling writer and journalist speaking. I thought you'd like it."

"Well they were right, only it was a bestselling author on *meditation*." My nose crinkles remembering the cringey lesson on how to connect with your *inner chi*.

"I thought it was enlightening," Holden adds, pressing ignore on an incoming phone call.

"You *would* say that, you're always cool, calm, and collected. The only time I ever hold still is when I'm asleep."

"Forgive me for trying to impress the woman I'm courting."

My body shifts to face him. The leather is cool on the back of my thighs as I scoot closer to him, smoothing out a slight wrinkle in his shirt. "I'm going to pretend you didn't just say the word *courting*. And I appreciate the thoughtfulness of the date, really. No one has ever done something like this for me."

"What's wrong with the word courting?" he asks, a confused look on his face.

Shaking my head, I let my cheek rest against his arm, snuggling into him slightly. "Holden, no one uses the word courting."

"I don't give a damn what word people use," he responds, a hint of a smile on his face.

I've decided I'm meant to live the lavish lifestyle. First, Nash made me a travel snob with his private jet, and now I'm not sure I can ever eat a regular meal again. I'm going to starve unless I can figure out how to afford a private chef daily. Okay, maybe that's a little much—I'd take only having one a few nights a week. That seems more reasonable.

A pasta noodle falls from my fork when I look up at Holden, realizing I've been enjoying my food too much to say anything.

"Good?" he asks from across the large dining table. I didn't know people casually ate at kitchen tables meant for ten, yet here we are.

"This is the best pasta I've ever had." The sauce is sweet and buttery with a hint of garlic. If fancy had a taste, this would be it. Not to mention, there's a bottle of red wine sitting between us that I'm nervous to even know the cost of.

"I'm happy to hear that," he comments, delicately twirling the pasta around his fork.

When I try to do the same, all of the noodles fall off before the fork makes it anywhere near my mouth and I revert back to my cave-woman style.

He busies himself pouring us another glass of wine, giving me the opportunity to peer around his swanky condo some more. When I first walked in, I'd made a comment about how it was the biggest apartment I'd ever been in. Holden politely corrected me, stating that it was actually called a *condo*. No matter what you call it, it's way too nice for someone to live in.

For starters, there's breakables in every direction. I'm stuck wondering how you can do anything in this house without being afraid of breaking something. Even at the table we sit at, there's a bunch of extravagant, unused glassware just begging to be broken. Every time Holden passes a dish or the chef brings a new one over, I'm too busy making sure my elbows don't bump into anything to pay a word of attention to what they're saying.

"I want to know more about you, Riley," Holden says, folding up his napkin and setting it next to his plate.

He leans back in his chair, waiting for me to answer. His gaze on me feels safe and warm.

I take one last bite of my food before pushing the plate slightly away from me, careful not to disturb any of the other dishes.

Sighing, I cross my legs and get comfortable. "I'm not all that interesting."

"Isn't that for me to decide?"

I don't hide my smile. "Well for starters, I grew up in a home that *never* had this many breakable items. I had too many brothers for us to have this many nice things actually stay nice."

"When I was ten I accidentally shattered my mother's favorite vase by playing lacrosse in the house," he interjects.

"Yeah, another fact about me, I have zero idea what lacrosse is."

It's extremely obvious that Holden and I had very different upbringings. My mother didn't even have a nice vase—at least not out where my brothers could reach it. The only sports I grew up watching were my brothers playing football in hand-me-down cleats. I hadn't even heard of lacrosse until now.

"I can't tell if you're being serious or not," Holden says, his eyes narrowing as if he's inspecting me.

My hand rests against my heart. "Cross my heart. I have no idea what you're talking about."

"You surprise me, Riley," he admits.

"Is that a good thing or a bad thing?" I ponder, running a finger along what I think is a dessert fork.

"Only time will tell. But I enjoy your company," he says, his smile contagious.

We fall into silence as we watch the chef prepare our dessert. It's an alcoholic coffee, lit on fire as he pours it back and forth between two glass pourers. The spectacle is just as good as the coffee itself—amazing. Just like everything about this evening.

As the night winds down and Holden drops me off at home with a chaste kiss, I can't help but think there's something missing. Holden ticks every box I thought I wanted in a man. He's sweet, attentive, and lets me do most of the talking—and I enjoy talking. Things with him feel... *comfortable.* Months ago, I would've gone to bed thrilled with the night I'd just had. But dating my boss shouldn't feel comfortable, it should feel scandalous and secretive.

Laying down in bed, I realize that apparently my new type involves men that are arrogant and possessive—men who have no intentions of ever dating or settling down. Because despite having a great night with Holden, when I pull out my toy to relieve myself, my mind drifts to Sebastian.

SEBASTIAN

Looking back on my life, I barely remember a time where I didn't have some sort of job. As soon as I understood the value of having my own money, I started working. It began with doing odd jobs for anyone that would pay a kid under the table. It wasn't much, but it was often the difference between going to bed hungry or not.

Later on, I got a job working at a local martial arts gym, and it was one of the best things that ever happened to me. I was allowed to train there for free as long as I was working, and between those two things I was almost never home enough to be my dad's punching bag anymore. It basically saved me.

Having to work from a young age taught me to have good work ethic, which helped when I started as a bodyguard and work was nearly twenty-four-seven. Now, as I sit alone in my apartment, I'm wondering if working all of the time was borderline unhealthy. Because with Nash in rehab after drunkenly falling off stage at a concert, and my job on hold, I have no fucking clue what to do with my spare time.

The couch cushions have perfectly molded to my ass as I aimlessly flip through different news channels. I pause on one at the mention of Nash.

My blood begins to boil when an entertainment channel that *claims* to be news blasts a video of an incoherent Nash stumbling around in front of the crowd. My stomach turns as the show hosts both laugh when he falls off the stage.

Even though it's been weeks now, I can still remember the exact moment it happened. I'd told Matt the entire concert that something felt different. Nash had seemed even worse than usual, something we weren't sure was even possible.

I'd been stuck to him like glue the entire day, trying my damndest to keep him as sober as possible. But I failed. And the moment he plunged off the stage, into a pit of screaming fans, it felt like I'd hit rock bottom as well.

I can't recall another time in my life when I've blacked out, but I don't have any recollection of making it to Nash. One moment I was standing next to Matt on the side of the stage, and the next I was down in the pit, shielding Nash with my body. I remember feeling like I was being ripped apart as rabid fans clawed at me in an attempt to get to Nash. I was being touched in so many different places that my skin felt like it was on fire. I was too worried about Nash to pay much attention to the frenzy of unwanted touching, though. Phone cameras blinded me as I tried my best to locate Matt and the rest of the concert security team.

It was terrifying. The sheer amount of people trying to take advantage of Nash at his weakest point, instead of helping him, had me shook. Especially the women that were tearing at his clothes as Matt and I carried him away. It was sickening.

It's a moment I never want to relive and yet here I am, watching two people who know nothing about the situation make idle comments as if the situation was no big deal.

Comments about *my* best friend.

To me and Matt, it was crushing.

We'd failed him. His whole team had, really. We thought we were letting him cope the only way he knew how, but we let it go too far. We let him get up on stage when it clearly wasn't safe for him to be up there. We're lucky all he wound up with was a concussion.

And in a weird way, falling off that stage may have been the best thing for him.

Somehow, after the team practically begged him to go to rehab, he agreed he would.

And even though I was elated that he was getting the help he needs, I learned that being alone, with no job or sense of duty, is not a good thing for me.

My first day off I slept all day.

The second and third I begrudgingly got some chores done.

But after a week, I started to realize I have no real purpose. I felt lost knowing Nash won't need me for months.

And weeks later, I'm still just as lost.

Annoyed by the TV, I turn it off. I'm left staring at a black screen, wondering what the hell I'm going to do these next few months. I can only hit the gym so much, I need something else to fill this new void in my life.

I've also got to get myself busy so I stop thinking about *her.*

The woman I have no business thinking of, but the one who won't leave my mind.

It'd be easier if I could blame her for what transpired between Nash and Nora. At least then I'd have someone to blame for the situation I'm in now. But the more I think about it—and I've had a lot of time to think—the more I don't blame her. She was loyal to her friend, just like I would have been if the situation was reversed.

But it doesn't mean I don't *wish* I hated her.

Maybe then thoughts of her wouldn't creep into my mind at night.

My phone breaks the silence, vibrating loudly from the arm of the couch. I lunge for it, not used to it going off much these days.

The screen lights up with an old friend's picture. I swipe to answer.

"What's up, Max?"

"Sebastian motherfucking Compton!" he shouts from the other line. There's loud cheers from somewhere near him as my name is chanted over and over.

"Having a good time?"

"It'd be better if you came out with us for once."

I stare at my reflection on the TV screen, wondering if I should finally accept his persistent attempts to hang out. Part of me regrets telling him I had some time off, but maybe this is what I need to get out of my funk. It *has* been awhile since I've been with a woman. The night at the gala with Riley, to be exact. And since then, a random hookup hasn't had the same appeal it used to, so here I am.

No matter what I'm doing, my mind goes right back to Riley.

It infuriates me.

Maybe what I need to wipe her from my memory is to find a new woman. One that's easier to forget. But the thought of being with a new woman—having to explain my rules *again*—sounds daunting.

"I don't know man," I finally answer. My eyes take in my pathetic excuse of a living room. Until recently, I didn't spend much time at home, if any. There wasn't any need for me to have that many decorations or things that made it a home. But now, as I sit on the phone waiting for Max to finish his inebriated conversation with somebody on the other end of the line, I discover just how sad this place really is.

"What the hell do you mean you don't know? Do you have something better going on?"

Just some pining after a woman like a lovesick teenager instead of getting my shit together like a grown ass man, I think to myself. My silence tells him enough.

"If you don't get your ass to this bar I'm going to come

grab you myself," Max demands. Seconds later, my phone is vibrating with a text message from him. It contains the name and address of the club, one not too far away from my place.

"You do know I could easily escape you right?" I deadpan. Max was a great friend back in the day, but anytime he wanted to roll around and spar, I completely kicked his ass. He's no match for me.

"Does you think I care? You're coming out. I don't care what bullshit excuses you come up with."

I'm just about to spit out one of those bullshit excuses when for some reason, I decide not to. "Fine," I answer unenthusiastically.

"*Fine?*" he repeats.

"Yes, Max. I said fine."

"Fine as in you're coming?"

I sigh, getting up off the couch and heading to my room. I don't think it's a good idea for me to go to a club in the clothes I worked out in a few hours ago. "Fine as in I'll see you soon." I end the call before he can say anything else.

MAYBE I SHOULD'VE STAYED at home.

I thought a night out with the guys is what I needed, but I was wrong. There's too many people in this club for it to be comfortable. Every time I go to grab a drink, I feel like I'm working an event--shoving my way through the crowd to make room. At least at an event the drinks are free. Here, I'm paying twice as much for a majorly watered down version of my favorite whiskey, just to sit at a table with Max and a bunch of his friends—guys I've never even met. You'd think I'd at least appreciate the music, but in light of recent events, pop dance music just makes me feel depressed.

Shit, I'm turning into Matt.

It shouldn't surprise me that Max has met a bunch of new

friends. He's always been the more outgoing one of us. We used to hang out with the same crowd in high school, but he went off to college and I'm never home anymore. It's tough to maintain friendships when you're never in one spot for too long.

Max has been talking about the girl he recently started dating for what seems like an eternity when he finally pauses to offer me a shot. I wave it off—the smell of vodka brings back way too many memories of smelling it on Nash's breath. There's a great chance that I'll never want to take a shot of it again.

Suddenly, like some cheesy romance movie, the air around me changes. A familiarity seeps into my bones. I've had it drilled into me from the moment I became a bodyguard. *Always be aware of your surroundings*. And I am. I'm aware as ever when suddenly, I feel her presence.

Riley.

I ignore every single word coming out of Max's mouth, my full attention on Riley as she walks into the club. My hands tighten into fists when I notice she's on Holden's arm. She looks comfortable there, making me wonder how long they've been together. The way he casually slides his arm down her back, feeling that delicious curve before reaching her ass, lets me know this isn't the first time he's touched her like that.

My pulse beats erratically, as if my heart might jump out of my chest and claim her as mine. The thought jars me. She isn't mine. I don't necessarily even want her as mine. But damn does it sound like a good idea now that I'm watching her with *him*.

Holden wears a sport jacket. It's hot as hell here in California and yet the douchebag with his arm around her wears a jacket to the club. He's completely different than me. My t-shirt is plain and boring. I'd rather let my body do the talking.

"And then we're going to honeymoon on Mars," Max says, briefly breaking my fixation on Riley.

"Oh so *that* gets your attention," he mutters, shaking his head at me.

Another guy from the group laughs, throwing a jab my way.

"I'm going to go get another," I tell them, ignoring all of their rude comments. I hold up my beer that's still half full. I don't think a single one of them buys my excuse, but I don't care. I get up and stalk toward the bar nonetheless.

I grab a barstool at the very corner of the bar. It gives me a full vantage point of the area, the perfect place to keep an eye on things. Riley and Holden wait patiently at the bar, seemingly deep in conversation. He watches her as if she's the most interesting thing in the world. It pisses me off. I want to know what she's telling him. I'm fascinated by the way she seems to just slightly shy away from his touch. I pay close attention to their body language, wondering if it's wishful thinking or if she really doesn't seem into him.

A girl slides onto the stool next to mine, saying something I don't quite catch. I don't give her the time of day, too enamored with watching Riley interact with the man who has the nerve to touch what clearly isn't his.

Watching them, I know one thing for sure.

It'll take the restraint of a goddamn saint for me to stay away from her tonight.

RILEY

HOLDEN AND I WALK OUT OF WORK TOGETHER HAND IN HAND. We've been dating casually for a bit now, and I'm wanting it to go to the next level. I *need* to take the next step with him. I'm hoping after we hit any base other than making it out, it'll give me more clarity. That I'll finally stop thinking about the arrogant bodyguard who wants nothing to do with me and I'll be able to fully invest in the man who is clearly ready to take me seriously.

"What's the plan for tonight?" I ask, my high heels loud against the concrete. I've been trying to ask him all day where he's taking me tonight, but all he keeps saying is that it's a surprise.

Usually I love surprises, but today, I just want to know what's in store for us. I'm hoping it involves finally seeing this fine specimen of a man without a shirt, and that it possibly ends in an orgasm or two for me.

"We're going to a club," he says nonchalantly, steering me toward his car with his driver.

I try to hide my shock, looking down at my work attire wondering if I looks okay. "A *club*? You wouldn't be seen in a club."

He rolls his eyes flippantly. "My whole post-grad experience while getting my master's was spent in clubs and bars."

"You're joking," I say playfully.

He shakes his head, squeezing my hand softly. "I'm not joking. I can have fun."

"Keep telling yourself that."

"I'm a little hurt you don't think I'm fun," he pouts.

"Last year for our Christmas party you planned for us to play *bingo.* Do you not realize that everyone who works in our office is under the age of forty? We don't play bingo."

"It was holiday music bingo," he states, taking up for himself.

I look at him triumphantly, sliding into the backseat. "I rest my case."

"I'll be sure to ask your opinion next time."

"Might be for the best."

"Tell me, Holden, why are we going to a club?"

"Because, *Riley*, apparently I need to let loose and have some fun. So fun I will have." He gives me a look that I haven't felt from a man in a long time. His eyes tell me he's interested. That he wants this—us.

There's no doubt that Holden will be the hottest man in the club. His cheekbones are sharp and defined. And don't get me started on those long, gelled locks of his. He's perfected how to put each one of those wavy, dark brown pieces in place.

My eyes rake over his outfit, admiring how good he looks in casual clothes. Well, casual for Holden—he still wears a sport jacket, but at least a casual t-shirt is underneath. The man looks hot in his business attire at work, but seeing Holden in a pair of jeans is a treat in itself.

"Fun *we* will have," I correct, trying to hint at exactly where I want this to go tonight.

His lip twitches, finally stretching into what could be categorized as a smile. "Yes, Riley. Fun, we will have."

As we pull up to the club, there's already a line weaving all the way around the building.

"Holden, I don't know if we're going to be able to get in."

Leaning over me to look out the window, he sighs. "You underestimate me, Riley." He opens his door, looping around the car to open mine.

We get our fair share of dirty looks as we walk past the people in line. Some of them make comments, others ask where we think we're going. Holden doesn't answer them, he just holds my hand tighter in his grip.

I like that he's holding my hand in public, not hiding it from anyone.

Sebastian wouldn't do that.

Even though every person in that house with us in Colorado knew we'd hooked up, he barely looked at me the next day. Sure he flirted, *some.* But the man flirts with everyone. He wouldn't be caught dead showing affection, not unless it was during sex.

Holden breaks my thoughts when he stops us at the bouncer, shaking the guy's hand.

"Nice to see you, Kip," Holden says politely.

"How've you been?" the bouncer, apparently named Kip, asks.

Holden looks at me, a gleam in his eyes. "I've been *really* good."

Kip looks at me briefly before turning back to Holden. "Good to hear. Get in there before anyone says anything."

I don't point out that it's probably too late for that. The people in line watching us walk in all make snide comments. Kip ignores them, moving the rope just long enough to allow Holden and me through.

The floor beneath me shakes to the beat of the music. It isn't particularly late, but the club is already bustling. Flashing lights illuminate the people on the dance floor.

Holden lets go of my hand, his hand sliding down my back until it rests on the small of my back. He gently steers me toward the bar. We have to squeeze into an open spot while the bartender helps someone else on the opposite end.

"What will it be?" Holden asks. "Wait, let me guess…a vodka cranberry?"

My nose crinkles in disgust. "Gross. I'll take a martini, extra olives."

"*Wow,* I really got that one wrong."

"We can't all be perfect." I flip my hair dramatically.

The bartender finally makes his way to us. Holden orders my drink and a tequila on ice for himself. While we wait for our drinks Holden keeps me close to him, listening intently to every word I say.

We find a booth in the corner to enjoy our drinks. I lose all track of time, unsure of how long we sit together in the booth. Holden is great at keeping the conversation going. He's extremely open about his life, his goals, everything that makes him, him.

As the night passes, his body gets closer and closer to mine. Before I know it, his hand rests on my leg, tracing small circles over my thigh. My dress has ridden up, allowing him free reign over the exposed skin.

The small touch gives me flutters. I'm anxious to see where else this night could lead, ready to erase Sebastian as the last man I was with.

"Dance with me?" I ask, biting back a smile.

"Is that even a question?" His long legs slide out of the booth. He holds a hand out, escorting me to the edge of the throng of people moving their bodies to the beat of the music.

Twirling me, Holden pulls me against his body. He's quite a bit taller than me, even when I'm in heels. His head comes to rest on my shoulder, our hips beginning to move to the rhythm.

Song after song goes by, the two of us too busy exploring the other's body to pay much attention to the people around us. Eventually, Holden leans in close to my ear. "I'm going to go get us another drink."

I turn so my cheek presses against him, having to yell over the loud music and people around us. "Okay. Come find me."

"I will," he breathes, laying a soft kiss on my shoulder. A small flutter erupts in my belly. "You can count on that."

He backs away, leaving me in the middle of the crowd. He doesn't look away from me until the throng of people swallows him up. Never one to be shy, I continue to dance, perfectly fine with dancing on my own.

A body brushes against mine, a voice speaking loudly next to my ear. "Didn't expect to see you here, trouble."

I jump, turning to find Sebastian standing there. He looks angry, not fitting in with the people around him having the time of their lives dancing.

"What are you doing here?" I ask, taking in the sight of him. He wears a simple t-shirt and a dark pair of jeans, it shouldn't look that good. *He* shouldn't look that good. But god, the way the clothes mold to him has me remembering things about his body that I shouldn't be thinking about.

"I could ask you the same thing." He slowly walks toward me, as I spin back around, getting closer until there's only a small amount of air between his front and my back. Sebastian pauses, as if he's waiting to see if I'll step away from him.

I don't. I should, but I don't want to.

When he realizes I'm not moving, his hand snakes around my waist and slowly rests against my stomach. There's a fabric barrier, but I still feel that small touch all the way down my body.

He's not gentle when he pulls my body against his. "Do you know what it's felt like to watch his hands on you all night?"

My stomach clenches, his comment catching me off guard. His hand drifts down my stomach, getting dangerously close to the spot my dress ends on my thighs.

"I saw you walk in with him. I was minding my own business, talking to one of my buddies when the two of you showed up. He took your hand like it was the most natural thing in the world. I hated it." His fingers brush against the hem of my dress, tracing the fabric delicately.

He needs to go. I need to step away from his hands before Holden walks up and finds us like this.

Oh god, *Holden.* I'm the worst person for not thinking of Holden until now.

Sebastian's hands on me have stripped me of any other thoughts. I can't think straight with his hand slipping underneath my dress. There's so many people around us, shielding us from any wandering eyes outside the dance floor, but it won't be long until Holden comes back.

"Sebastian," I breathe, my body melting against his.

"I've watched you all night. I've watched *him* all night. Tell me, trouble, did it feel this good when he touched you?"

His knuckle brushes the inside of my thigh. "Use your words, Riley." The brush of his lips on the spot behind my ear makes my skin break out in goosebumps.

"No," I answer truthfully. All night he's been at the back of mind. I hate it, but my body doesn't respond to anyone's touch like it responds to his.

"Good girl," he responds, his finger dangerously close to the line of my underwear.

I swallow a moan when he applies pressure to my inner thigh, it feels like he's claiming me, trying to leave his fingerprints in a delicate spot.

I know that I'm wet when I shouldn't be, my body reacting the moment he pulled me against him.

He kisses the back of my neck tenderly. It feels more intimate than anything we've ever done together. I despise the feelings it elicits from me.

Sebastian keeps skirting around my inner thighs, curling his body around mine as if to shield me from the world. I'm incredibly turned on by the guy I did *not* arrive with, surrounded by people as he takes his sweet time familiarizing himself with my body. I shouldn't be doing this. I'm breaking every rule in the book, but my body won't listen to my brain.

I've missed his touch since the gala. And now that I'm getting it again, I'm not strong enough to walk away.

Even if everything about this is *wrong*.

He continues to lay kisses across my skin, each one more intimate than the last. Sebastian works his way from the base of my neck, to my shoulder, to the side of my neck. He's gentle, not biting me like our first night together. Between the tenderness of his lips, and the way his finger teases me, never quite reaching the spot I want him most, my senses are on overdrive.

"This right here," he gently taps the soaking wet spot on my underwear, "is mine. *You're* mine, trouble. Not his."

His words bring me back to reality. The possessive claim pisses me off. Coming to my senses, I push him away, trying to create distance between us in the mass of bodies.

"Fuck you, Sebastian," I say angrily, turning to face him.

He looks shocked. His hand runs over the front of his jeans, bringing attention to his large bulge.

"What's your problem?" he asks, trying to take a step closer to me.

I laugh. "My *problem*? Oh, that's cute," I tell him sarcastically. "My problem is that I'm not yours. You want nothing to do with me until you see me with someone else."

Moving my hair out of my face, I look around, trying to see if I can find Holden. Luckily, he still hasn't come back with our drinks. I don't know if I could ever look him in the eye again if he'd found us like that.

What the hell am I doing?

It's not like Holden and I are anywhere near exclusive—hell we've made out a handful of times and that's it. Still. The fact that we've only made out doesn't make me less of a shitty person. I'm letting another guy near me, allowing his hands on me, while I'm on a date with Holden. I *want* to know where things with Holden will go, but I have to leave Sebastian fully in my rearview mirror to do so.

"When did I say I didn't want anything to do with you?" Sebastian stares at me intently, his brown eyes watching me carefully.

"I'm not doing this." I try to find a gap between the people on the dance floor, needing to get away from him so I can think straight again.

Sebastian grabs me by the elbow, turning me toward him. "Riley, wait. We need to talk."

Rolling my eyes, I pull my arm from his grasp. "We have nothing to talk about, Sebastian. What just happened… shouldn't have happened. I need to go."

I dodge a couple making out, losing Sebastian in the process.

I don't look back over my shoulder as I make my way toward Holden. He stands at the bar, chatting with a guy next to him. He smiles when he sees me heading his way.

"Riley," he says, reaching his hand out. "What are you doing out here? Meet one of my friends from grad school, Thomas."

Thomas gives me a nod, holding his hand out.

I take it. "Nice to meet you," I mumble, too wound up to pay much attention.

"Everything okay?" Holden asks, looking at me worried.

I nod my head. "Yeah, I just don't feel good."

"Want to go home?" he asks, stepping away from the bar.

He begins to say goodbye to his friend, but I interrupt him. "You stay, Holden, catch up with Thomas. I'll catch an uber home."

Holden shakes his head. "No way. I'm not letting you leave alone."

I sigh, thankful that he's being a good guy, but flustered because I can barely look him in the eye right now. There's still wetness between my legs, elicited from another man.

"Okay. Let me just head to the restroom first."

His eyes scan over me, before he nods. "I'll meet you at the front."

Breaking away from the bar, I make my way toward the back in the direction of the restrooms.

When I'm there, I pull out my phone, thankful that an uber is nearby. As soon as the little car icon gets closer, I leave the bathroom and sneak out the back door before Holden can find me.

I know what I'm doing is shitty, but right now I need space to gather my thoughts and I can't do that with Holden around. He's too kind and observant, he'd know something was wrong instantly and I don't want to put up a front with him.

I look for the white sedan of the uber driver, sending a text to Holden to let him know I ran into a friend who was also leaving. I'm not sure he'll believe my lie, but I need some time to myself.

I need time to process what in the hell just happened.

Finally spotting the uber, I walk up to the window and confirm the name of the driver before opening the back door. I climb in, letting my head fall back against the headrest, the emotions from the night flooding me all at once.

Before the driver can pull away, the door across from me opens and Sebastian slides in.

SEBASTIAN

"What the fuck do you think you're doing?" Riley seethes. Her hand extends to the door handle, she tries to open it but the door doesn't budge.

"We need to talk," I demand, repeating myself from earlier.

"Uh, do you know him?" the uber driver asks uncomfortably. The guy can't be much older than twenty. He's watching me as if I'm some serial killer that just slipped into his car. The fear in his eyes contrasting the rage in Riley's.

"No."

"Yes."

Her head swivels, her eyes screaming with anger. "Get out of my uber."

"Listen, do I need to call the cops?" The guy in the front picks his phone up from the cup holder.

My hands fly into the air. "Jesus, Riley. Tell him he doesn't need to call the cops."

"Not until you get the hell out of this car."

I run my hand over my mouth in frustration. "I just want to talk to you. Please," I add softly.

I was seeing red the moment I spotted her walking into the club with him. In the time since the gala, I'd wondered if something had transpired between Riley and her boss. I guess tonight is my answer. Seeing her walk into the club brought back all of my bullshit feelings, sending them straight to the forefront of my mind.

"Fuck you," she says, breaking me from my thoughts.

"Maybe later, trouble," I mutter under my breath. "You can go now," I tell the uber driver, settling deeper into my seat.

The guy looks over his shoulder to Riley. "Is that okay?"

A frustrated breath leaves her mouth. "It's fine. Just help me hide his body when I murder him, okay?"

"This better be a good tip," the driver says so quietly I almost don't catch it. He pulls into the flow of traffic, leaving both Riley and me trapped in the car together.

"I'd love to see you try," I toss out, folding my arms over my chest.

She looks at me, narrowing her eyes. "Don't tempt me."

"Everything okay back there?" the driver asks nervously. He's got both hands on the wheel and he's holding it the way I imagine a kid on the first day of driver's ed would. His knuckles are white and he's bound to get a kink in his neck if he leans any closer to the windshield.

"No. I've been kidnapped," Riley snaps, turning her body to face the window. She's basically glued herself to the rear passenger door. She's made it so she's as far away from me as possible.

"I think we're being a little dramatic," I say under my breath.

Her head swivels. "*Dramatic?*"

"Just a little."

"Oh that's great coming from the man who just ruined my perfectly good evening."

"Funny, it couldn't have been that perfect if you ran out on it."

She opens her mouth to say something, but the uber driver slams on his breaks and we jolt forward. "Will the two of you shut up for two seconds?" he shouts.

His outburst manages to do the trick. Riley and I sit speechless as the kid regains his breath.

"I'm trying to drive and the two of you arguing is distracting. Just don't talk for the rest of the ride."

"He started it," Riley mumbles, otherwise following directions.

I choose not to respond, not wanting to stress this kid out any further. Plus, I'll have plenty of time to get my words in the moment we make it to her place.

The tension in the car is palpable, even with neither of us speaking a work to each other for the duration of the ride. I know the moment we get out of this car, she's going to let me have it. And I'm fully prepared for it.

Fighting with her is better than watching some other man have his hands all over her.

The car is barely in park before Riley is opening her door and darting out onto the street like a bat out of hell. I go after her, not letting her out of my sight. She bursts through the doors of her building, not giving anyone a second glance on her way to the elevator.

On the ride up to her room, she looks at me with disdain. "If you make my uber rating go down I'm going to cut your dick off."

Her comment gets my attention. I look at her, eyebrows raised. "Are you into knife play, trouble?"

"You're annoying." Turning to face the opposite side of the elevator, Riley tunes me out for the remainder of the ride up.

I follow her silently all the way to her door. Keeping my mouth shut as she unlocks it and angrily waves me inside.

The apartment is dark, and for the first time since I climbed in a car with her without any kind of plan, I wonder where Nora is.

Walking over to flip the light on, she takes a deep breath. And then she unleashes all of her pent up rage.

"I can't believe you followed me home like a damn stalker!"

"Is it technically being a stalker if you knew about it?"

"Sometimes I hate you."

"Weird, I vividly remember you saying my name in pleasure as I went down on you."

She sets her purse down on the counter. "Just tell me whatever the hell you want to tell me and then leave. I'm tired."

My feet bring me toward her until she has nowhere to go. I make sure to leave some space between our bodies, but not much.

"I want to talk," I tell her, reaching out and running my index finger down her arm.

She lets out a frustrated sigh. "Talk about what, Sebastian?"

"Talk about how you shouldn't be out with him."

"And how I should be out with you instead?"

"Maybe. What's so wrong with that?"

"Nothing is *wrong* with that, Sebastian, except for the fact you've never once made it seem like you wanted to go on a date."

"Because I didn't think you wanted to go on a fucking date. You knew the rules. You didn't seem like the kind of girl who wants flowers." I point to the vase sitting behind her.

"No, you're right. According to you, I'm the girl you fuck in secret and pretend doesn't exist after you've had your needs met."

My teeth grind against one another. "I never said that."

"I liked the flowers," she tells me defiantly, plucking one of the long-stemmed daisies from the vase. She lifts the flowers to her nose, inhaling deeply.

"He can buy you flowers. But will he give you what you *really* want?"

I close the remaining distance between our bodies, needing to feel her pressed against me. My hands find her hips, lifting her and setting her down on the counter behind her.

Taking the flower from her hand, I begin to run it along her leg. The petals brush softly against her calf. "You're not the kind of girl who wants flowers, Riley. You're the kind of girl who wants excitement, a thrill. You don't want goddamn flowers."

Grabbing her neck, I pull her face to mine, devouring her the second I come in contact with her mouth. I throw the flower to the ground, the petals scattering at our feet.

The fight in her from earlier is forgotten—at least for now. Her lips work against mine powerfully. I'm relishing in the feeling of her fingers running against my scalp, gently tugging my head into the position she wants it.

I take her bottom lip between my teeth, pulling her legs so they wrap around my waist. Her heels fall to the ground with a soft *thud.*

Arching her back, she pulls away. "Why does it have to feel this way with you?"

"I keep asking myself the same damn thing."

"I don't want to watch you leave in the morning, Sebastian."

Her words hit me hard, making me pause before kissing her once again. "Then I won't."

"You can't mean that." Her voice is just a whisper against my lips, but by the way it wreaks havoc in my head—and in my heart—it may as well have been a scream.

"If you're telling me you want me to be here in the morning, then I'll be here in the morning. But don't be surprised if I want *you* for breakfast."

Her head falls forward, resting against my shoulder. The hot air of her breath permeates my thin t-shirt when she speaks. "I don't think I would've stopped this even if you said no."

My hands wrap around each side of her face, my thumbs

resting on her angled cheekbones. "This is different for me, too. I won't promise anything other than I'll be here in the morning."

Leaning down slowly, I land a soft kiss on her pink lips. It's the softest kiss we've shared, but it messes with my mind the most. It tastes like promises and new beginnings and I don't know how to feel about it.

Time passes as the two of us do nothing but kiss. Our hands don't have ulterior motives, we just let go, enjoying the feeling of our mouths pressed against one another.

Eventually, I can't take it anymore. *I need more.* I need to taste every other inch of her, to feel her come apart from my touch. I need to know I can still drive her wild.

"Do you trust me, trouble?" I ask, moving a blonde lock of hair out of her eyes.

She nods, biting her lip in anticipation.

"Then lay down."

She looks at me in alarm, running a hand over the cold granite. "Right here?"

"Right here."

"What is up with you and countertops?" she says under her breath, still following my direction. She holds her body up by her elbows, looking at me in anticipation. I lightly pull on each one of her legs, bringing them up so the balls of her feet rest on the edge of the countertop. Then I slide her feet until her legs are spread wide open for me.

"You rip this thong and you're dead," Riley says, adjusting her hips.

I smirk. "Tempting, trouble. I don't want anything to do with these." I reach up, hooking a finger in the fabric and pulling it down her thighs. "You put these on thinking that boring little boss of yours would actually appreciate them. What a shame that I'm the one ripping them off you tonight."

With her thong discarded somewhere at our feet, I find her wet, willing and ready for me to taste her.

I lean in, planting a kiss on the inside of her thigh right next to the part of her that's dripping for me and only me. My lips tease her skin as she writhes underneath me, trying to steer my mouth to her center.

Still a little pissed off from watching her with another man all night, I make her wait. I let my tongue take one lap of her before I pull away.

Her angry eyes find mine.

"You didn't think it would be that easy did you, trouble?"

My feet take me around the island, my body now up by her head. I let my hand pet the soft tendrils of her hair, moving some of it out of her face.

"You got all dressed up and put on your prettiest pair of underwear for another man." I tsk, pulling at the neckline of her dress. "You're going to pay for that. You let him touch what's mine."

"I wasn't under the impression I was yours."

Her comment stops me. I look at her, trying to get a reign on my possessiveness. "Let me be *very* clear. I don't want anyone else touching you but me. Understood?"

"You don't get to say things like that, Sebastian."

"Watch me."

Riley doesn't respond, she's too busy watching my every move. It's not often that this woman is speechless. I pull one arm and then the other through the sleeves of the dress, leaving the thin fabric bunched around her waist. Her tits lay heavy and ready.

I'm about to take one of her peaked nipples in my mouth when I get an idea. She looks at me curiously as I pull one of the daisies from the vase not too far from her head.

I stand next to her, spinning the stem of the flower between my thumb and index finger. One of the petals falls off, fluttering in the air until landing on the counter. "Are these what you want, trouble?"

Bringing the flower to my nose, I inhale. "You want pretty

flowers that will wilt and die? Is that what you want from a man?"

"They're pretty." Her voice is strained, the words laced with want.

I hum in understanding. Running the petals of the flowers over her lips. "Since when did you want pretty things, trouble?" I trace the petals of the flower down her throat, over each collarbone.

"You didn't seem to want *pretty* that first night we were together. If I remember correctly...you didn't like pretty, you liked sloppy."

"I just—" her words fall flat when I circle the soft petals of the flower around her nipple. Goosebumps pop up all over her skin.

"How do you think it makes me feel," I begin, giving attention to her other nipple, "when I see some prick's hands on you?"

"He's not a prick," she moans, arching her back off the counter as I circle the petals around her belly button.

I stop, lifting the flower and letting it dangle in the air. "Yes. He is. Any man that thinks he'll possibly be able to bring you the pleasure that I do is a stupid prick."

"Last I checked, you don't give a shit about me." Her legs fall open once more as the flower skirts over her wetness.

I use the daisy to draw loops on the tops of her thighs, looking her straight in the eye. "That's false, trouble. I'm afraid no matter how much I don't want to, I give a shit. And I have no fucking idea how to handle it."

One of her knees begins to fall inward, blocking my view of her. Placing my hand on the inside of both her knees, I push her legs open so all of her is in front of me again. The flower falls out of my hand, discarded on the floor, right where it belongs.

"For now, I'm going to make you remember why the fuck

you don't care about flowers." My middle finger enters her, feeling just how ready she is for me.

When I pick up pace, she begins to writhe underneath me. Judging by how much she's moving, I can tell she's close.

"If you're going to come, you're going to come on this dick or on my face, trouble." I steady her by wrapping an arm around her thigh and pressing down on her midriff. Holding her in place, I seal my mouth against her pussy.

It doesn't take long before her moans echo off the surrounding walls. She claws at my hair, riding the waves of her orgasm.

Standing to my full height, I lean over her until we're face-to-face. When I look down, I find a bead of sweat traveling down her sternum.

"That was…"

"Better than flowers?" I finish for her, not bothering to hide the smirk on my face.

"Way better than flowers."

The timid smile on her face does so many things to me. Foreign things. Things that can't lead to anywhere good with my fucked up perception of love or feeling.

I feel a feather-light touch against my oblique. It's so light I almost miss it. It's just strong enough to register. Slowly, she applies more pressure until the tips of her fingers are branding the small sliver of skin showing between my t-shirt and the waistband of my boxers.

"I want to do the same for you," she announces, getting braver with her touch.

It's the first time I've let a woman touch me like this. Or at least, the first time I've let someone *willingly* touch me like this.

Growing up with a piss-poor father did a lot of things to fuck me up. One of those things being how I view women. He'd have a new woman at our house every night. They'd get high together. And sometimes, when it was a good night for me, he'd trade in taking shots at me for a tumble in the bedroom with them.

Other nights, he thought it was funny to have those women make a pass at me. It started when I was thirteen. I was tall for my age, and where puberty had my peers breaking out in zits and still looking scrawny, it did other things to me.

My muscles began to become defined, my baby fat all but lost. The women frequenting our house started to take notice. They'd ask my dad how old I was—if I wanted to join in. This humored him—until it didn't.

He'd let them run their hands all over me, no matter how many times I said no. But I tried to respect the women. I didn't know what to do in those moments. I couldn't just shove them off. Eventually, I learned fighting back would only make me even more of a punching bag for my dad.

Sometimes, the women would get *too* interested in me. Then it would really set him off.

There were nights that I gave in, succumbing to the scrape of a woman's fake nails all over me just so I didn't take a beer bottle to the head. Unfortunately, most of those nights, the woman became a little *too* into it. And then my dad would get jealous and take it out on me.

Until one day, after spending years doing martial arts, I decided to hit back.

Harder. In the places that hurt the most.

After that, I never gave him the opportunity to touch me again. I never gave *anyone* the opportunity to touch me. Not unless I told them *where* and *how* to do it.

Until now—and at this moment, I want to feel her touch anywhere and everywhere.

I don't know if I've ever felt shy a day in my life. It just isn't who I am. But right now, sitting on this kitchen counter, my hand timidly exploring Sebastian's bare skin, I'm the most cautious I've ever been.

I hold my breath, just waiting for the other shoe to drop. Waiting for him to push my hand away and say something smartass before he distracts me by touching me somewhere. It's what he's done in the past.

But the more my fingers feel the slopes and ridges of his abs, the more his eyes become hooded. His forehead drops to my shoulder, the muscles in his body relaxing with my touch.

"Trouble, trouble, trouble." His voice is strained and muffled by my hair. "Your touch is intoxicating."

A shaky breath leaves my body.

I've become so accustomed to the brutally honest, cocky Sebastian that this vulnerable version of him throws me off-kilter.

I don't know how to proceed. I don't know what we're doing.

But for tonight, I want to forget all the reasons that he and I could never work and pretend that for once, this unattainable man might actually want more than just my body.

Slipping my hand in the waistband of his jeans and briefs, I let my hand travel down his warm skin. My fingertips brush his tip. Curiously, I wrap my fingers around him, paying attention to his every reaction when he lifts his head to look at me.

A muscle ticks in his jaw, the flutter matching my racing pulse. As soon as I begin to pump up and down, he closes his eyes. After watching him react to every rise and fall of my hand, I decide I want more.

The backs of my thighs slide against the countertop as the tips of my toes hit the floor. Dropping to my knees, I pull his jeans and underwear down his hips, completely freeing him.

"You don't have to," Sebastian says softly, his fingers brushing the hair from my face.

"I don't have to do anything. I want to, desperately." My fingers wrap around him, stroking his shaft as I lean in closer. The tip of my tongue explores his head before I take his full length in my mouth.

I take him as deep as my throat allows. His fingers that gently moved my hair aside now tangle tightly in the strands. He doesn't force my head down, letting me decide the pace as I bob up and down on him.

I'm surprised at how long he lets me take his length in my mouth, exploring with my tongue. Eventually, he takes control once again.

"You can suck my cock again later, trouble," he says. His hands pick me up from underneath my armpits. The second I come face-to-face with him, he's attacking my mouth with his. We make out, my legs wrapped around his middle as he walks across the kitchen.

He balances me in one hand, turning the knob on the door when I look up.

"This is Nora's room," I state, pointing over my shoulder to my closed door.

Sebastian pauses, as if he's contemplating continuing to her room anyway. He sighs, turning around and making his way to my room. The door bounces against my wall loudly when he throws it open. Wasting no time, he carries me to my bed and we fall down onto the plush comforter together, neither one of us wanting to break apart.

His weight pushes me into the mattress as his lips work wonders against my mouth. I've kissed plenty of men in my life, but none of them hold a candle to Sebastian.

The moment he pulls his lips off mine, I'm already begging to feel them once again. Sitting back, he grabs the bunched up fabric around my waist. He pulls the dress off in one fluid motion, leaving me completely naked.

Acting as if we have all the time in the world, his eyes roam over every exposed inch of me. I try not to squirm as his heated stare focuses on each of my nipples, and then on the pooled wetness between my legs.

I've never been one to be super self-conscious about my body, but it's not hard to feel uncomfortable when every bare inch of you is on display for someone. I know there's lines on each of my breasts, my boobs going up a couple cup sizes the summer I got my first period.

My stomach varies from day to day, fluctuating based on what I eat.

But in this moment, none of my insecurities come to light with his stare on me. They're all but forgotten. It seems impossible for anyone to feel insecure about themselves when a man as sexy as Sebastian is looking at them the way he's looking at me.

He makes me feel like the most beautiful woman in the world.

I just wish that feeling could last longer than a night.

"I could spend every waking minute of my life getting to know each and every curve of your body," he marvels, his fingertip brushing against my ribcage.

With the way he's looking at me right now, this doesn't feel like *just sex* anymore. No matter how hard I want to fight against it, I know deep down I'm developing feelings for him. I want to crawl inside my own heart and cut each one of those little things before they can mature anymore. My mind is wise enough to know a man like Sebastian won't give me what I want long-term.

He admitted it himself. He's the guy that you have fun with, the guy that teaches you things about your body you didn't even know yourself. But he's not the guy that keeps you forever, his heart forever unattainable.

I know it with every fiber of my being—I've caught feelings for Sebastian. It transcends just sex now. But I know I either need to fight them tooth and nail, or let them stay unspoken forever. Neither option leads to more time with him.

"Do you want to know what I thought when I first met you?" he says, pulling me out of my thoughts.

"That I need to stop flirting with the hot pilot?"

He laughs. "Okay, the *second* thing."

"If you're about to say something inappropriate…"

"I joked, in my head, that I already loved you. Your sharp tongue, the way you didn't try to impress Nash when you first met him. *I was so turned on by it.*"

"I for sure thought you were going to comment on my rocking bod." My hands run down my torso, catching his glance.

"You're more than your body, trouble." Taking my breath away, he leans down and kisses the stripes on my hips. His breath is hot as he lets his wet tongue run across my abdomen and up to the lines on my breasts.

This man.

Casual fuck buddies shouldn't be kissing every piece of you that makes you insecure.

His hands slide underneath my ass. He lifts me by the hips, lining me up perfectly with his mouth. Again, he's ravishing me with his tongue, taking me places I didn't know existed until him.

I thought multiple orgasms was some kind of magical fantasy that never happened for women. Hell, even with my trusty purple friend I can't typically get one right after the other.

Sebastian's finger slips from tracing my clit, down my seam until he gently circles a place I've never had someone touch. I jerk, unfamiliar with the pressure on that part of me.

"Relax," he whispers into the dark, only pulling away long enough to say those words before his tongue gets back to work. The tip of his finger slowly enters me. With the feeling of the unfamiliar pressure and his tongue still working meticulously, I know I'm close to coming again.

"I'm going to come," I moan.

He answers by both his tongue and finger working faster, harder. In no time, I'm writhing against him. His fingertip bores into the fleshy part of my ass as he holds me against him, making sure I get every last bit of pleasure from this one.

Setting down my hips, he crawls across my body until we're eye to eye again. He uses the back of his hand to wipe the evidence of my arousal from his face.

It's *so* fucking hot.

Seeing what he's done to me still lingering on the perfect lines and angles of his face is intoxicating.

"Not complaining about the orgasms or anything," I breathe, reaching down to shove his pants the rest of the way off him. "But can we skip to the part where you fuck me now?"

His lips quirk, a smile finally following suit. "I love it when you boss me around, trouble." Sliding off the bed, he steps out of his shoes and yanks his pants off.

He wastes no time coming back to the bed. Settling between my legs, he looks at me, the gleam in his eyes a promise of what's to come. "Do you want me to fuck you, trouble?" Teasing me, he rubs the tip of his cock down my wetness. I try to align my body with it so he enters me, but he foils my plan.

"Use your words."

"Yes, Sebastian," I moan. "Fuck me, damnit."

He isn't gentle when he sheathes himself fully in me. At first, he stays upright as he drills into me over and over. I have nothing to grab onto, his body too far away from me to reach in this position. My fingers twist around the fabric of the comforter, needing to hold onto something to keep me steady.

Just as I feel another release building, he slows down his rhythm. Shocking me, he leans down. Our fronts now completely pressed against one another, my hands free for the first time in this position.

Cautiously, I let go of the comforter, bringing one of my hands to rest on his lower back as he pushes into me.

He doesn't jump at my touch, or push my hand away. He does something worse. He looks me in the eyes, those brown eyes of his looking more vulnerable than I've ever seen them. "Touch what you want," he says, running a fingertip across my lip. "I want you to make it go away," his voice is raspy as he utters the words against my throat. "To replace the bad memories with *this.* With the feel of your touch. Erase it all."

Pressing my palm deeper against his skin, I take my time running my hand over the taut muscles of his back. My fingers dance over the tattoos on his arms, the black ink creating designs spanning both arms.

He moves in and out of me slowly. Each one of his thrusts seems deliberate, as if he's trying to make this moment last forever. I let him, not knowing if he'll ever give me this opportunity again.

It feels weird to have *vanilla* sex with him. My arms aren't locked over my head, and he doesn't have me testing my flexibility in some unique position. There is something pure and perfect in his vulnerability that makes me want to hold onto this moment forever.

SEBASTIAN

I CAN COUNT ON ONE HAND THE NUMBER OF TIMES I'VE WOKEN up to find a woman in bed with me. And that includes now.

I've never really been one to invite someone back to my place. In high school, it was because my dead-beat dad was always home. The last thing I wanted to do was subject those poor girls to him. As I got older, it just became routine. I'd become accustomed to never inviting a woman back to my place, even when I lived alone.

The great thing about sleeping over somewhere else was how easily I could sneak out in the middle of the night. Every woman I've ever hooked up with has known that I'm not looking for anything serious, but that doesn't mean some don't think they'll be the one to change me. Leaving early prevents those awkward conversations and broken promises of another meeting that'll never actually happen. But with Riley, it's never been that easy.

After the first night Riley and I hooked up, I spent thirty minutes in the morning watching her sleep. Some may call it creepy, but I couldn't help myself. I was intrigued by the woman next to me. I spent the whole time trying to figure out what was so unique about her.

What made me want to stay in that bed?

I couldn't put my finger on it. All I knew was something was different with her. We were cut from the same cloth—

both loyal and stubborn. If the two of us were magnets, we would completely repel each other. But instead, despite all logic and science, I find myself being pulled into her force-field, unable to fight the attraction.

But just like with so many women before her, the moment Riley began to stir after our first night together I found myself in a familiar spot, sneaking out of the room we'd shared.

Because I knew better.

I knew I was already toeing a boundary by sleeping with Riley—someone I almost certainly would see again. Sex can complicate things, and I shouldn't have mixed business with pleasure. Not with someone so close to my boss. Not with the intention of never wanting more from her.

At least, I hadn't expected to want more.

Now, I'm met with another opportunity to watch her sleep, another morning I don't want to leave her bed, and another chance to second-guess myself—to further complicate things.

If the last few weeks have taught me anything, it's that my job is one of the most important things in the world to me. Nash has hit rock bottom. He's gone *past* rock bottom. I can't help but wonder what he would think about Riley and me. The last thing I want is to be in a position where I have to choose between two people I care about.

Furthermore, I know I shouldn't be doing this for the mere fact Riley deserves more than what I can give. It was a lot for me to promise to stay in the morning. It's completely out of character for me and breaks every single rule I've set for myself. But me promising to stay doesn't change my stance on relationships. I don't have any idea on how to approach a relationship, and Riley deserves better than that. Apparently, I don't care too deeply about that, either, because I still don't find myself leaving her bed.

This is new territory for me. I have zero fucking clue what I'm doing. I don't do *morning after* breakfast. Yet here I am, wondering if she likes eggs and bacon or if she'd prefer to have waffles.

Her blonde hair is in knots, the tendrils having a mind of their own as they fan out in different directions on her pillow. She looks adorable lying next to me. Her knees are pulled all the way into her chest. I had no idea that someone could sleep in such a tiny little ball. It looks terribly uncomfortable to me, but clearly it's working for her. She hasn't stirred at all the entire time I've been watching her sleep.

Trying not to disturb her, I slide off the bed. I use the morning sun breaking through the window to find my discarded underwear from the night before. We spent most of the night getting reacquainted with each other's bodies. It wasn't rough and hurried like it was at the charity gala. It was slow—and something much more. Neither one of us had bothered to put on clothes, knowing that they wouldn't stay on for long before we were tangled in the sheets once again.

I narrowly avoid stubbing my toe on her dresser as I make my way out of her room. The floor creaks underneath my bare feet as I head toward the kitchen. Riley had told me last night that Nora shouldn't be home until tomorrow night, giving me time to pretend I'm not messed up a little while longer.

Opening the refrigerator door, I begin to rifle through the contents. I can't help but wonder how two humans are surviving off the measly amount of food in this fridge. I scan my eyes over some of the contents—three eggs left in a carton, a half-eaten container of blueberries, and a super-size bottle of ranch. I desperately search the other items, noting they don't have much else. There's a few leftover containers shoved in the back of the fridge. One thing they do have a good amount of is wine bottles. There's four half-drank bottles taking up most of the space. When I open the freezer door, I find microwave dinners and various ice cream cartons, and nothing else.

I pull ingredients from various locations until I *think* I have enough to make a decent breakfast. It figures, the first time I try to cook a woman breakfast and I'm stuck with little to nothing to work with.

I'm reminded of those weird cooking shows where contestants are only allowed to use certain ingredients to make a delectable meal. The only difference is, I don't win a bunch of cash if I do well here. Nope. The stakes are much higher.

I try to give it my best shot however, wanting to do something nice for Riley. Something to prove to her that I'm not breaking my promise from last night.

I open every cabinet in the kitchen before finally finding the one holding exactly *one* frying pan. One. I'm a bachelor, I'm almost never home, and I still manage to have a full set of pots and pans.

How do the two of them live like this? I wonder, setting the pan on the burner.

I've made an absolute mess of the kitchen by the time Riley pads down the hallway. She yawns, clearly still trying to fully wake up. She's somewhat tamed her hair into a messy braid. She's thrown on my t-shirt from the night before. It's large on her, coming down to her mid-thigh. When she aims a sleepy smile my way, I feel things deep down that are totally new.

"Did you make breakfast?" she asks softly, closing the distance to where I've laid the meal out on the island.

"I attempted to," I begin, suddenly self-conscious of the spread in front of us. "It was a little hard considering you had absolutely no fucking groceries to choose from."

Riley plucks one of the blueberries from a plate, plopping it into her mouth with a smile. "I've been too busy to go shopping."

My eyebrows pull together in a scowl. "Too busy gallivanting around with your boss?" I say, a slight edge to my voice.

She eats up my jealousy. "A lady never kisses and tells, Sebastian."

I reach out to pull the plates from the counter. "Well in that case, I'm eating all of the breakfast."

Riley hits me on my bicep. "Give the food back right now."

Holding a plate in each hand, I bring them over my head, out of her reach. "I'm making breakfast for a woman for the first time in my life and I'm being thanked like this?"

She mulls my words over. Stepping closer to me, she cautiously runs a hand over my cheek. "I was just joking. It wasn't because of Holden."

I watch her carefully. She looks sincere, and even if she wasn't joking, it's not like I could blame her for moving on with her life.

"If you say his name again, I'm going to bend you over this counter and fuck you until you forget he even exists."

"You make that sound like it's a bad thing."

Her eyes rake over the food on the plate. There weren't a lot of options, so I had to get creative. An over-easy egg sits on her plate. I have no idea how she takes her eggs, so I just took my best guess. I had to use the butt end of the loaf of bread to make a pathetic excuse for french toast. I tried making it look more appetizing by putting a scoop of ice cream and some fresh blueberries on it, but the ice cream has slowly melted and now it's just a big, gooey mess.

She dips her finger into the melted ice cream. She knows exactly what she's doing when she licks it off the tip of her finger, pulling her cheeks in.

"You really made this for me?" she asks, grabbing the fork and taking a bite.

I nod, too busy watching her take her bite to fully respond.

Riley moans, closing her eyes in pleasure. "This is delicious."

I look at her suspiciously. "You're lying."

"No I'm not. This is so fucking good."

"I had to make it out of the butt of the loaf of bread, it can't be *that* good."

She cuts herself a heaping bite, shoveling it into her mouth. She talks through a mouth-full of french toast. "What if I love the butt?"

I roll my eyes, taking a bite of my concoction. I discover she may not actually be lying. The french toast isn't half bad, all things considered. The large mass of ice cream melting all over it probably helps.

We eat our food, engaging in a casual conversation the whole time. It's the most mundane of things, but it feels powerful. It gives me a small glimpse of normalcy. It makes me want more mornings eating french toast with her. The realization is slightly terrifying.

"I'm so full," Riley says, pushing her plate away from her. Her shoulders hit the back of the barstool. "I can't eat anything else."

Grabbing her plate, I eat the remainder of food she left on there, having emptied mine five minutes ago.

"I'm glad it wasn't a total disaster."

"It was amazing. Be careful, Sebastian. Between the mind-blowing sex last night and breakfast this morning, you might have me believing that I actually *mean something* to you." She exaggerates the last part, throwing my words from months ago right back at me.

"Well, now that you bring that up…" I begin, feeling uncomfortable. I've been waiting for this to come back up. I need to explain myself more, I just haven't known how to bring it up myself.

"We don't have to talk about it, Sebastian." She takes a drink of water, probably to keep herself busy or ignore the awkward feeling in the air.

"I want to talk about it, I do. I'm just shit at talking about things like this."

"Your feelings?"

I scratch my head. "You could say that."

I'm hoping she'll help fill the silence, give me more time to approach the topic, but she doesn't. She just watches me expectantly, making it clear she's waiting for me to make the first move.

Sighing, I try to form the right words. "That night of the hometown concert, I said some things I shouldn't have. I was pissed at Nora for what she did, and I took it out on you instead. Since you knew..."

"I'm not trying to make excuses for myself," she interrupts. "I know keeping her secret was wrong. But you have to understand that I'd known about her true feelings. About how much she wished she hadn't done what she did. About how in love with him she was. I knew she regretted her choice the minute she got to know him. I'm not trying to make excuses for her either, I'm just saying there was more to the story. Not saying we were in the right, but..."

"Something can be *not* wrong, and *not* right. It can just be..."

"In the gray area?" she finishes for me.

"Yeah. Anyway, when I found out you knew, it was more disappointing than anything. I saw something different about you and I wanted you to be better than that. At that moment, it didn't feel complicated. It felt like what you did was just —wrong."

"I'm sorry, for what it's worth."

"I'm sorry, too."

"So you're saying our night together wasn't so meaningless after all?" A playful smile overtakes her face. The sun hits her cheeks perfectly, the sight of her in the morning light absolutely breathtaking.

I scoff, tapping the tip of her nose. "I don't think anything with you could ever be meaningless, trouble. Things would be a lot simpler if they were."

My finger brushes over her top lip and she playfully nips at the tip of it. "You mean things between us aren't simple?"

"Do you want it to be simple?" I question, trying not to act as nervous as I feel.

I feel like I'm under a fucking microscope as her eyes roam all over me. I've asked something vulnerable, something I never do. Something I've actively avoided for years. It makes me feel itchy—vulnerable.

She takes forever to answer me, probably just to fuck with my head. This push and pull seems to be our thing, the two of us constantly battling for the upper hand.

"No. I don't need simple. I'm not a fan of things that are boring."

"Really?" I ask, feigning surprise.

"You know what *wouldn't* be boring?" She quips. "Your mouth on mine."

"I whole-heartedly agree." Moving closer to her, my hands find either side of her face, pulling it close to mine.

And then I kiss her, not giving a single fuck that nothing about us will ever be simple.

I'M IN TROUBLE. BIG, *BIG* TROUBLE. WHICH IS IRONIC, BECAUSE that also happens to be Sebastian's nickname for me.

I'm in the biggest of pickles.

After spending an entire day with Sebastian, I've come to the conclusion that I, without a doubt, have feelings for the asshole.

It wasn't a secret that we were already familiar with each other's bodies before today. But now that I've gotten to know his mind, I'm in deeper than I'd ever intended.

We've spent two hours building a sheet fort. I'll say that again, *a sheet fort.* Our first attempt was going to be in the living room, but the furniture was too spread out to make it work. We settled on my bedroom, piling up pillows and scrounging up sheets and thin blankets from every corner of the apartment until we had fashioned the most perfect of forts.

It's weirdly romantic and cheesy. I don't typically do cheesy, and I certainly didn't peg Sebastian as the type. The one time a man actually bought me flowers, Sebastian had to go and point out all the reasons I've never been the biggest fan of them in the first place.

But today, I'm afraid, is the definition of cheesy.

The two of us lay inside the fort, admiring our work in

silence. The string lights that are strung across my ceiling shine brightly through the sheets, creating a soft glow around us. Sebastian lays next to me, only a pair of jeans on his body. When he'd tried to put on his t-shirt, I'd snatched it from his hands, deciding it looked better on me.

I'm staring at the sheet above me, wishing that this day never had to end and that Sebastian and I could hide out here in this fort forever, when Sebastian speaks.

"This is the first fort I've ever built," he confesses.

My head swivels to look at him in shock. "Are you joking right now?"

He shakes his head sadly. "I didn't exactly have the *build-a-fort-in-the-living-room* type of family."

Turning to face him, I rest my cheek in my palm, watching him closely. He stares at the sheet above us, seemingly lost in his own world.

"Want to talk about it?"

His lip twitches. "Not at all." His head turns slightly to look at me. "But for you, I will."

The stupid thing in my chest flutters at his admission. Blood rushes to my cheek and I feel like those five words hold so much meaning.

For the next few minutes, I lay still as a statue as Sebastian explains his upbringing. My heart hurts for the little boy who was never shown love. For the teenager who had to choose between having boundaries and getting abused. My soul breaks for the man next to me, who is so clearly damaged from his past that he's too scared to let anyone in again.

"So yeah," he says, letting out a long breath. "That's why I sometimes get set off by being touched when it's unwanted, or when I'm not expecting it."

When you first meet Sebastian, his boyish charm and natural swagger pulls you in. You'd never know all the shit he hides behind that confident smile.

"I don't blame you," I whisper quietly. I desperately want to reach out and comfort him, but I don't know if it's a good idea when he's clearly thinking about all the times his dad used and abused him for humor.

"It was years ago. I should be over it."

Sitting up, I think my next words through carefully. "That is something you can't just get over, Sebastian. The one person in this world who was supposed to love and care for you above all else was the worst possible parent to you. No parent should *ever* put their child in the position you were put in. It makes sense why you're still dealing with it today..."

"It's not as bad as it used to be. Not with you. You touch me and I still feel in control—or for once, I don't mind losing that control."

He pauses for a moment.

"If you could be anywhere in the world right now, where would you be?" Sebastian asks, his finger tracing circles over my shoulder as he changes the subject. Part of me wants to keep asking him questions, but I don't want to pressure him into divulging more. I'm content with the small tidbits he's given me today.

Nestling into his chest, I think about his question. "Anywhere?" I ask. My foot brushes against his underneath the blanket.

"Anywhere."

"God, that's so hard. There's so many choices. I want to go anywhere and everywhere. It's always been my dream to experience different places—to see the world."

"But if you had to pick *one* place."

"Tahiti," I say, smiling into his chest. "I've heard the water is so blue and clear you can see down to the ocean floor."

"It *is* pretty fucking blue."

"You've been there?"

He turns my head so our eyes meet. "Yep. Nash vacationed there once. He took both Matt and me. We weren't needed for a lot of the trip, so it was actually pretty fun."

"I'm so freaking jealous."

"You should be. It was pretty epic."

I groan, playfully swatting his chest. "Stop rubbing it in. I've barely been anywhere cool in my life."

"Being a bodyguard does have some perks."

"How did you get into being a bodyguard anyway?"

"It was kind of a lucky break. I had trained at a martial arts gym for years and years. I actually worked there so I could train for free. It was my first *real* job. After a while, I got pretty good at defending myself. One day I was doing some sparring when Matt showed up. Apparently he and the owner had been friends for years and Matt was looking for some new muscle." He flexes his biceps with a smile. "He offered me the job as soon as I got off the mat."

I roll my eyes. "It was that easy? How did he know you were qualified?"

He laughs. "I'm glad you have so much faith in me, trouble. It was a long time before I was given any kind of responsibility when it came to Nash. They really just wanted someone around Nash's age to keep an eye on him discreetly. Matt is intimidating and stiff. He looks like a bodyguard. If someone were to see Nash and me walking down the street, it might not catch their attention as much. We'd just look like two friends hanging out."

"I still feel like I'd notice if I saw you and Nash walking down the street."

"Yeah, we don't go many places without being spotted. But that was the hope when I was hired, at least. Plus, I may not come off *as* intimidating as Matt, but I can kick some ass if I need to."

I think through his words, wondering what it's like to be responsible for keeping someone safe. I can barely keep a succulent alive, I could never imagine being responsible for somebody's safety.

"Close your eyes," he says.

Confused, my eyebrows pinch together. "What?"

Smiling, he reaches to put his large hand over my eyes. He gently slides his palm over my eyelids, reminding me to close them.

I do as instructed, not able to hide the smile on my lips. "Is this about to get sexy?" I tease, wiggling my hips against him.

"Picture you're standing on a beach—on a wooden dock jutting out from the sand. When you look out over the horizon, there's just a large expanse of crystal clear water."

The vision takes flight in my head.

"You can feel the ocean breeze on your cheeks." His breath tickles my cheek, the sensation similar to the one he's describing.

"You can smell the salt of the sea, mixed with the sweet smell of your sunscreen."

I chuckle, keeping my eyes sealed shut. "Safety first."

His hand inches underneath the shirt I'm wearing. "Of course. You have to protect this soft, beautiful skin of yours." He pushes my shirt up until the cold air meets my exposed stomach.

Opening my eyes, I find him about to lay a soft kiss near my belly button. Sebastian looks up, clicking his tongue. "Close your eyes."

He hovers over my skin until I do as I'm told. The moment my eyelids flutter close, his lips meet my skin.

"Imagine I'm there with you." His wet lips circle my belly button, one of his hands drifting underneath my hips to hold me closer to him.

"What if I didn't invite you? This is my fantasy we're talking about..."

This earns me a soft nibble to the top of my thigh. "Don't

be shy, trouble. I know I'm involved with every single one of your fantasies."

"A little full of ourselves aren't we, Sebastian?"

"You love it," he says, his lips trailing down my body. His mouth is almost where I want it when an annoying knock thumps against my door.

A KNOCK ON THE DOOR CATCHES OUR ATTENTION. RILEY POPS up on her elbows, looking into the hallway from her open door.

"Do you think it's Nora?" I ask.

"I don't think so. She has a key."

I'm about to continue going down on her, letting whoever is at the door come back another time. Or never. Doesn't matter to me. But then another knock sounds against the door, this one louder.

"Ugh," her hands rub down her face in frustration. "It may be my crazy neighbor. He'll never stop until I answer."

I look up from between her thighs. "Paul?"

Riley laughs, "No, not *Paul.* I had to break things off with him the moment I got back. You ruined me."

She sits up, pulling her legs out from my reach. Standing up, her shirt—my shirt—falls back down her body. She leaves me alone in our fort. I stay inside to begin with, not needing her crazy neighbor to see the bulge in my pants.

I can't see outside of the fort, but I can hear her rustle around her room.

"Why is it so hard to find pants?" she mumbles under her breath, the sound of a slamming drawer following suit.

"You could just ignore the knocking and come back to let me finish what I started."

The knocking begins again, the frequent taps draining blood from my lower-half.

Cock-block.

The sounds of her hurried steps get further and further away from the fort. I hear the door open, followed by Riley's overly chipper voice.

"Hi," she says. Her voice gets quieter. "What are you doing here?"

Her words pique my interest. If it was her weird neighbor, why did she suddenly get quiet?

A confident, arrogant tone begins to speak. "I wanted to make sure you were okay after last night."

"Right. Yep! Doing great." Her voice raises by an octave. The hurried way she gets her words out has me crawling out of the fort to see who's at the door, although I think I already know the answer—and I don't like it.

"You haven't answered my texts. I've been worried. May I?" As soon as I make it down the hallway, I find her pompous boss stepping through the doorway.

The second I come into view, his eyes widen. He stares at me before looking back at Riley. "Feeling better?" he asks, his tone dry.

"Holden—"

"What a shame. I thought you were better than this, Riley. Better than *him.*"

"What the fuck did you just say?" I respond angrily as I move closer to the two of them.

"I said what I said." He gives me a disgusted look, before dismissing me and looking back at her. "You deserve a man that will take you on a date, Riley. Not this—not him."

We're chest to chest now, my face inches from his. "How about you don't tell her what to do?"

Riley's hand slides between us, her body wriggling between us to create a gap. "Both of you—stop it."

Looking over her head, I make eye contact with the fucker.

"Clearly she doesn't want you, bud. She's mine. Run along back to the country club."

He laughs, having the nerve to smile.

Riley speaks before he gets the chance to, shouting to get our attention. "Cut the shit! Both of you." She looks at each of us. "Holden. I'm sorry. Things just got…complicated. Can we talk?" Riley points to the hallway outside her apartment.

"Are you kidding me?" I ask, wondering what the hell she needs to talk to him about.

"I just need one minute, Sebastian." When she looks at me, I can see regret all over her face. It stops me in my tracks, feeling like a straight punch to the gut.

Understanding washes over me. I walk to her kitchen, grabbing my belongings and putting on my shoes.

"What are you doing?" Riley asks.

Holden stays quiet as he waits in the doorway.

"I'm letting you talk. Talk as long as you want. I'm out."

"Don't just go," she pleads, catching me by the bicep.

The last thing I want is for her to be alone with this guy, but I'm not just going to wait here and look desperate.

"I'm not going to sit here and wait for you to go stroke his delicate ego," I say, lashing out at her.

"My ego is nowhere near delicate. I know I'm the better man here. When you figure that out Riley, just let me know," he says coldly as he turns and walks out the door.

"Holden! Wait!" Riley shouts, chasing after him.

"Don't go after him."

She looks toward me. "Stop telling me what to do and let me think for one minute!"

I amble toward her, but she puts her hands out to stop me. "What the hell do you need to think about?" I ask.

"You. Him. Everything!"

Her words take me by surprise. "I was unaware there was much to think about here."

"Just stay right here, please!" she says over her shoulder,

already running after Holden.

"You've got to be fucking kidding me," I say under my breath, slamming the door shut.

Pacing back and forth, I consider leaving. This is exactly why I don't do relationships. I'm not interested in being a backup guy for her. But something stops me. Today has been different. I need the chance to talk to her. I need to attempt and get my head on straight.

My body presses against the door as I peer through the hole at the top. They stand a respectable distance apart. Riley looks guilty as she explains something to him. He nods, his eyes looking over her head for a moment before focusing on her again.

Whatever he says back to her must hit home, because when Riley looks back to him, she looks sad. She looks remorseful. The look on her face stops me in my tracks.

That look says so many things. It reminds me of all the reasons we shouldn't be doing this. It reminds me she isn't really mine, and why—because of how I am—she never will be. Not really. Not in the way she deserves.

The sadness in her eyes also reminds me of all the ways I'm being selfish and leading her on. She's changed so many things for me. She's finally started to get me to open up, to face the bullshit of my past. But despite all that, I still don't think I'm capable of giving her what she wants.

Commitment is terrifying, and eventually, that's what she'll want. And it's the one thing I don't know that I can give. There's a loss of control in doing that, and I'm not prepared for it. At least I don't *think* I am.

When it comes to her, I'm so messed up in the head I don't know where my boundaries lie any longer.

The two of them finish their conversation. He steps forward like he wants to hug her, but my jealousy reaches its breaking point. The door slams against the wall loudly when I yank it open.

"Time's up, pal."

"Remember what I said." Holden holds her eye contact for a few moments longer before he relents. Both Riley and I watch him retreat down the hallway.

"What in the hell was that?" she seethes. There's a fire in her eyes I haven't ever seen.

"What are you talking about?"

She points out into the hallway. "You know exactly what I'm talking about, Sebastian."

"Enlighten me."

"You just all but dangled the fact that you and I hooked up in front of him!"

I shrug. "Was it supposed to be a secret? He should know that you aren't interested."

She throws her hands up in anger. Stalking toward the open door, she shuts it, giving the two of us privacy in her kitchen. "I am interested. I *was* interested, until you came back into the picture."

"I had to let the uppity fucker know he doesn't have a chance."

"Oh and why is that? Because I'm *yours?*"

Yes. No. Hell, I don't know.

I want her to be mine, I just don't know how to deal with the shit that comes with that territory.

She laughs sarcastically. "God, why am I so naive when it comes to you? I'm not typically this girl, Sebastian, and I *hate* that you make me this girl."

"What kind of girl?"

"The girl who thinks she'll be the one to save the guy." She shrugs. "It's cliché and it never happens. Yet here I am, desperately wanting to be the one to change it all for you."

"I'm not sure anyone is capable of changing me, trouble."

It's silent. She stares at me and I stare right back. There's so many things I could say right now. Things that could maybe make this better. Things that could ease her fears, but I don't want to make empty promises. Not to her.

The truth is, I want to change everything so she *does* become that girl. She basically already *is* that girl. But I can't tell her that. I don't want to give her hope before I know what I'm doing first.

"You've got me fucked in the head," I finally admit, desperately trying to give her *something* to hold onto.

"You've got me fucked in the heart," she responds instantly.

"Don't say things like that."

"I'm just telling the truth. We're playing a dangerous game. Anytime I'm around you I lose all sense of myself and it has to stop. I can't do this. I'm not the girl who leaves her date to go hook up with somebody else. I hate myself for doing that to him."

"Who cares what he thinks."

"I care!" she yells. "I care, Sebastian."

I'm trying to think of something that could make this better. To make it *not* feel like we're ending things when we haven't even *begun* something. Unfortunately, I don't think of something soon enough.

"I want you to leave. Right now."

I'm left staring at her, wrestling with my head and heart about what to do. I want to stay here and fight with her until I get my point across. I need her to know how much it took for me to tell her about my dad today. I'm opening up as quickly as I can.

But instead, I'm silent, because deep down I know that I can't give her what she needs.

At this very moment, I'm unable to make any promises to her.

So I do exactly as she asks me to. Exactly as I've done a hundred times before. I leave. Only this time, I'm wishing I wasn't.

SEBASTIAN

I'M UNCOMFORTABLE WITH THE AMOUNT OF WHITE THAT surrounds me in this room. No matter what direction I look in, I'm met with different variations of white. Even the pamphlets fanned out on the white table in front of me are devoid of color with a simple, black font.

And then there's green. Towering green plants in pots sit in almost every corner. A leafy plant sits on the end table to my left, the soil freshly watered.

My thumbs fiddle in my lap nervously. Normally right now I'd scroll mindlessly through my phone, but they took it at the front desk when I arrived. It didn't matter how many times I told them I worked for Nash, or explained I have no reason to film him or do anything to leak his presence here. They didn't care, cheerfully smiling as they placed my phone next to a few others.

At least I know they're doing their best to make his safety a priority here. His six-month stay is coming close to an end, and they've done a great job keeping his whereabouts on lock down.

I have to hand it to Monica, this off the grid *wellness retreat* for celebrities seems to be legit.

"Sebastian Compton?" A nurse in sage green scrubs emerges from a hallway, her eyes scanning over the waiting room.

I pop up, the only person waiting in this room. "That's me."

She smiles. "Mr. Pierce is ready to see you."

"Let's do it," I mutter, trying to tame my nerves.

This will be my first time speaking with Nash since he checked himself in here. We've spoken briefly on the phone, but this is totally different. Now I'll actually get to see if this place has done him any good—if he's truly healing or if he'll break the moment he leaves.

The nurse's pristinely white sneakers squeak on the floor as I follow her down a hallway. We walk past small sitting areas, some empty, some with groups of people occupying them.

I try not to do a double-take when I swear I see a top selling female pop artist, Merit Winter, sitting at a table playing chess with a nurse. She and Nash had a hit single together a few years ago. I could be seeing things, but I would bet money that it's her.

The nurse stops in front of a glass door. Looking through it, I find Nash seated on a long, leather couch. He's staring down at his lap, appearing to be scribbling in one of his journals.

The sight makes me nervous. Nash typically writes songs when he's either in a deep, dark hole or he's in a really good place. When he's in between he's typically staring at his journal or the wall angrily, without any lyrics free-flowing to his head.

"You can go in," the nurse says nicely.

My feet stay planted, my mind racing. I've never been one to stay quiet. In school I was always the kid in trouble for talking too much. Right now, my mouth feels dry. I'm nervous to face my boss.

Selfishly, I need him to get better so I can have a job again, so I can have purpose.

The last few months have been hard—being in the dark

about how he's *truly* doing. The updates from Monica, and even the brief conversations with him, didn't give too much insight on his mental state.

I'm anxious to discover if Nora has ruined him completely. And even knowing how hurt he is, I've started developing feelings for her best friend—just another reason to be nervous. I don't know how he's going to feel about that, either. Shaking my head, I force all thoughts of Riley out of my head. That's over. I should be thinking about Nash, not her.

Before the nurse resorts to shoving me through the door, I reach for the handle. A wall of frigid air hits me in the face, the room noticeably cooler than the hallway.

The sound from the door has Nash looking up from his journal. When his eyes land on mine, his face breaks out in a familiar smile.

"There's my second favorite bodyguard," Nash jokes, standing up from the couch and closing the distance to me. He pulls me into a hug, patting me on the back.

"Hey, Boss," I respond, gripping his neck for a moment before ending the hug.

Taking a step back, his eyes take me in. Smiling again, he says, "Man. It's good to see that ugly mug."

My hand runs over my face. "Better looking than yours."

He scoffs, waving his hand in the air. "Keep dreaming, Bash. There's a reason this face has graced Times Square."

Nash leads me to the sitting area, gesturing for me to take a seat. I follow his lead, taking a deep breath. "I just haven't been discovered yet."

His eyes almost roll back in his head. "Fuck, did I miss you and those dumbass comments. Like I said. Keep dreaming."

A tray sits on the table in front of us. A pitcher of water with cucumber and lemon sits on top. Two glasses sit pre-loaded with ice next to it.

"It's so good to see you, Boss." My eyes roam over the

room. It feels like we're sitting in a big, glass cage. No matter the direction you look in, the walls are see-through. They're giving us the illusion that we're alone, but I wonder if somewhere someone still has their watchful eye on us. I'm trained to know every single thing going on around me, and I'm confident the person cleaning the blinds in the room next to ours is there for more than one reason.

"What's it like out there?" Nash asks, pointing outside.

"Fucking hot as hell," I respond, not a huge fan of the Arizona heat. It's torturous. I'm not sure why anyone would want to live in a place that seems as hot as satan's asshole.

Nash laughs, "It is, isn't it? Part of my *healing* is yoga outdoors in the morning. And let me tell you, it's still hotter than fucking hell bright and early in the morning here."

I can't help but laugh at the mental image. "Nash Pierce… doing yoga? That's a picture I'll never get out of my head."

He shakes his head. "Oh, blow me. I actually don't hate it. You should maybe try it instead of spending every single one of your workouts beating the shit out of a bag or wrestling around on a mat all day."

"First of all, those are both great ways to exercise. And second, I've done yoga before. But fuck doing it in the heat."

Nash raises his eyebrows, clearly surprised. "Well, I know who my detail will be when I continue being a yogi even after I break out of rehab."

There's an awkward silence. Nash has now addressed the elephant in the room. He's in rehab, and we're both aware that I want to know how the rehab is going.

He looks a lot better now than he did before he came here. His eyes aren't as sunken in from exhaustion after his constant benders. He actually looks well-rested. There's even some color to him, as if he's been able to get some sun while here. The biggest thing I notice is his smile. He smiles freely, not because of alcohol, or drugs, or because he's performing in front of tons of people. Now he's smiling on a normal weekday afternoon, and it's the first time since the plane touched down in Arizona that I've had hope that he truly is better.

"Never known you to be the quiet one, Bash. That's Matt's job."

Matt and I were both a little shocked when Monica called, telling us Nash had requested me as a visitor. Matt had been with him longer than I had. He has kind of a weird father-figure, older brother type of vibe going on. And if he wanted to talk security, it was typically with Matt, not me—which made me wonder if he wanted to talk about other things.

Like if he somehow knew about Riley and me.

"A quiet Sebastian freaks me the fuck out," Nash continues. He bends over the table, pouring himself a glass of water.

"Sorry," I breathe. "Just taking it all in."

Noticing my stare, he lifts the glass. "I've traded vodka for flavored—oh, excuse me, *infused*—water. It's actually pretty good."

I busy myself by making my own water, taking a large gulp of it when I start to wonder if now's the time he tells me he knows I've been sneaking around with Riley. Fuck, I'm paranoid.

"Well, before this gets any more awkward, I'll start out by saying I'm doing good, Bash. I'm doing really fucking good."

"Yeah?"

He nods. "Don't get me wrong. It was a wild fucking ride to get here. Detoxing was…fuck, it was awful. Having to face the mess I made of my life sober, to come to terms with everything dry as a bone, it was almost torture. But I did it. I fucking did it, Bash."

"Good for you, Boss," I tell him honestly.

He smiles back at me, taking a sip of his own drink before setting it down. He then pulls his journal from where he set it on the couch earlier.

"I've been doing a lot of coping through this." He shakes

the journal in the air, some of the pages falling open. I can't make out any words, but the pages are written in.

"I'm stoked to hear that."

Nash thumbs through the pages until he lands on one about halfway through. He traces his fingers over the words on the page.

"How is Nora?" he asks, his voice a little less confident than before.

I try not to choke on my own spit as I gulp.

"I don't know," I lie.

"I've missed her."

"I'm sorry," I get out, not knowing what else to say. Looking down, I cross my arms in front of my chest to stop my hands from shaking. I want to change the conversation to anything else on the planet.

"Don't be, I've forgiven her."

My neck snaps back up as I look at him quickly, disbelief covering my face. My reaction catches him off guard. He brings his hands up defensively.

"I know, you think I'm crazy. But look..." He holds the journal up once again, showing off the page from earlier.

There's a long message written, the handwriting much neater than his typical chicken scratch.

"She left me a note. She told me the truth before Taylor did. Or, she wrote about it…"

He thoughtfully looks over the words written on the page. I assess his every move, trying to figure out his mental state. If it were six months ago, he'd be losing it at even the mention of Nora's name. But right now the only emotion I get from him is peace, and it's throwing me for a damn loop.

"I was writing lyrics one day—about her, shocking I know."

I laugh. "You don't say?"

"Then this page flipped open, and I got to read all the things she was too scared to say. I understand why she did what she did. I don't agree with it—she caused some major fucking damage—but I don't hate her for it anymore."

"Good for you, Boss," I say, relieved. It feels like the smallest of weight has been lifted from my chest at his words. "I think that'll make it a lot easier to move on," I add, letting my shoulders hit the back of the couch. I've been sitting so rigid, my nerves going crazy, it's a miracle Nash hasn't called me out on it.

"Move on?" Nash asks in disbelief. "I'm not moving on, Bash. I'm going to get her back."

I've mastered being able to hide my emotions. I've learned to not let anything phase me. But at his admission, it's impossible *not* to let him see my shock.

"What?" I stutter, unable to get anything else out.

From the way Riley has made it sound, I don't think Nora has truly gotten over Nash, either. But the last thing I expected was him telling me he still wants her, especially after all the healing crap he went through here.

"I'd rather forgive Nora and still love her than hold a grudge for the rest of my life and never have her again."

His words spin around in my head. Every time he speaks of love, my mind flashes back to Riley. I have no idea what it means to really, truly love someone. I haven't ever wanted to. But the more time I spend away from her, the more I'm faced with losing her, the more I think about how she's someone I want to fight for.

SEBASTIAN

I listen as Nash tells me about his master plan to get Nora back. I have to bite my tongue so I don't ask him if it should be the other way around. She's the one who hurt him, shouldn't she have some big plan to try and win *him* back?

I let him explain everything he's had to do here in rehab to improve his mental and physical health. Apparently the first week or two was just him yelling at everyone in sight, his body experiencing withdrawals from the alcohol and drug concoction he'd been on.

And then there was a long period of time where he stooped very low. He had to deal with his thoughts completely sober.

"It took a lot of therapy," Nash says, pausing for a moment to gather his thoughts.

His body relaxes as he continues to recount the past few months. There was a point in time when he hated Nora, but he hated himself more for not being completely over her.

"I begged Monica to let me call her," Nash tells me. "She told me calling Nora wouldn't help—no matter how many times I pleaded with her."

I sigh, wondering if that was Monica's call to make. She was also part of the reason he hit rock bottom. "She did?"

He nods, stretching his arms above his head, not seemingly bothered to be having such a deep conversation. "Yep.

She told me that if any of my doctors called her saying they thought it would be best, she'd arrange it. She's ruthless man, but in this case, it paid off."

"So she isn't on your shit list?" I tease.

He laughs, moving a piece of hair out of his eyes. "Monica forever pisses me off but I think she does have my best interest at heart. She's shit at showing it, but I know now that contacting Nora would have been detrimental to getting myself clean and healed."

I run my hand over my mouth, smiling. "Monica Masters saving the day? I'll be damned."

"Don't tell Aiden I said that. He'd never forgive me for giving Monica a compliment."

I gesture zipping my lips, pretending to throw the key over my shoulder. "Your secret is safe with me."

Nash looks at me suspiciously. "You fucking suck at secrets."

"It was *one* time," I say, thinking about the time I accidentally told Nora where Nash was taking her for their first date. In my defense, he hadn't made it seem like it was supposed to be some huge surprise.

"I can think of like ten things you've spoiled off the top of my head."

Rolling my eyes, my arms cross over my chest. "Whatever."

"So enough about all of my bullshit. That's all I've talked about for months. I want to talk about someone else for a change."

"Great, let's chat about Aiden. How's your brother doing?"

"Stop avoiding talking about yourself. I want to know how *you* are doing. I'll talk about Aiden with Aiden."

"There's not much that's new with me."

He stares me down. His body language shows that he doesn't believe a word I'm saying. "You're telling me that you've essentially been off for months and *nothing* interesting has happened?"

"I got a dog."

He raises his eyebrows. "No you didn't."

"No I didn't. Would it be more interesting if I did?"

Nash shrugs. "Maybe. Not sure you live the best life for a dog. Maybe try a fish instead."

"I'll pass."

"Stop avoiding the topic. Tell me what the hell you've been up to. I want to live vicariously through your adventures the last few months."

He sits forward, ready to listen. His forearms rest on the tops of his thighs, his hands clasped in front of him. He watches me expectantly.

Oh, I've just been in some sort of friends with benefits scenario with Riley. Turns out our one night stand turned into multiple nights.

My mind races with all the different ways I could come clean to him. He seems in a healthy enough place to hear it. But I hold back. I don't want to do anything to jeopardize the way he's feeling.

Or our friendship.

Or my job.

"Just been doing this and that, Boss. It's been utterly boring if I'm being honest. I'm ready to be kept busy again. I hate this whole sitting around thing."

He watches me carefully. I'm wondering if he's going to call me out when he finally speaks.

"It was hard for me at first, too. Ever since I was in middle school my life has been planned out to the minute. And then I got here and it was so…*not* planned out. I had a schedule for the day but nothing long-term the way I do at home. Yoga, therapy, group sessions, things like that. But there was still *so much* down time. I hated it in the beginning."

"And now?"

"And now I find that I crave the downtime. I used to hate

being alone with my thoughts, and now I know it's good for me."

I scoff. "Yeah I don't think downtime is my thing."

"Probably because you never stop talking," he teases.

"Someone has to keep things interesting. Between your brooding, Matt's lack of personality, and Monica's constant pestering, *someone* has to be the fun, energetic one."

"It'll be good to leave here. To get the crew back together," he says thoughtfully. His fingers twitch around the journal he's holding.

"I'm ready to get busy again. What's the plan for when you leave?"

"Keep my shit together," he laughs. "Get my girl back."

"You really love her don't you?"

He nods right away. His back straightens with confidence. "With every part of me. Even the parts of me that are hurt by her. For worse or for better, she's the one I want by my side. The money, the fame—I don't want any of it without her. My rain show."

"Rain show?" I ask, confused.

"It's something she wrote in here, and it resonated. Rain shows are my favorite to put on. They're wild and epic. She's my rain show."

I hum, thinking his words over.

"Have you been in love?" he asks.

"Nope."

"Oh, that's right," he says. "And you don't ever want to."

It turns out, he wasn't too drunk to remember the conversation we had in the hotel room—which feels like an eternity ago now.

Shrugging, I can't come up with anything to tell him. The thought of falling in love is the most terrifying thing I can think of. I've faced my raging dad, drug dealers with loaded guns, and hordes of screaming fans trying to claw their way to Nash. But the thought of giving someone everything and allowing them the opportunity to break you into a million little pieces, to rock you to your very core—that's the scariest shit in the world.

The thought of becoming vulnerable with someone, telling them about the parts of me that make even my skin crawl, seemed impossible. I didn't want it.

And then came Riley. My *trouble*. And now, falling in love doesn't seem as bad as it once did. We've only stolen moments here and there with each other, but even the small moments can mean the most, because I've given her pieces of myself I've never given to anyone.

I can't help but wonder what would happen if we weren't in this situation.

"You'll find it one day. And I can't fucking wait to meet the girl who manages to tame Sebastian Compton."

Maybe you already have.

I'M LYING IN BED WHEN A TEXT POPS UP ON MY PHONE. At first, I ignore the notification, knowing that I've got to be up early for work tomorrow.

I'm not exactly on the best terms with my boss right now, so the last thing I need is to be late. Surprisingly, things haven't been terribly awkward with Holden, despite everything. He hasn't been overly friendly, but I'm still doing actual work instead of fetching his coffee every morning, so I can't complain. It's been a couple weeks since the apartment incident, and I don't want to do anything to make us back-pedal. Well, nothing more than leaving a date with him to go have sex with the man I can't seem to shake.

A reminder notification dings and my curiosity gets the best of me. Flipping over, I pull my phone off the nightstand.

A text from Sebastian pops up on my phone. Curious, I open the notification, unable to ignore it.

Sebastian: Miss me, trouble?

I don't miss the way my heartbeat picks up in my chest.

Me: Who is this? ;)
Sebastian: Does someone else call you trouble?
Me: What if I'm into that?

Three dots pop up, showing me Sebastian is typing. I watch them disappear and reappear multiple times before a message finally comes through.

Sebastian: Meet me outside?
Me: Now?
Sebastian: *photo*

I look down to find a smirking Sebastian standing in front of my apartment building. The look on his face a cocky one. His eyebrow is arched, that same unforgettable smirk on full display—as if he already knows that I won't be able to deny him.

Me: Wrong building.
Sebastian: Should I just come up there then?

My stomach drops. Nora is sound asleep in the room down the hallway. Sebastian would definitely wake her up if he came pounding on the door. My phone vibrates again.

Sebastian: I'm going to see you, trouble. If you don't get down here, I'll come up there, no matter who else is in that apartment with you.

This text has me jumping out of bed. Partially in fear, knowing he means what he says, and partially in anticipation. It's been weeks since I've seen him and we didn't exactly part ways on the best terms. We haven't spoken aside from the time he texted me a few days ago to let me know he'd be out of town visiting Nash. It isn't lost on me that I'm probably one of the first stops he's made since being back in the city.

Reign it in heart, I remind myself.

I slide my feet into a pair of sandals before opening my bedroom door softly. Sticking my head into the hallway, I look in both directions, making sure the coast is clear. I pad softly to our door, opening it as quietly as possible.

When I step out onto the sidewalk in front of my apartment building, I find Sebastian standing at the curb.

His hands sit in both of his pockets, his eyes trained solely on me. I'm wearing a large t-shirt and a pair of thin shorts, nothing special. But the way his eyes scan from my toes all the way to my head makes me feel like I have on the sexiest pair of lingerie.

"There's my trouble," he states, meeting me halfway.

Both of his hands slide into my hair effortlessly. He pulls my face against his as if it's the most natural thing in the world. The moment our lips meet, I remember how much I enjoy kissing him. His lips on mine remind me of how much I've missed him while also warning me how dangerous that thought is. Dirty little secrets aren't meant to be exposed.

"I thought you were with Nash?" I ask, pulling away.

His forehead falls against mine. "I was. I'll be back down there again. Matt and I fly down this weekend to prepare for picking him up. He gets out shortly after that."

I nod, reveling in the feeling of his fingers tangled in my hair. I take note of when Nash will get out, wondering if I should tell Nora about it. Surely once he's out it'll be all over the news, there's no way she'll miss it. I'm just not sure if it'll be better or worse for her to know ahead of time.

"Why are you here?" My hands brace against his stomach as I push off, looking up into his eyes.

I missed him more than I care to admit—especially after spending that unforgettable time with him, building our sheet fort and talking about his childhood. I realized I really was catching feelings for him. There's something about the way he slowly opens up to me that has me coming back for more, despite the glaring red flags of his aversion to commitment and questionable possessiveness.

Sebastian shrugs. By the way he scratches the side of his head and avoids eye contact, I wonder if he's nervous.

"I didn't really think about it. I got in and wanted to see you..."

It's hard to calm the racing of my heart at his admission. He hasn't said much, yet his words feel monumental. He's letting me in, being vulnerable, and I can't resist.

"You did?" I ask, trying to hide the hopeful tone in my voice.

He nods, moving my hair off my neck. Bending down, he lays a chaste kiss to the place between my neck and collarbone.

"Sebastian," I whisper. "I can't keep doing this. The push and pull, it's exhausting."

He doesn't stop, his lips trailing up my neck. "I'll leave if you tell me you don't want this, that you don't feel this."

I should be pulling away from him, but I do the opposite, my body leaning into his. "Of course I feel it, Sebastian. Feeling hasn't ever been an issue with us, but I can't keep hooking up and pretending it doesn't mean anything to me..."

"It means something to me, and I hope like hell it means something to you, too."

"I need more. I need more from this, I need to know I'm the only one. I need to know this has potential. I just need to know you're not going to freak out the moment things get real."

He cages my face between his hands, roughly turning my face to look up at him. "Things are already real between us."

"Do you mean it?"

"I mean it. I'm giving you everything I'm able to give right now."

"It's hard to believe you. I can't figure you out. I want to believe you, but sometimes it seems like you only want me so somebody else can't have me."

His fingers are hot against my skin. Even if I wanted to turn my head, I wouldn't be able to. His grasp on me is desperate. "Listen very carefully to my words, trouble. I don't want *any* other man to even look in your direction, let alone touch you. The thought of that makes me go mad. It's because I'm so damn crazy about you, because I already know that I need you more than you need me, and it's the scariest position I've ever been in."

"Oh, Sebastian," I cry, standing on my toes to kiss his cheek.

"Come to my place," he says against my ear. My skin breaks out in goosebumps despite the California heat.

"Your place?"

"I need you, trouble. I thought about you the entire flight home. Whatever's happening between us, I can't stop it. I won't."

His hands are back on either side of my face, steering my face gently so I looks up at him. His face is serious.

"I don't want to stop it, but…"

So many questions fly through my head, but they all disappear when Sebastian wraps me in his arms. He's pulling me against his chest before I have time to think about what he's doing. He's seen me in almost every single intimate position imaginable, but somehow, my head against his thumping heart feels ten times more intimate.

"I'm done questioning what this thing is between us. I know that when I'm not with you, you're all I think about. And that this is more than sex for me." He pauses, as if he's just had some kind of epiphany. "I think it's been more than sex for a while for me."

"Sebastian, don't say things you don't mean."

He looks at me sincerely. "I mean every single word I'm about to tell you. Riley, you were trouble the moment I met you, but in the best possible way. I've never had a girlfriend before, so forewarning I could be the shittiest boyfriend imaginable, but…"

"But?" I interrupt, hanging on every single one of his words.

"But will you be my girlfriend, trouble? Teach me all about how to do the whole boyfriend gig?"

I laugh, shaking my head in disbelief. "I've barely ever had a boyfriend."

"Good. I was going to make sure you forgot about them anyway."

"A bit possessive, are we?"

"I told you that night at the club, you're mine. You were mine before I even realized what that meant."

"Will you buy me flowers?"

"Absolutely not."

I stick my lip out dramatically. "But what if I love flowers?"

"Well then, *maybe*, but I can give you something better."

"And what's that?"

"Mind-blowing sex with french toast afterward."

I moan, remembering the epic french toast he'd made. "Deal. Take me back to your place, boyfriend?"

His eyes light up, a smile overtaking his face. "Yeah? Boyfriend and girlfriend?"

"Don't make it weird."

"Oh, I'm going to make it weird."

Grabbing a hold of his neck, I tug until his head is level with mine. I don't think twice about making our lips crash against one another. There's a million things we still have to figure out, but for right now, giving into the temptation feels so right.

SEBASTIAN

RILEY'S EYES TAKE THEIR TIME ROAMING OVER MY APARTMENT. It feels like I'm under a microscope as she takes in every detail of my living space. I don't know why I feel so nervous. Having her in my home, in my space, it just feels different. This moment feels important for some weird reason.

Thinking about it, it's probably because I've never brought a girl here.

I'm not home much, my life revolves around Nash's. There's many times that I just stay wherever he is. But even on the nights I do stay at my own place, I don't bring women here. I typically don't like people in my space at all.

Until Riley. My *trouble.* Coming in and making me change the way I've always done things.

"It's nicer than I was expecting," she states, letting her purse fall onto the entryway table.

I look around at my home, nodding my head to agree with her. "Yeah, it was my favorite one—well, at least from the options I was given."

"Options?" she asks, shocked.

"Yep. I had to live somewhere close enough to get to Nash's if need be. He sent me this place or another one and let me choose."

Riley runs a finger along the back of the large couch. Her fingertip leaves a small trail down the suede fabric. Not shocking me at all, she walks around my space as if she owns the place.

A large TV is mounted on the wall to my right, a sectional way bigger than I'd ever need aligned in front of it. There's even a rug in the middle of the living room, one I had no part in picking out. I still don't know who exactly picked it out, I never cared to ask.

To our left is the kitchen. It's three times the size of the dingy one I grew up in, fully equipped with top of the line appliances.

She steps into the kitchen, twirling in the gap between the oven and island. "Is this where you'll make the french toast?"

"I have to make you come first. Rules are rules."

This stops her, her head swiveling to look at me. "Something tells me you've always been one to break the rules.

Putting my hand over my heart, I shake my head. "Oh no, trouble," I say, walking to her. "I was a *total* rule follower."

"You're such a liar."

For every step I take forward, she takes one back. The pattern continues until her back bumps into the counter.

"I'd never lie about something so serious. I told you I'd make you come before getting french toast. I take this very seriously."

One of my knees hits the hardwood floor, followed by the other. My face lines up with her stomach. Her t-shirt bunches in my hands as I lift it, exposing the tan skin of her abdomen.

"How would you like me to make you come, Riley?"

"Just getting straight to it, are we?" she huffs, bracing herself by grabbing onto my shoulder.

I look up at her. "Would you like me to stop?"

She smiles, trying to act nonchalant. "Might as well get to work while you're down there."

I lay a kiss against her stomach, kissing the spot right above the waistband of her shorts. My hand trails up the back of her thigh, enjoying being able to touch her once again. To feel her come undone underneath my touch.

Her body relaxes as she uses me for support. When I pull away, I look up at her with a grin. "You didn't tell me how you wanted me to make you come, trouble."

"Anyway. All the ways," she pants.

Standing, I pick her up, loving the feeling of her legs wrapped around my waist. "As much as I love having you spread open for me on a kitchen counter, I'm going to take this to the bedroom."

I guide us to my room, setting her gently on my bed before taking a step back.

She sits up on her elbows, looking at me with messy hair and rosy cheeks. "What are you doing?"

"Taking in the sight of my girlfriend on my bed."

This shuts her up, her mouth snaps shut as I pull off each of her sandals.

"Do you know you're the first woman to be in my bed, trouble?"

"I already told you, you're a bad liar."

Crawling up the bed until I hold my weight over her, I caress her cheek. "No lies here. It's never felt right. Not until now."

"Sebastian—"

I kiss her before this can get any deeper. Where we're at now is already a lot for me. It's the furthest I've ever been with a woman emotionally, the most I've ever opened up before. I need to take baby steps before I go and fall in love with her, or do something else incredibly stupid.

The kiss deepens. I throw every single thing I'm scared to admit into it. I'm desperate for her to know how twisted up she has me.

I slide my hands underneath her shirt, memorizing the slope from her back to her ass. My fingers grab onto the hem of her shirt. I pull it up and over her head, only allowing our kiss to break for a brief moment before my mouth is on hers once again.

My hand snakes up her back, surprised to find nothing underneath her shirt.

"You're killing me," I groan, grabbing one of her heavy tits in my hand. Her back arches at my touch, her lips becoming even greedier when I pinch her nipple.

"Good. I want it that way."

I take her nipple into my mouth while my hand plays with her other one. Riley squirms underneath me, her hands grasping onto my back.

I move from one side to the other. "I'm not going to say this again, Riley. Tell me how you want to come."

Her fingernails dig into my skin. "I said any of them, or all of them, I don't really care," she pants.

I tsk, playfully biting her nipple. "You greedy, greedy girl."

My hand slides down her middle with purpose, my fingers lifting up the waistband of her shorts. I run it along the band over and over, knowing it isn't the place she wants my fingers.

"You need to use your words. Tell me, should my finger, my mouth or my dick make you come first, baby?"

"Mouth."

"Good choice."

My body slides down the bed until I'm even with her lower half. Grabbing onto either side of her shorts, I rip them off, letting them fall somewhere in the sheets.

She's bare, waiting and ready for my mouth.

My finger plays with her wetness, gearing her up for my tongue. Her hips buck at the first touch.

"I'm about to show you how much I've missed you, trouble."

And then I do. I'm lapping every ounce of her pleasure until she's riding out an orgasm against my face. I don't stop working her with my mouth until I feel her legs relax.

Sitting up, I find her already looking at me.

She smiles. "That was a *great* choice."

"Was it?"

Bringing her legs to her chest, she leans forward and crawls to me. It's the sexiest thing I've ever seen. She stops in front of me, extending up on her knees.

"Now, Sebastian. You're going to choose. My mouth, my hand, or my pussy?" She doesn't waste time getting my clothes off. The second she pulls on the hem of my t-shirt, I'm grabbing onto it and pulling it over my head. She begins to work at the button of my jeans, pulling the denim down my legs as soon as the button is undone.

"Can I choose two out of three?" I tease, rubbing up and down my length.

"Now who's getting greedy?" she asks, her fingers replacing my own.

My head falls into my bed, basking in the feeling of her small hand pumping up and down my cock.

Her other hand reaches over her shoulder, moving her blonde hair onto her back and out of the way. She bends down, her lips wrapping around me. It takes everything in me to resist the urge to nut right here on the spot—the feeling of my cock in her mouth again sending a shiver down my spine.

Fuck, I've got it bad for this girl. Her head bobs up and down and some of her hair falls forward with the movement. Grabbing onto it, I twist it around my fingers, getting it out of the way. I let her set her own pace as she works me up and down.

When I'm too fucking close, I pull on her hair, pulling her off me.

She gives me a dirty look. "I wasn't done."

I smile, deliriously obsessed with her. "Come here. Sit on my face, trouble."

She wastes no time inching closer to me, but it still isn't quick enough. I need to taste her again like I need to breathe.

I'm grabbing her roughly by the hips and aligning her pussy with my mouth.

"Grab onto the headboard, baby. You're going to need the support."

She does as she's told. The minute my tongue runs up and down her slit, she's falling even deeper onto my face.

I'm having my way with her when she pulls herself free. Before I can ask what she's doing, she swings both her legs over me, turning around so her perfect ass is on display right in front of my face. She lowers her hips so she's even with my mouth again before bending over so she can take me in her grasp once more.

"Oh fuck, baby," I moan. "How did you know math was always my favorite subject?"

I ravish her with my tongue. Gripping her asscheeks, I spread them open as I move my tongue in and out of her. She continues to work on me, pumping her hand up and down and rubbing my tip with her nipple. I take her into my mouth and suck just as she does the same to me, the two of us writhing in mutual pleasure. She rides my face, grinding back and forth until she screams, coming all over me.

When the orgasm is done, she falls onto the bed, clearly spent.

Leaning up, I crawl over her body until I'm on top once again, pushing hair out of her face.

"Done so soon?"

She answers by grabbing me and lining me up with her entrance. "Hell no."

I'm about to push in when I stop myself. "Fuck, I need a condom."

She sighs in annoyance. "Then be quick with it."

I extend my body until I can reach the drawer of my nightstand. I rip the packet open and sheathe myself in it as quickly as possible. Coming back to her, I place us in the same position as before.

She's ready for me, helping me ease in the moment I'm lined up.

I push in and out of her, unable to restrain myself. I know with the way my hips hit her that I'm not being gentle, but our punishing pace seems to only turn her on further.

Grabbing her neck, I make her look at me. "Tell me that it's never felt like this with another man." Slowing down, I push in and out of her at a tantalizing speed.

"It's—" she moans, her words cutting off when I push all the way into her.

"Trouble," I warn, sliding out until just the tip of me is in her. "You better fucking tell me right now that it's never felt like this for you. Not with Holden or any other fucker who had the nerve to try and have you before me."

"Only with you, Sebastian." She rocks her hips, allowing me even deeper inside her.

Her words mixed with her movements are my undoing.

"Only ever me," I say before kissing her with everything I have in me.

RILEY

My legs kick at the foot of the bed as I watch Nora dart across her room in a frenzy. She paces from one side of the room to the other, her anxiousness beginning to make me nauseous.

"I mean, I shouldn't do it," she mutters, biting at her fingernail. "Going to visit Nash as he gets out of rehab is just a little *too* stalkerish. Right?"

"Personally, I don't see a problem with it," I tell her, swinging my legs back and forth.

"I don't either!" Lennon yells from FaceTime. Typically she's the quiet one between the two of them, but the second you get her on the phone she thinks she has to yell to be heard.

"I'm just wondering, at what point do I cross the line from being romantic to just being creepy?"

I wave my hand dismissively. "Honey, you've got a long way to go before you approach being creepy."

Nora looks at me, unsure. She chews on her lip, thinking my words over. Finally she says, "I'm not sure I agree with that. Besides, how do we know he won't just flat out ignore me?"

"At least then you'd know for sure," Lennon offers.

"I'm with her," I agree.

"I'm feeling ganged up on," Nora says, looking at her closet as if it holds all the answers.

"You've stalked Monica for months," I point out. "You've been desperate to find out where he's at and now that you actually *know* where he is, you aren't going to go?""

Nora chews on her lip. "Well, when you put it that way…"

"So it's settled!" I cheer.

"My sister is going to win back Nash Pierce," Lennon finishes for me.

Nora lets out a long breath, her eyes still focused on the closet. "Holy shit. I'm going to track down Nash."

"And say a little prayer that he doesn't hate you," I joke.

This earns me a dirty look from Nora.

"Riley!" Lennon scolds from the other end of the phone.

My hands fly up in surrender. "Sorry! I'll read the room better next time."

Stepping up to her closet, Nora stands on her tiptoes, pulling a large duffle bag from one of her shelves. She begins to throw in one article of clothing after the other. I'm wondering if she's paying any attention to what she's throwing in the bag, or if she'll get to Arizona and learn that she packed all shirts and no pants.

"Don't forget toiletries," I remind her, focused on picking at one of my cuticles.

"Do you need tampons?" Lennon asks. "Oh my god, some guy just heard me ask that," she mutters quietly into the phone. When I look at the screen, I can see her cheeks are red from embarrassment.

"No, she doesn't," I say, knowing Nora's cycle because it's exactly lined up with mine.

At the same time, Nora says, "Nope. Had my period last week."

Excuse me, what?

My eyes fly to her, quickly trying to do the math in my head.

There's no way she had a cycle last week, unless she was suddenly irregular. Our cycles have been synced since high school.

Lennon says something to Nora, but I'm too stuck in panic mode to pay any attention. Trying to be as discreet as possible, I pull out my phone. Pulling up my calendar app, I count the weeks since the last time I had my period.

I find the date, counting the weeks it's been since then.

Holy fucking balls.

I'm late.

I've never been late.

The blood drains from my face as things begin to click in my head.

I sort through every sexual encounter Sebastian and I have had in the last two months. I remember us using a condom most of the time, but things are fuzzy the night he followed me home after the night club.

I'm sure he did.

I'm just overreacting.

We've been safe. Really safe. I'm absolutely positive we've wrapped it every single *other* time, so there's no way that we just happened to forget that *one* time.

Right?

I still can't calm my nerves because I know I've been feeling off lately. Yesterday I bawled my eyes out because they were out of my favorite pastry at my local coffee shop.

And my boobs have been hurting.

This can only mean one thing.

Fuck, am I pregnant?

"What do you think, Riley?" Nora asks loudly, catching my attention. She holds up a summer dress in front of her body.

I think I might be pregnant, I say in my head, not daring to utter those words out loud.

"I think it looks great!"

Nora's eyebrows pull together suspiciously. "You hate it?"

My eyes bulge. "What? *No*, I love it."

"Then why is your voice all weird?" Lennon asks.

Even though she's in another state and only visible through the small screen, I give her the evil eye. The girl barely speaks up, and when she does she decides to call me out.

Not cool, Lenny.

"I really do love it, Nora. And better yet, I think Nash will love it." I try to act as nonchalant as possible, while on the inside I feel like the room is spinning.

My brain is trying to come up with any other possible scenario that could explain my period being late and the weird symptoms—one that *doesn't* involve me being pregnant.

The whole time I assist Nora in packing her bag for Arizona, I'm only halfway present. The other half of me is counting down the seconds until she's gone so I can run to the closest store and grab a pregnancy test.

The three of us continue to plan out what she's going to say to Nash when she sees him. I can tell she's nervous by the way she keeps trying to talk herself out of the plan, but Lenny and I don't let that happen.

Plus, by the little bit Sebastian told me, I think it'll go better with Nash than she thinks. And I'm praying it does—for her sake and mine. It means Sebastian and I won't have to sneak around anymore. We could finally be open about our relationship instead of feeling guilty.

It would all add up perfectly. Well, except for the one small blip that I could have a child growing inside of me.

Yeah, that's just a slight *uh-oh*.

The seconds tick by agonizingly slow until I'm essentially shoving Nora out our apartment door.

"Just like we rehearsed. You got this!" I send her off with words of encouragement.

I do think it'll go great. It has to. I don't even want to think about what might happen if it doesn't.

I wait five minutes, staring out our kitchen window until I'm confident I won't be running into Nora outside. Once I feel like the coast *has* to be clear, I run out of our apartment as quickly as my legs will take me.

I don't even think twice about what I'm wearing, too hurried to give a shit about my appearance.

The clerk at the convenience store greets me, but I'm too busy sprinting for the pregnancy test aisle to reciprocate the sentiment. When I find the aisle, I'm overwhelmed by the wall of boxes staring back at me.

Why are there so many options?

Do I do strips or digital?

An ovulation test wouldn't be it, right?

Fuck, I'm not qualified for this. Pulling my phone from my back pocket, I try to google which brand is the best, but my shitty service foils my plans.

The screen doesn't move.

Good ol' Google abandoning me in my time of need.

Not wanting to waste another second, I pull box after box off the shelf. I shove them in my arms until I'm confident I've bought every damn brand and type of pregnancy test this store has.

I walk to the cash register, wishing like hell there was a self-checkout so I could buy these discreetly.

No such luck.

In the time it took me to choose a pregnancy test—or twenty—a line has formed in front of the counter.

I think back to high school when I always had to buy sanitary products for Nora. She was embarrassed to check out with them because the clerks were always guys we knew from school. Me, on the other hand, I didn't give a shit if they knew I was buying tampons or not.

But now, standing behind an elderly couple, I feel like I'm doing a walk of shame.

A lady holding a toddler stares me down, eyeing the heaping pile of regret in my hands. I hold one of the boxes up. "My husband's a doctor. He wants to be *real* sure."

"Next," the clerk calls.

Stepping up to the counter, I let the mass of boxes fall to the surface. They ricochet off one another.

"Do you think it takes that many, dear?" she asks in a snarky tone. There's beep after beep as she rings one box after another.

"Oh, uh, just wanted to be real sure, you know?" I respond, wondering why the hell she has to bring attention to this.

She grunts.

Luckily for me, she keeps any other remarks to herself. I'm able to pay and leave the store in peace with two full grocery bags in tow.

I hold the bags awkwardly close to my chest as I ride the elevator up to our apartment. The second I get in, I'm sprinting to my bathroom.

Cardboard flies everywhere as I rip open box after box. I pull out one of every brand and type. Reading the directions, I learn I can either pee on the sticks or stick them in a cup of my own pee.

Realizing there's no way I have enough pee to spray every single one of these sticks, I opt for the cup option. Running to the kitchen, I search through our cabinets. All of our normal cups are dirty, so I grab a coffee mug.

It's got a handle. It was made for this.

I'm dropping my pants and sitting on the toilet in no time. My hand is shoved awkwardly between my legs, holding the cup steady. Except now, I can't make anything come out. I'm too nervous. After pushing until my abs are sore, a steady stream falls into the mug.

I set the mug on the counter, pulling my pants up and washing my hands. Taking a deep breath, I begin to dip test after test into my urine.

There's a line of pregnancy tests along my counter. I stare at the lineup, my heart hammering in my chest as I wait for the results.

Time ticks by incredibly slowly, and then suddenly, one finishes.

I stare at the two pink lines.

My eyes flick from the test directions to the results and back again, even though I already know what those two little lines mean.

Pregnant.

I'm fucking pregnant.

One-by-one, all of the other tests show that I'm pregnant. Some of them have two pink lines while some others flash a big bold *pregnant* in my face.

There's no denying it.

I'm pregnant.

Nash and Nora make out in the backseat of the SUV while Matt tries to exit the airport parking lot.

"I'm really happy you guys are back together and everything," I say, holding onto the handle as Matt swerves away from a car full of paparazzi. "But could we have done this reunion a little *less* publicly?"

Nash stops sucking Nora's face for a moment. "Blame, Rose here. She had to go and run before I had the chance to respond."

She hits his knee playfully. "You let me walk away! I thought you hated me."

"I was just trying to think of what to say," he responds.

"Yeah, well, maybe better communication next time?" I offer.

"Agreed," Matt says, still focused on the road.

"So when do you think we'll be getting a call from Monica?" I ask Matt. It shouldn't take long for the photos of Nash and Nora to end up all over the internet.

Anything that has to do with Nash ends up everywhere, but a very public reunion with Nora immediately after spending six months in rehab? I'm shocked we haven't already gotten a call from Monica.

As if she read my mind, her name pops up on my phone.

"Why is she calling *me?*" I panic, a little terrified of her.

"Shouldn't she be calling you?" I turn to Matt and then to Nash.

Nash is too busy whispering sweet nothings to Nora to pay attention to me.

Matt lets his face break into the slightest smile. "She probably already tried Nash, and she knows I'm the one who always drives." He nods to the phone ringing in my hand. "Better answer it."

I bring the phone up to my ear hesitantly, nervous for what version of Monica I'm about to get on the other line.

"Hello?" I ask, clearing my throat.

"So it worked?" she asks bluntly.

"What?" I blurt, trying to keep my head from hitting the window as Matt whips the car around in a U-turn as if he's auditioning for a Fast and Furious movie.

I look over my shoulder, thinking his move may have actually worked. For the time being, I don't see anyone following us.

"Did it work? Are Nash and Nora back together?"

My eyes flick to the lovebirds in the backseat. "Yes, they're together. Did what work?" I ask confused.

Monica sighs in frustration. "The plan, Sebastian! The plan to make Nash happy again. For him and Nora to reunite."

My mouth hangs open. "You knew?"

She scoffs as if my question is the most asinine thing she's ever heard. "Clearly you don't know me well enough. I know everything, Sebastian."

Turning toward the window, I whisper into the phone. "You wanted Nash back with Nora?"

"Of course I did. She made him happier than I'd ever seen him. I'm not a *monster*," she says it like she actually believes it.

I stare out the window in disbelief. I was wondering how Nora knew where Nash was, but I didn't have too much time to think about it. But now that I know Monica had a hand in it, I'm shocked.

The wicked witch may have a soul after all. Or at least some semblance of a conscience.

"Are you there?" she asks. I can hear the tapping of her nails against something.

"Uh, yeah. I was just a little shocked to discover you actually have a heart, if we're being completely honest. I thought you were the Grinch."

"Doesn't the Grinch end up having a heart in the end?" she huffs. "I just had to know for myself if it worked. It turns out if I had just waited one more minute, I would've found out for myself that it worked." She pauses. "These pictures are something else."

Turning around, I face Nash and Nora, the two of them finally separated—slightly.

"You're in trouble," I tell them with a smile.

Nora's eyes widen at the same time Nash returns my smile. Holding his hand out, he gestures for the phone. I hand it over to him, watching carefully as he begins to speak with Monica.

She must not give him time to get a word in. Before I know it, Nash is handing my phone back to me, an unreadable look on his face.

When I go to speak to her again, I find she's already hung up.

"What?" Nora asks, resting her hand on Nash's thigh.

"Monica just told me she was…happy…for us."

His sentence even gets Matt's attention. His eyes dart to the rearview mirror, watching Nash as he processes this whole thing.

"Are we that shocked? She did help me find you," Nora points out.

"Yeah, we're shocked," I answer for all of us.

Never once have I heard Monica name an emotion of hers, let alone one like *happiness.* To be honest, I didn't know she could be happy. I've always kind of wondered if she was some kind of robot or some shit like that.

"She did give me shit for the whole public display of affection for the world to see."

I laugh at Nash's words. "Now *that* sounds like the Monica we know."

My phone vibrates, and looking down, I find a text from Monica.

Leaning forward, Nash looks over my shoulder. "And that should be the hotel Monica booked us for tonight. The jet flies out tomorrow."

Nodding, I plug the address of the hotel into the car's GPS system. It's a pretty quiet ride to the hotel. Nash and Nora spend the whole time whispering to each other in the backset.

Watching them together makes me wish for Riley. She's the first girlfriend I've ever had, so while it's a foreign feeling, it's still not hard to admit that I miss her.

I want to tell Nash everything that has transpired between Riley and I while he's been away, but first I need to discuss things with her. Ideally, I'd like to tell Nash and Nora about Riley and me *with* Riley. If they could see how happy we are together, they should be happy, too. I don't see why they wouldn't be at this point. Nash and Nora have figured things out. We can all go on with our lives.

MONICA ENDED up booking us three rooms right next to one another. It isn't ideal. Typically we book a penthouse that allows for Matt and me to have rooms in the same space as Nash, but Monica couldn't find one where we're at. This time, Matt has an adjoining door with Nash and Nora. He grills them about making sure the door stays unlocked in case of an emergency. Nash humors him, nodding as if he's listening to a word Matt says.

I, on the other hand, know Matt is wasting his breath. There's no way Nash is going to leave the door unlocked tonight. This is a reunion for him and Nora, there's no way he's allowing Matt the opportunity to open the door whenever he pleases.

"Let's leave them alone," I chime in, cutting Matt off.

He gives me a dirty look. It appears he wasn't done with his whole safety lecture, but if he knew Nash at all he'd know that it isn't worth it. Nash knows the drill. He'll call one of us if someone gets creepy or if there's an issue, but I doubt that'll be a problem. We snuck him and Nora into the building. No one should know they're here, which also means nothing should happen, and if it does, Matt and I will be ready.

Something tells me Nash and Nora won't be leaving the room at all tonight, so they shouldn't be running into any trouble.

Matt throws one last look at Nash before walking toward the door connecting their rooms. "You call one of us if you need something."

Nash salutes him jokingly. "Yes, sir. Now get out of my room."

There's a loud giggle from Nora and then the door is slamming in our faces. Matt looks at me annoyed, sighing and crossing the room to his bed. Picking up his phone, he glances up at me suspiciously. I don't bother to ask. Instead, my feet carry me to the armchair sitting in the corner of his room.

Falling into it, I sigh. "Fuck, I'm tired."

Matt grunts, too busy on his phone.

"Not going to lie, when we went to pick Nash up today I wasn't expecting for it to end up like this." He still doesn't answer me, but it doesn't deter me. I could talk to a wall if I had to. "But I'm happy for them. They look happy, don't they?"

This finally gets his attention. He looks up from his phone. "Yeah. They do."

"Do you have a problem with it?"

He thinks over my words for a bit. "It's not entirely my business. I just don't want him to be blinded by his love for her. I don't want to see him go right back into the hole he just crawled out of. If anything will send him on that path again, it's her…"

"And you don't trust her?"

He shakes his head. "No, not yet. Not after what she did."

I nod in understanding. Months ago, I'd been in the same boat as Matt. But because of Riley, my eyes have been opened to the other side of things. I don't agree with what Nora did, I never will, but I don't hate her for her decisions either. If Nash can forgive her and move on from it, then that's good enough for me.

Looking down at my phone, I get the urge to talk to Riley. I haven't heard from her all day. I'm trying not to be a hovering boyfriend, but it feels like I should've heard *something* from her by now.

Maybe I was supposed to text her first? Is that how this works?

Fuck if I know.

"Care if I go to my room for a bit?" I ask, standing up and stretching.

Matt shakes his head. "Go for it. I'll let you know if you're needed."

The minute I get into the privacy of my own room, I'm clicking Riley's name on my phone.

I'm wondering if she's going to send me to voicemail when she answers.

"Hi," she says.

"Hey there, trouble." I take a seat on the bed, scooting backward until my back rests against the headboard.

She doesn't answer me, the silence makes me nervous.

"How was your day?" I ask, crossing one ankle over the other.

"Uh, it was good."

"That's good..." My voice trails off. This is weird. Why does it feel weird?

"What are you wearing?" I tease, trying to break the tension somehow.

This gets a small laugh from her. "Are you for real?"

Nodding my head, I pull my phone from my ear. I click on the FaceTime button, waiting to see if she'll accept.

When she does, I find her lying in bed. The only things illuminating her face are the light from the phone and the moonlight pouring in from her window.

"Hi," I say again, happy to see her face.

She gives me a soft smile. "Hi, Sebastian," she whispers.

"I miss you."

"I miss you too, surprisingly," she adds.

"Ouch."

"I'm kidding. How did today go?"

"It went well. Nash and Nora are once again."

"Nora hasn't texted me back. Both Lennon and I are blowing up the group text."

"Oh, trouble, I don't think she'll be answering you tonight. I'm sure she and Nash are a bit...preoccupied." I grin.

She catches onto my words, her lips parting. "Oh."

It's silent as I wait for her to continue, but she doesn't.

"Did you have a good day?" I prod, trying to get more information out of her.

She stares at something off the screen, whatever it is, she seems focused on it. Her eyes are blank as she stares off into the distance.

"Riley?"

She jolts, her eyes connecting with the screen. "What?"

"Is something wrong?" I ask. I can tell something's up by her mood. She seems anxious and fidgety, both things that are out of character for her.

Her teeth dig into her lip. The phone shakes a bit as she

stands up, judging by the background it looks like she may be pacing in her room. "I'm totally fine. Just tired."

I know she's lying. It's clear as day something is bothering her, or at the very least—something is definitely on her mind.

"You can talk to me, trouble," I say quietly—anxiously. Her mood has me nervous that she's second guessing our relationship. I can't help but wonder if something has happened since the last time I saw her that has her thinking twice about being my girlfriend.

"I told you I'm just tired, it was a long day."

Nodding, I try to hold my tongue. I've spent enough time with her to know when she's telling me a lie, and right now, I know she's suffering from more than fatigue.

"I thought I'd hear from you today," I say, changing the subject before I can think too much into her somber mood.

"Sorry," she mumbles, slightly smiling. "I was busy."

I let out a long whistle, sitting up in bed. "Well, I can let you go then."

"Sounds good, we'll talk later."

I'm about to say bye, but she hangs up before I get the chance. My phone sits limply in my hand as I stare at it, wondering what the hell that just was. Riley is never that quiet and distracted. If I were in LA, I'd already be in my car driving to find out what is going on. But considering I'm all the way in Arizona, I don't have that option.

So instead, I'm stuck sending her text message after text message like a crazy person.

Sebastian: What was that?
Sebastian: Are you sure everything is okay?
Sebastian: ?
Riley: We can talk when you get back.

I try calling her again, desperate to know what she wants to talk about. My stomach has made it all the way down to my feet from nerves. I fear that she's having second thoughts, or maybe even regrets about us. And if that's true...I definitely didn't see it coming. When we made it official, I expected things to go smoothly for us—at least a little while. I definitely didn't think she'd be the one pulling away first.

For the rest of the night, I can't seem to shake the pit in my stomach.

I'm not going to let her walk away from this without putting up one hell of a fight.

My feet pace the same pathway in my kitchen over and over again. Sebastian should be here any moment, and I'm miserably anxious about what I'm about to tell him. I don't know the right way to tell my brand new boyfriend that I'm pregnant with his kid, but springing it on him first thing in the morning probably isn't the best idea…unfortunately, I can't wait another second.

I wanted to tell him about it last night, but this isn't something you say over the phone. This kind of news changes everything, and it isn't something that should be shared anywhere but in person.

But now that he'll be knocking on my door any second, I'm terrified. I have no idea how he'll react. We haven't talked about the future at all. Hell, we've barely been able to talk about the past and present. The thought of kids hadn't even begun to cross my mind.

I don't even know if he wants kids.

I don't even know if *I* want kids—not that it matters now.

I still need to schedule an appointment, but I don't know if that's something Sebastian would want to go to so I've put that off until I talk to him. Now I'm worrying about whether I should have waited and officially confirmed the pregnancy before telling him.

Maybe I just had false positives?

There's no time to back out now, because his knock rattles the door, making me jump. I stare wide-eyed at our apartment door, trying not to have a full-blown panic attack.

I glance at the present I wrapped on the counter. Suddenly, I'm self-conscious about it, wondering if the presentation is too much.

He knocks again. My socks slip against the hardwood floor as I jog to answer it. As soon as I open the door, he's stepping through the entryway and pulling me into his arms.

It's comforting, having his arms wrapped around me again. Feeling his toned arms around me brings a small amount of peace.

His hand finds the back of my neck, holding me even tighter to his chest. He takes a deep breath in. "Fuck, I missed you, trouble."

"Not as much as I missed you," I mumble against his chest.

"Careful there, trouble," he teases. "You may just have me believing you're catching feelings for me."

I laugh sadly against his chest. We're past feelings at this point.

Stepping away from him so I can see his face, I find that confident smile I've loved from the moment I met him. My eyes close the moment his lips touch mine in a gentle, sweet kiss. It's just what I needed.

"We need to talk about what was wrong last night," he says.

"Wait," I respond, pushing off his chest. "First, I have to give you something." My voice breaks at the end, my nerves getting the best of me.

His thumb runs over my cheek. "Hey. You okay, trouble?"

I nod, faking a confident smile. "Totally." Walking toward the counter, I grab the gift. I'd searched all over the apartment for wrapping paper. The plain, brown butcher paper was the only thing I could find.

Now staring at the small box in my hand, I'm wondering if I should've gone to these lengths. It just felt weird to throw a stick I peed on at the guy, I wanted to at least make it a *little* less awkward.

"Is this for me?" he asks, staring down at the box in his hands.

"I didn't wrap the gift for myself," I joke.

"Sorry," he laughs awkwardly. "I'm just not used to gifts."

The comment makes me sad, remembering what he said about his upbringing. My heart is a sledgehammer against my chest as I watch his fingers begin to pull at the tape.

"Wait," I say, reaching out to put my hands over his.

He looks confused, watching me with trepidation. My hands shake, overlapping his.

"Can I open it?" he asks carefully.

I pull my trembling hands away, only managing to nod in response.

He rips into the paper, the white box underneath now exposed.

I'm questioning my entire plan as he lifts the top of the box off.

The moment his eyes connect with the pregnancy test, his mouth pops open.

"Is this?" he asks in disbelief.

"I'm late," I answer immediately. "I took like eighty tests, and well…"

"You're pregnant?"

Nodding, I study him carefully. Part of me wonders if he will run. I'm kind of expecting him to run. This is a lot. We've been dating an insignificant amount of time, adding an unplanned pregnancy to the equation probably tips the scale against us.

"Wow," he breathes. Taking a step back, he sets the box on the counter and pulls out the pregnancy test. He studies it carefully, flipping it around in his hand.

"When did you find out?" he asks.

"Two days ago."

"Does anyone else know?"

I shake my head. "I didn't want anyone else to know before you."

"I don't know what to say."

"Say anything," I plead, wanting to take a step closer to him but not having the nerve to do it. He's too focused on the test in his hand. I can't figure out what he's thinking.

"I'm just... I'm going to be a dad?"

I nod, trying to swallow a lump forming in my throat.

"I don't know a goddamn thing about being a dad, trouble," he says sadly.

A tear escapes from my eye. It's wet and tickles my cheek as it makes its way down my face.

Setting the test down, he braces the kitchen counter. His muscles are tense as he grasps the lip of it tightly. Slowly, he lays his head against the cold granite, taking a deep breath in.

"I'm sorry you had to find out alone," he finally says, his head still down. "I should've been here."

"You're not mad?"

Turning his head, he looks at me. "Why would I be mad at you? I was just as involved in this process as you. How could I be mad?"

"I don't know. I thought you'd be mad, or scared, or run."

"It's fucking terrifying. I'm just trying to process all of this. We just started dating and now you're having a baby..."

"*We* are," I correct, taking one small step closer to him.

"Of course. We are. I'm sorry, Riley. I'm trying not to freak out here."

"I'm freaking out too," I admit.

This catches his attention. Stepping away from the counter, he closes the distance until he's standing in front of me. His hands find either side of my face. "We'll figure it out. Whatever happens, we're a team now. We'll figure it out. I'm with you, trouble." His thumbs trace each of my cheekbones delicately. Tears begin to well up in my eyes. I try to blink the moisture away, but some end up betraying me and spill out.

He wipes each tear away. I can't read the look on his face as his eyes watch me carefully.

"Tell me what you're thinking," he whispers.

Shrugging, I look away, having no idea what I'm thinking. I can't sort through my thoughts quick enough to verbalize them.

"Try for me?" he pesters, not letting go of my face.

Making eye contact with him, I swallow the lump in my throat. "I'm scared, Sebastian. I didn't know if I wanted kids. I haven't had time to even put much thought into it. I've never been serious enough with anyone to even *play* with that idea."

"I know, trouble. It's soon."

A weak laugh escapes my lips. "Soon? We've barely even started dating. I don't think we've even been on a first date and now…" I look down at my stomach at the place where apparently I'm growing a human.

"And now things have gotten real. But I'm here for you, Riley. You know that right? It may seem fast, but that doesn't change the fact that things have always been different with you. I want to see where life takes us. I want to tackle it all with you."

"If it's real, if I'm pregnant… I need you to know I think I want to keep it. And if you don't then—"

He cuts me off. "I want that, too."

Shaking my head, I let my body relax into his. His hands find my hips, pulling me flush against him. "This is fast. Too fast. Totally unconventional."

Stroking my hair, he rests his chin on the top of my head. "I know it is, trouble. But when have things ever been conventional between us?"

"Never. But we could've been a little more normal."

Guiding my face away from his chest, he tilts my chin up

so I look at him. "I don't want normal. Normal is boring, remember?"

He doesn't give me time to respond, instead he pulls my face to his, giving me the most tender of kisses.

Once we break apart, he looks down at me. "How are you feeling?"

"Like shit. No food sounds good and my boobs hurt so bad."

He takes a look at the boobs in question for a moment. "When was the last time you ate?"

Looking at the ceiling, I try to remember what I ate last. "I had crackers this morning, other than that… I don't know. I've been kind of in my head, not thinking about food much. Plus, nothing sounded great."

Pulling his keys from his pocket, he begins to head toward the door. "I'm going to get you food."

"You're what?"

"I'm going to get you food. What sounds good?"

"I don't know…"

"So nothing?"

I shake my head. "Not nothing. Food sounds good. I just don't know *what* sounds good."

"Well, okay then." His hand is on the doorknob to the apartment door until he suddenly turns around. Taking large steps, he barrels toward me.

"Forget something?"

"Yeah," he breathes, before pressing his lips on mine. This kiss is filled with promises and emotions, things I never thought that would happen with Sebastian.

But things I'm desperately wanting.

"I'll be back, trouble. How about you lay down and I'll be back with food."

Speechless, I watch him walk through the door.

Telling him went vastly different than I was expecting. It was better than I could've ever hoped for. And that thought petrifies me. If he would've reacted badly, if he would've ran, it would be easy to reign in my feelings for him.

But instead, his reaction was utterly perfect.

And now I'm afraid no matter how much I guard my heart from him, that it's too late. He's made it his, he's carved his name deep on my soul.

SEBASTIAN

A BABY.

Riley is going to have a baby—with me.

I'm going to be a dad.

Taking a deep breath, I open the door to the restaurant. I try to act casual while my pulse thumps irregularly. I've never given much thought to being a dad—but growing up with such a shitty excuse of a father, I know the importance of being there for a kid.

Until Riley gave me that pregnancy test, I didn't know if I wanted kids. But something odd happened when I looked at that test, when I heard her words. Amongst all the fear, trepidation and worries, I felt calm. I knew I would do everything in my power to be the best dad possible to our child.

I wish we had more time just the two of us, but no matter what, I'm ready to do this with her. To be there for her, to help with whatever she needs.

The hostess asks my name, and I tell her the name for the to-go order, waiting for the food. I repeat the process at four more restaurants until I feel like I have a good selection of different options.

I'm lost in my thoughts on the car ride home, still trying to process that Riley's pregnant. We were safe for the most part, but all it takes is one time of not wrapping it up. Her missed period and pregnancy symptoms are proof of that.

I debate knocking on her door when I make it back up to her apartment, but decide to walk right in. If she's asleep, I don't want to wake her up by knocking.

Trying to free one of my hands, I'm finally able to get the door open without dropping one of the take-out bags. I quietly step into the apartment, the sound of the TV spilling from the living room.

Setting the bags on the counter, I find Riley fast asleep on the couch. Her hand is tucked underneath her cheek. She looks peaceful, so I let her sleep. I feel bad she's been having to process this news on her own while I was working, so if she needs to rest, I'll give her the time for it.

I get to work pulling out the various food from the bags, laying out each container on the island. I'm happy with the variety of choices, hoping one of them will sound appetizing to her. There's a mixture of aromas filling the kitchen. When I look up, I find Riley stretching on the couch.

Yawning, she stands up, slowly making her way toward the array of food.

"What's all this?" she asks quietly, her eyes jumping from one box to the next.

"Food," I answer, smirking.

She narrows her eyes. "Really? I would've never known. What *kind* of food?"

Looking down at the food in front of us, I point to a small white box. "Well, here we've got fried rice as well as sesame chicken." My finger stops at the next container, a black styrofoam box. "And here is chicken parmesan with garlic bread. We've also got a cheeseburger, chicken tenders, and a cobb salad." I point to one box after another, finally making it to the final one. "And this is a breakfast scramble with some toast."

Swallowing, she looks from the food to me. "You got me all of this?"

"Well, I didn't know what you wanted…so I figured I'd give you options."

"Options," she repeats under her breath. She reaches to open the box with the pasta inside. Pulling out the garlic bread, she takes a hesitant bite, chewing slowly.

"How is it?" I pluck one of the spaghetti noodles from the box, dropping it in my mouth. Reaching into one of the bags, I pull out a set of wrapped plastic silverware. I open the package, handing her the fork.

She takes it silently, dipping the fork in the spaghetti and twirling the noodles around it.

"It's delicious," she says around a mouthful of pasta.

I open the other boxes, making sure she knows she has the other options as well.

"You didn't have to get all of this."

"I wanted to."

"It's too much, Sebastian."

"You don't have to eat it all."

She shakes her head, frustrated. "No, this." Her finger points from me to her. "This is too much. We just found out I'm pregnant, shouldn't there be more drama, more talking, more—"

"More what?"

The fork falls out of her hand, landing with a small *smack* against the island.

"I don't know!" she says, raising her voice.

"It just feels like we should talk more about this, about what this means for us. We're freshly dating, we're just going to bring a baby into this and pretend all of this is normal?"

"Why are you so focused on this being normal? Why can't we just be us?"

"How are we going to tell Nash and Nora?" she asks, reminding me of the fact Nash doesn't even know I've been seeing Riley behind his back.

I pause, somehow that fact had slipped my mind until

now. I was too focused on being there for her. I haven't even thought of telling Nash—not since I held that pregnancy test.

"I don't know, Riley. It's kind of bigger than them at this point. They're together now, it shouldn't be too big of an issue."

"And if it is? You basically live with Nash. How are you going to keep your job and take care of a baby?"

I open my mouth to respond, but she throws her hand up, stopping me.

"I think I need a little space." She looks me dead in the eye, the look of determination in her eyes hitting me in the chest.

"Space?" I ask, my voice breaking.

Nodding, she looks to the floor. "Yes. I just need to think all of this through, process it more. I was expecting you to react differently, and now you're just acting..."

"Acting how?" I interrupt.

"Acting perfect!"

A sardonic laugh falls from my lips. "Oh, I'm sorry that I didn't react the way I was supposed to. Could you please enlighten me on what you were expecting? For me to tell you I won't be present for a child? For me to tell you to figure it out on your own? Jesus Riley, what kind of person do you think I am?"

"I didn't think you'd do that! I just didn't…"

"Didn't what?"

"I just didn't expect for things to have to get so serious for us so fast. People are supposed to love one another when they have a baby…"

"Well I never said I didn't love you," I say under my breath.

"What?" she asks in shock.

I don't want this to be the moment I confess my feelings to her. Not with all this uncertainty in the air, not with her looking at me like I've done something wrong. "Nothing, Riley. Absolutely nothing."

"Why are you acting so cool about this? Shouldn't you be freaked out after—"

"After what, Riley?" I cut her off. "After not having a dad myself?"

"I don't mean it the wrong way, but yeah." There's a long pause as she gathers her thoughts. Her next words hurt worse, knowing that she had time to think them through, and yet she still says them. "You didn't grow up with a dad and now you're being forced into being one."

Her words sting. I don't want her using my lack of a father against me. The sins of my father don't define me. If anything, the way he treated me as a child is the reason why I'm confident I won't make the same mistakes as him.

Taking a deep breath, I try not to lash out at her in retaliation. I don't know what the last few days have been like for her, especially with finding out this monumental news alone. I don't want to fight, I just want her.

"That's the thing," I start. "It doesn't feel forced to me. It seems fast, but not forced. Forced has such a negative connotation around it, as if I don't want this baby—as if I don't want you—but I'll be here anyway. I'm not letting you do this right now," I say, rounding the corner to stand in front of her. Tilting her face up to look at me, I find unshed tears in her eyes.

Her bottom lip shakes. "Do what?"

"You're not using the things I've confided in you against me. That isn't you."

"How am I using it against you if you've been the one to say it all along? It's *you* who was apprehensive at being able to handle a relationship. Now all of a sudden *you're* ready to have a relationship and a baby? What's up with the sudden change, Sebastian?"

The answer is simple. It's her. "You," I say confidently.

"What?" My hands fall to my side the moment she steps away from my touch.

"You're the sudden change, Riley. Everything about you has changed it all for me. I haven't wanted to ever give anyone the time of day, but for you, I do. For you, I want to give everything. I *will* give everything. Why is that hard for you to understand?"

"I don't know, maybe because for months the only time you gave a shit about me is when you saw me with another man, or when I was underneath you. For the longest time you didn't even let me touch you, Sebastian."

Closing the distance, I pull my shirt up and flatten her palm against my chest. "Touch me wherever you want, trouble. You've branded yourself so deeply inside me that my body, my mind, my *soul* is yours. There's not a part of me that doesn't have your name written all over it. Is that what you need to hear?"

She stares at the place her palm lays against my heart. I wish I could say the three words that would change this all. Maybe an *I love you* would convince her that I'm not going to run. I just can't bring myself to say something so colossal in the middle of an argument. Plus, part of me wants her to be confident in the promises I've already made to her, not needing more than that right now.

Her hand trembles against my chest. I want to pull her into me and forget about the last five minutes. I want to forget about all of her concerns for me. I want to pretend that she has faith in me and that she believes in me—but I can't. She's hurt me, it's clear she doesn't trust me, not fully. How can we do this if she doesn't even trust the things I'm saying to her?

"I'm sorry, Sebastian," she says, her voice scratching. "I want to believe you, I do. I believe that you *think* the words you're saying are true, but I'm scared that once this sinks in—once it really sinks in—everything will change."

My lips find her forehead. I close my eyes, committing the

smell of her to memory. I memorize the feel of her body against mine, feeling her warmth against me. For a few moments, we're stuck in the embrace, and for a short moment in time, I forget about all the things stacked against us.

Pulling away, I begin to walk toward her door, needing a moment apart from her before I say something I can't come back from. She clearly needs space and time to think about this, to realize how serious my words are.

"Where are you going?" she questions, her footsteps echoing behind mine.

"I'm leaving. You wanted space, remember?"

"Sebastian, wait."

Turning on my heel, I look down at her. "I'm not going to apologize for wanting to raise our child with you. I refuse to apologize for giving this thing all that I've got. But first, Riley, you need to figure out if this is what *you* want. Because as much as I hate to admit it, I'm wondering if you want something different."

"It sounds perfect. Too perfect."

"You know how I feel. I've told you my intentions. I want you. I want this baby. I want to be a family, and I mean it with the entirety of my soul. But you're going to have to trust me to do that. Call me when you've figured out if that aligns with what you want."

It takes everything in me to leave her standing alone in her entryway. This wasn't how I envisioned this day going after she told me. And it hurts like hell.

It takes forever to get an appointment with a decent OB in this city. Either they're always this busy, or I'm pregnant along with every other woman in LA, because it takes me three weeks to snag an ultrasound appointment. Which, if my pregnancy calculator app is correct, would make me almost ten weeks by the time of the appointment. I was told to go into my general practitioner's office to take a pregnancy test there, which was glaringly positive. And now I'm in a waiting game to see the baby growing inside me on a screen.

Nora has barely been home and I'm somewhat grateful for it. Life has become almost robotic for me. The days run together. I go to work, come home, binge watch TV shows, go to bed—wash, rinse, repeat. Luckily, I'm only nauseous first thing in the morning. As soon as I'm able to get water and food into my system, I feel more like myself. Except feeling extremely tired no matter what I do.

I'm not proud to admit I've been avoiding Sebastian.

I don't know why I'm doing it, and I know there's no reason I should be. He's doing everything possible to make this work. He's perfect, *too* perfect. It makes me fear that eventually, the perfect will just…fade away. I'm scared he'll realize that being a father and a partner aren't the things he wanted for himself, and that he'll leave me and the baby. And right now, I can protect my heart enough from that to survive him leaving. But the more time we spend together—the more I'm able to see the pieces of his heart he's kept guarded from the world—the more I fall for him.

I slow down, trying to find an empty space in the busy apartment parking lot. Today was a long day at work, and all I can think about is taking a nice, warm bath.

Finally, I'm able to snag a spot. I whip my car into the space quickly, making sure no one can steal it from me. Putting my car in park, I grab my purse and start the walk toward my building. This spot happens to be at the very back of the parking lot. My aching feet protest as I make the trek to my apartment.

I'm halfway regretting choosing heels when a familiar body stops me in my tracks. Leaning against a light pole is Sebastian. His back is to me, but I would recognize that tall frame anywhere.

When I first met him, he seemed bigger, having more weight on him. But in the time that Nash was in rehab, he spent hours in the gym, regaining the toned, muscular body he claimed to have had in high school. The way the light hits his arms showcases those defined muscles.

I get flashbacks of the times I had a front row seat to the ripple of the tendons in his arms. Stopping, I take a moment to get a hold of myself before alerting him of my presence.

I don't know what I want to say to him but I'm getting tired of avoiding him. I'm sick of living in fear that this man can—and will—hurt me. The growing baby inside me deserves for their parents to give it a shot at being together. My fears of getting my heart broken for the first time shouldn't stop me from giving this a shot, and yet, I can't seem to get over *his* fear of commitment.

"Sebastian?" I say quietly.

His back tightens when I say his name. Quickly turning around, his eyes connect with mine for the first time in weeks.

"There's my trouble." The smile on his face could bring

any woman to her knees. His charm is effortless. He's too good looking for his own good. No man should be allowed to have a smile that conveys so much confidence.

I try not to be awkward, my feet coming to a stop in front of him. My hands twist in front of me as I wonder if I should give him a hug, or what the protocol is here.

Catching on to my awkward energy, he stuffs his hands into his pockets. I wonder if it's the only way he's able to refrain from reaching out and touching me.

"What are you doing here?"

The wind picks up, ruffling the short strands of hair at the top of his head. He gives me a sheepish smile. "I've had to resort to stalking you…"

I can't hide the smile that forms on my own lips. "I can see that."

Letting out a pent up breath, his face turns serious. "I needed to see you. We need to talk about this, Riley."

I'm not shy about re-memorizing the slopes and planes of his face. The weeks have added up, and I'm left marveling at how handsome he is all over again. A perfect combination of rugged and handsome.

"What if I say no?"

His head tilts up as he eyes the building up and down. "Then I guess I'd have to find a way to climb up to your balcony."

I laugh. "I don't have a balcony."

He scrapes at the pavement with the toe of his shoe. "I'll throw rocks at your window, then. Pester you until you have no choice but to talk to me."

"How would you know you're throwing rocks at the right window?"

"I guess I may have to piss off a fuck ton of people to find out."

"You're ridiculous," I sigh. The air around us is quiet, the sound of distant cars filling the void. The two of us take time to look at each other. I know that if I wanted to, I could close the distance to him and get wrapped up in his warmth. He hasn't been shy about his feelings, about what he wants. I'm just still trying to figure out if that's what he *actually* wants or what he *thinks* he wants.

"About that talk, trouble," he says, his tone getting serious. He keeps his hands in his pockets as he looks at me expectantly.

My mind reels with so many different things I could say. Before getting pregnant, I was willing to live off any scrap of affection or promise he could give me. Now that I'm going to have a baby, things are different. It's opened my eyes on what I want. I want someone who doesn't run from their feelings. I want to be part of a relationship where I'm not always having to guess where we stand. So far, the entirety of my relationship has been guessing with Sebastian.

"I'm not ready. I'm still trying to wrap my head around all of this," I finally get out.

His jaw clenches. He nods, looking at something over my shoulder.

"Will you ever be ready?" he asks.

I shrug, playing with the hem of my dress to give me something to do with my hands. "I just don't know if I can give you what you want, Sebastian."

"And what do I want?" he responds immediately.

"You want me to trust you."

He falters for a moment. "You don't trust me?"

I scrape my hands over my face, letting out a frustrated groan. "I do but I don't."

"You're going to have to elaborate." There's resignation in his face. For so long, it seems like he's let me in to see small slivers of who he really is. Now, I'm afraid that my reluctance to jump into things with him is the reason he's guarding his heart once again.

"I just don't want there to be resentment. I don't want you

to feel trapped. You can be a great dad and not have to be in a relationship with me."

"Is that what *you* want?"

I chew on my lip, shaking my head. "No. Not at all."

He reaches out to touch me, but stops seconds before his arm lands on mine. "Then I don't see the problem here."

"Because I'm still not confident that you won't end up resenting me. That this won't be too much for you too fast. I know how important being a good dad is to you, after everything with yours. I don't want to pressure you into also figuring out how to be a romantic partner at the same time."

"Do I get a say in any of this?" he says, his voice low, with an aggravated tone. His brown eyes are angry when they look at me. "Because I've told you time and time again that I want both. I want it all with you. It's *you* that's running, Riley. Not me."

"But everything with your dad…"

"That doesn't mean I'll make a shitty father."

"I never said that, Sebastian."

He runs a hand through his hair. It's not often he loses control of his emotions, but right now, he's looking a bit unhinged. His hair sticks up in different directions from where he's ran his fingers through it. The muscle in his jaw ticks incessantly, letting me know he's mad.

"It sure seems like you are. Do you want me to make things better with my dad? Is that what it will take for you?"

"No, of course not," I answer, my voice cracking.

He pulls out his phone, waving it in front of me. "Because I will. Right now if you want me to. If that's what it'll take for you understand that I'm *all fucking in*, I'll do it."

"That's not what I meant."

"He's been calling me recently. I haven't answered any of his calls because, quite frankly, I don't give a damn about what he has to say. But if that's what *you* need—if you need me to forgive and forget about every abusive, belittling thing he did to me—I will. I'll call him right now."

Taking a step closer to him, I lay a hand on his cheek. "That isn't what I need at all."

His fingers cover mine, holding my hand to his face. He looks at me sadly before pulling my hand off him. Before he lets go, he lays a kiss on my palm.

"I can't do this with you, Riley. I can't keep trying to prove my worth—*my word*—to you. You need to figure out what you want, and you need to do it soon. I won't keep putting myself through this. I'm not going to keep chasing you down. If you want me, you know how to reach me."

He drops my hand and stalks back to the parking lot before I can say anything else.

The moment he leaves, I'm left wondering what I'm afraid of more—losing him after falling in love with him or never actually having him at all?

SEBASTIAN

Not talking to her is torture. There are so many times I almost cave and call her, but I manage to fight the urge. There are only so many times I can handle her rejection before I'll give up.

Her lack of faith in me is unnerving. I've only ever been upfront with her about my take on love and relationships. I guess maybe I'd been too honest, because that same honesty is biting me in the ass now. I don't know why she can't get it in that thick skull of hers that she's changed it all for me.

I'm not repulsed by her touch, I crave it.

I'm not going to run from her, I *want* to stay.

I'm not scared of loving her, I already do.

All of these things I'd tell her, but she just isn't ready. Right now, she's more scared than I am and I'm going to give her time. I'm going to prove that no matter how long she avoids me that my feelings for her don't change.

I'm all in for her, she just has to let me be.

All of these things run through my head as I check my phone for a message from her. Just like all of the other times, there's nothing. It was a long day at work, and all I can think about is going home. I wish I was going home to Riley, but instead, it's another night of returning home to my empty apartment.

Pulling into my parking lot, I can't help but wonder what Riley is up to tonight. I want to know how she's doing, if she's feeling okay, but I haven't reached out to her. I know that my texts or calls would go unanswered, so I don't try. I did at first, after I left her standing alone in the parking lot. For days I called and messaged her, but she never responded to me. So I stopped. Eventually she'll come to her senses, and if she doesn't—I don't even want to go there.

I'm pulling my keys out of my pocket when I notice someone standing near the front door of my building. They wear an old ball cap, one that is forever seared into my mind.

"You've got to be me fucking kidding me," I mutter under my breath. He hasn't spotted me yet, he's too busy looking at a piece of paper in his hand, so I could make a break for my car before he spots me.

I think about my options for a moment, but think better of running. Clearly he's aware of where I live, so I need to face the inevitable and tell him to get lost.

"What are you doing here?" I say, my voice raised.

My dad startles, almost dropping the paper in his hands. When he looks at me, I'm shocked at how different, yet familiar he looks from years ago.

The last time I saw him was after we'd had a huge fight. He'd thrown a beer bottle at my face to wake me up from sleeping on the couch. I'd been passed out from working my ass off to be able to pay our rent that month. He'd spent all of our money on drugs. He was pissed that I was taking up the entire couch and he thought it was a good idea to nail me in the eye with a bottle.

It wasn't the first time, but I made damn sure it was the last. I wasn't some little kid that had to take his shit anymore. I was bigger than him. I could hit back—and hit back hard. I saw red and it became an out of body experience. One moment I was laying on the couch, holding my eye, and the next his head was flying backward from the impact of my punches.

I left him bleeding on the carpet as I packed my shit and left. I never looked back.

I hadn't planned on ever seeing him again, but apparently fate hates me.

"Sebastian," he says.

His voice sends creeping, crawling tingles down my spine. I used to hate it when he said my name, I preferred when he was passed out high or drunk to when he'd acknowledge me. Nothing good ever came from him noticing me during my childhood.

"I'm going to ask again. What are you doing here?" I say through clenched teeth. Blood angrily pumps through my veins.

He tucks the piece of paper he was looking at into his pocket. "I was looking for you, son."

"I thought the ignored calls were enough of a hint that I want nothing to do with you."

Even though years have gone by, he looks better now than he did the last time I saw him. He looks sober. His eyes are clear and not sunken in, and there's actual color to his skin. There's new wrinkles on his face, and his beard has grown out more than the last time I saw him. The hat sitting on the top of his head hides his hair, but I'm wondering if he's fully gray by now. Or bald.

"I have so much to say to you, Sebastian. I wrote it all down." He pats the place where just stuffed the piece of paper.

"Save your breath," I say, walking past him. "I don't want to hear it. It's too late."

He grabs my arm. "I just need one minute, son."

Turning quickly, I rip my hand from his grasp. "Don't ever do that again," I say through clenched teeth.

He takes a few steps away me. His eyes are wide with fear.

His lip barely trembles, but I notice it. Good. I feared him for a long time, it's about damn time that I return the favor.

"Please?" His voice is shaky.

Deep down, I hate that there's a tiny part of me who wants to hear him out. No matter how fucked up it is, it seems like it's ingrained in kids to love their parents, even if those parents don't deserve their love. For a long time, I loved my dad. Even though there wasn't a single part of him that deserved my love, I still did. But there's too much history between us now. There's too much bad blood. So even though some dark, twisted part of me wants to hear what he has to say, I can't handle it. Not now. Not while I'm still reeling from my last conversation with Riley. Not while he's responsible for my trust issues—the very reason Riley won't talk to me.

I step closer to him, close enough to make our height difference obvious. I'm not shorter or smaller than him, not anymore. I'm a head taller than him, my muscles a different contrast to his skinny stature.

"Let me be clear. I don't give a shit about what you have to say to me. I don't want a reunion. I don't want to see your face. Leave me the hell alone."

I don't give him time to respond. Rushing to the door, I pull it open and disappear inside the building. I'm not able to take a deep breath until I make it into the safety of my apartment. I don't know if he knows my exact apartment number or just the building, but I don't risk it. I slide the deadbolt into place, making sure I take the extra time to lock the door.

Stepping away from the door, I clutch my chest. My lungs feel tight from holding my breath and tensing up.

He'd been calling for a while, but I figured he would give up once he realized that I wasn't going to answer. That I wasn't going to give him money or whatever else he wanted. Never did I imagine him showing up at my place—especially sober. I don't recall a day of my life that my Dad's eyes weren't glassy from drugs or booze. He seemed to have more weight on him than he used to. He seemed *healthy*. The sight was more jarring than if he would've been strung out.

I try to go about my normal nightly routine, but I can't stop thinking about what he could possibly want. If it isn't money for drugs, then what is it? I know my Dad. There's no way that after neglecting me my whole life he finally wants to try and be a father.

The hot water from the showerhead beats down on me. Seeing my dad has set me off in so many ways, but not in the ways I expected. The reason I was angry with him was because of the situation I now find myself in with Riley. I hate that my insecurities, the reasons I'm so messed up, are because of him. And now those are the reasons Riley won't accept my love. And right now, what I need most in this world is for her to believe me—to trust me.

When I'm supposed to be thinking about Nash and how to keep him safe, I'm thinking about her.

When I'm supposed to be upset about something, all I can remember is how she laughs and a dimple appears on her cheek in the most unusual spot.

There are so many things about her that I'm obsessed with. I want to feel her touch for the rest of eternity. I want to spend my life making memories with her. Now all I need is to convince her of these things.

I devise a plan as I get ready for bed. Seeing my dad only fueled my fire. The shit he messed up in me will not be the reason I don't get the girl of my dreams. I will do whatever it takes to prove to her that I'm in this forever, that I love her and that I'm ecstatic at the thought of creating a family with her.

Before my head hits the pillow, I send her a text for the first time in a couple of weeks.

Me: I'll be at that first OB appointment. You wouldn't have told me the date and time if you didn't

want me there. I'm going to prove to you that it's you I want forever, trouble. Get ready for it.

I don't wait for a response. Instead, I go to bed with a game plan.

I'm going to win my girl back, and then I'm never going to give her a reason to doubt me again.

My stomach drops the moment Sebastian's car pulls in next to mine at the OBGYN office. I can't remember the last time I felt nausea in the afternoon, but seeing him next to me, I suddenly feel sick. I sent him a text telling him the time and date of my first OB appointment so he could come. I wanted him to be here—I still do. My nerves are just on fire between seeing him *and* seeing our baby.

He steps out of his car, walking around my car until he stops at my door. Pulling the door open, he gives me a cocky smile. "Miss me, trouble?"

More than I'd care to admit.

"Hi, Sebastian," I say, taking his out-stretched hand. He pulls me out of the car a little too hard, knowing exactly what he's doing by throwing me off balance. I have no choice but to fall into his hard chest.

"Sorry," he smirks. "It was an accident."

Rolling my eyes, I turn and grab my purse from my passenger seat.

Once I'm ready, he holds his hand out once again. "Let's go see our baby."

I stare at the hand, wondering what he's thinking. We've never been the couple to hold hands, and now suddenly he wants to walk into this office and pretend we are?

Sighing, he grabs my hand, wrapping his fingers around

mine tightly. "It'd be a whole lot easier if you just admitted to yourself that you want this."

I stare at his back blankly as he pulls me in the direction of the office. All I'm left to do is follow him. If I wanted to, I could pull my hand from his grasp. I know that he wouldn't try again if he realized that I didn't actually want this. But that's the thing. I *do* want this. I want to hold his hand, to feel his skin pressed against mine. I was deprived of it for so long that even something as small as this feels significant. I'm just so freaking scared. I am so, *so* scared.

Thoughts of us fade to the back of my mind when another fear creeps in the closer we get to the doors. I come to a complete stop. "What if something's wrong?"

My feet stay planted, my arm pulling him away from the building slightly. There's a weird sensation in my stomach, making me feel like I could vomit at any moment.

He squeezes my hand tightly. "Hey, don't think like that."

I watch closely as a woman who looks like she could pop out a baby any day walks into the building. She waddles from side to side, her body disappearing behind the tinted front doors.

I look at him anxiously. "I can't help it. Bad, terrifying thoughts are just running through my head right now."

His finger is cold against my face when he brushes a strand of loose hair away. Shortly after his finger leaves my cheek, he's bending down, pressing his lips to the spot the hair just was. "I've got you. No matter what. We get to see our baby, trouble."

God, I missed him. His touch. His words. Everything about him.

He gently pulls on my hand, leading me through the automatic doors. Being in the waiting room is like being in a different universe. There's women in various stages of pregnancy surrounding me. I know that OB's do other things but deal with pregnant people, but you wouldn't know that looking around this room. There's only one other man besides Sebastian in the waiting area.

Sebastian must be thinking the same thing I am. His eyes are wide as he scans the room carefully.

"You're severely out-numbered," I whisper underneath my breath.

Shaking his head, he grins at me. "The things I do for you."

We get checked in with the receptionist. She tells me to go back to the bathroom so they can gather a sample. I give Sebastian a look, not knowing they still needed my pee for anything.

I hurry in the bathroom, trying not to pee on my own hand as I fill the tiny sample cup. I speed back to Sebastian, wondering if peeing in the cup is going to be a normal occurrence.

My hands sweat way more than they normally do as we wait for them to say my name.

Sebastian flips through a pamphlet. "How do you feel about circumcision?"

My eyes bug out of my head. A woman side-eyes us from across the waiting room.

I snatch the pamphlet from his hand, stuffing it into my purse. "Did you really have to say that so loud?"

He looks around the room. "Why does it matter?" He lifts a hand at the people around us. "They're having to make the same decisions we are."

"Yeah, well, we don't have to discuss it here," I say through gritted teeth.

He spends the next ten minutes collecting every single pamphlet he can find in the place. He even grabs a magnet with the phone number of the OB office—*just in case*—as if somehow it slips his mind that we can save the contact in our phones.

After they call the name of almost every single person in

the waiting room, finally a woman in purple scrubs opens the door, clipboard in hand.

"Riley?" she says sweetly, her eyes drifting around the room.

I bolt up, almost tripping over Sebastian's long, outstretched legs in the process. "Present!" I say awkwardly, cringing at myself on the inside.

"*Present*," Sebastian mocks under his breath.

I elbow him in his middle.

"What the hell," he says, plastering a smile on his face when we stop at the nurse.

"That's me," I correct, hoping she didn't catch my earlier statement.

"I'm your sonographer," she announces. Her finger points down a long hallway. "We're down this way, second door on the right."

Nodding politely, I follow her. She looks over her shoulder. "How are you today?"

"Nervous," I tell her honestly.

"Psyched!" Sebastian says at the same time.

She smiles, directing us to the room. "You can take a seat on the table. We're going to try and see if we can get a view from the stomach first. If not, you'll have to undress."

Undress? I wonder.

Following her directions, I take a seat in the chair. I pull my t-shirt up and unbutton my shorts.

She types on a contraption next to the bed, chatting away as she does so. "We're going to have to do measurements with the probe, but you may be far along enough for us to get a view of the babe with an external ultrasound."

Sebastian takes a seat in the chair next to me. He instantly grabs me by the hand, his eyes taking in every single movement of the sonographer. In this room, it doesn't feel like we're not together. It feels a lot like the complete opposite, and I like it—a lot.

"This might be a little cold," she warns, squeezing a jelly onto my stomach. It actually feels warm against my skin.

She types one more thing on the machine before grabbing a probe, and holding it in the air. "You ready?" she asks cheerfully.

I grasp Sebastian's hand for dear life, nodding my head. There's a pit the size of Texas in my stomach, I'm nervous something won't be normal when she places that probe on my stomach.

"Don't mind the pressure," she warns, pushing it into my belly.

At first, there's nothing on the screen. There's a lot of black and white blobs, but nothing that resembles anything like a baby.

And then…suddenly, there is one.

"There we go," she says, doing something on the computer that makes it zoom in.

"Oh my god," I breathe, marveling at the screen in front of me.

Floating around in a sea of black is what looks like a teeny, tiny baby. It looks more like a tadpole than a baby, but there's no mistaking what it is.

Our baby.

Misty-eyed, I look to my side at Sebastian. I find him staring at the screen in awe. The baby inside me twirls around, two nubby little legs bicycle kicking repeatedly.

"That's it?" he asks, his voice shaking with nerves.

"Yep," she answers. "Just one in there!" A line shows up on the screen. She clicks from one side of the little dancing tadpole to the other.

"Measuring about ten weeks and two days. Right on par with the date you listed."

For a moment, I have no words. I can't stop looking at the baby on the screen, only able to look at Sebastian's reaction.

The look on his face seals the deal for me.

I'm obsessively in love with this man.

The father of the child on the screen in front of us.

He must feel my eyes on him. He looks down, a huge smile on his face.

"That's our baby," he whispers.

Not able to hold back, I squeeze his hand tightly. "I want what you want," I admit, loud and proud.

The sonographer continues to do different things on the machine, but for the moment, I'm not paying attention. I'm too caught up in the look on Sebastian's face.

Pure bliss.

The skin around his eyes crinkle as he breaks out into the biggest smile ever. Leaning down, he kisses my hand over and over.

"I've been waiting way too long for you to say that."

It's difficult to swallow all of the emotions I'm feeling. My throat feels like it's closing up. When I look up to the woman bearing witness to our confessional, I find her watching us closely.

"Sorry," I choke out, "all these hormones."

"Oh don't apologize. This happens all the time."

I nod, going back to look at the wiggling blob on the screen. The nurse might be used to couples getting all mushy when they see their baby, but this is a surreal moment for us.

We're going to give this a shot. I can't deny him for any longer. I have to give us a chance. I have to give *him* the chance to stick to his word.

Walking out of the office, I feel like I'm on cloud nine. The two of us come to a stop between our cars.

Sebastian pulls me into him, cradling my head against his chest. "What made you come around?"

I take a deep breath, ready to bare it all to him. "Seeing our baby made me realize I can't be scared of loving you forever."

"I'm happy we're no longer stalling the inevitable, but I

still want to talk about all of this, Riley. Fuck, I don't *want* to at this point, I *need* to."

"What exactly do you want to talk about?"

He looks at me as if I'm out of my mind. "I've been going crazy the last few weeks, thinking about us. Thinking about this pregnancy. About what I want for you and me…and our baby." His last sentence is quieter than the first ones.

"And what exactly do you want for us, Sebastian?" I ask timidly. My teeth dig into my lip nervously as I anxiously await his answer.

"I want us to be a family," he answers honestly. "I never had a family, and I've had weeks to realize how bad I want this. How bad I want what I didn't have."

"Aren't we rushing into things?"

A sarcastic laugh falls from his chest as he merges into a lane. "We've rushed things from the moment we met."

"I just don't want *you* to feel rushed. For you to one day regret living this simple life with me."

"Oh, trouble," he says, his hands framing my face. "You're still thinking that?"

I shrug helplessly. "Maybe. I just don't want you to feel the pressure of saying something you—"

"Stop right there." His voice is strong, confident. "Never would I ever say something I didn't believe in. When I tell you I want us to be a family, I mean it."

His finger finds my chin, tilting my head up. "And when I say that I've felt things for you that I've never even dreamt about feeling for a woman, I mean it."

"You do?"

His free hand timidly lays flat against my stomach. "I mean it with every-fucking-thing I have, trouble. I'd tell you I was in love with you if you were ready to hear it, but you aren't. So for now, I'll tell you I want us to be a family."

A tear leaves my eye. I try to wipe it away before he notices it, but I'm not fast enough. He grabs my wrist, blocking me from being able to wipe away the wetness. "Let me see those tears, trouble. They give me some kind of hint that you want what I want."

I stare at him, his body blurry due to the tears. "I'm ready for you to tell me."

"I'm going to spend the rest of my life convincing you that my heart is yours. It will only ever be yours, and that I don't want to be anywhere you aren't."

"You swear?"

He nods his head, pulling my face close to his. Our noses touch. "Yes, I swear, with everything that I am.

"I'm still waiting for you to tell me," I whisper.

Shaking his head, he kisses one of my tears. "Fuck, do I love you, trouble. I love you with every part of me, even the deepest, darkest parts. I love you with those the most."

"I love you too," I say. "I love you so much that it scares me."

"I love you," he repeats proudly. "And I'm so happy that I don't have to pretend that I don't."

We're in love.

We're having a baby.

Everything in this moment is perfect.

"Close your eyes, trouble."

His breath tickles my forehead, but I do as he says. People walking by are probably wondering what the hell we're doing, but I don't care. They can stare. I'm just happy to be in his arms once again. To be done pretending.

"Imagine our life together. Imagine the family we'll create. The adventures we will go on. Picture us old and grey and bickering because no matter how much I love you, you're stubborn as hell."

I laugh, opening my eyes. "It seems like a beautiful life."

"It will be, trouble."

For a moment, we stay locked in an embrace, neither one of us wanting to pull away from the other. Finally, my feet start to hurt so I pull away, grabbing my keys from my purse. Sebastian plucks them from my hand the moment I go to unlock my car.

He opens the passenger door. "Get in," he instructs.

I point to his car behind him. "What about your car? I can drive myself…"

"Nope. I just got you back, I'm not letting you go so easily. I'll get my car eventually."

I do as I'm told, sliding into the passenger seat. He gets in quickly, pulling the car out of the parking lot and getting on the highway.

"I'm never letting you out of my sight again," he says.

"We both have jobs."

"Yeah, well, I'm never letting you out of my sight when we're not at work."

"I still can't believe we're having a baby," I tell Sebastian.

He chuckles. "At least we know the kid is bound to be funny—and incredibly good looking."

"Did you just admit that I'm funny?" I tease.

He lifts one of his shoulders slightly. "It's possible."

"Mhm, you're just too scared to admit that I'm way funnier than you."

"Keep dreaming, baby."

We fall into a comfortable silence. I stare at the string of images we were sent home with, admiring the teeny tiny human growing inside me. The radio plays softly in the background.

One of Nash's new songs comes on, one about Nora, and suddenly I'm brought back down to earth.

"Hey, Sebastian?"

He looks at me from the corner of his eye. "Yeah?"

Sighing, I look down at the images in my hand. "I think it's time we tell our friends about us…"

"Are you sure you're feeling okay?" I ask Riley, navigating the car to the front gate of Nash's house. One of his home security guards, Ron, recognizes me instantly, waving and pressing the button to open the gate for us.

"For the fifteenth time, I'm feeling fine," she answers.

"But are you *really* sure?"

"Sebastian!" she yells. "I'm feeling *great*. We aren't going to back out of this. Get it together. We're telling Nash and Nora that we're together and having a baby."

The car stops in front of his gigantic house. Looking over at her, I try to fake a smile. "I just wanted you to know we could bow out if we wanted to."

Her eyes roll into the back of her head. "No. They need to know, Sebastian." She points to her stomach. "I'm not going to be able to hide this bump for much longer."

Bending down, she pulls her purse from the floorboard and reaches to open her door.

"Wait!" I demand, hustling out of the car. Running around it, I open the door the rest of the way for her. "You're supposed to wait for me to open the door."

"I can open my own damn door," she huffs.

"You're too stubborn for your own good," I groan, following her toward the front door.

There's a few cars parked in front of the house. Nash and

Nora are hosting a dinner tonight. I'm sure a lot of his inner circle will be there, as well as a few people close to Nora.

It wasn't our intention to tell everyone at the same time, but getting a chance to speak to Nash and Nora together has been damn near impossible. I spend most of my days with the couple for my job. But it's been harder than we anticipated to come up with a way for Riley to be there as well.

When Riley planned a dinner for Nash, Nora, and herself, she and I decided I would just insert myself into the equation so we could spill the beans together. But Nash, apparently quite the host now, insisted on making it a big thing. So now, we get to tell everyone that not only are Riley and I dating, but she's also three months pregnant.

Surprise.

Playing it out in my head only makes me more nervous.

One of Nash's staff, Glenda, greets us at the door. "Hi again, Sebastian," she says, turning to face Riley. "I'm Glenda, you must be Riley. Nora talks about you often."

Riley takes her outstretched hand. "It's so nice to meet you."

"How's it going?" I ask.

"It's a full house in there," Glenda comments.

She directs Riley to a place where she can put her purse. There's music softly spilling from the speaker system around the house. Voices can be heard coming from the sitting room.

"Fantastic," Riley says in mock excitement.

"Are you ready for this?" I ask through my teeth, careful that Glenda doesn't hear.

"As ready as I'll ever be. Really wish I could take the edge off with a drink."

"Oh, good idea."

Spinning around, she gives me a dirty look. "You suck."

"You'll be the one sucking later," I tease, getting in one quick ass-grab before we are faced with a slew of people.

"I cannot deal with you."

"You'll be dealing—" I'm not given time to finish my sentence. We're met with a large group of people mingling about, the initial shock of the crowd cutting me off.

Nash has his arm around Nora while they talk with Lennon and Aiden. Landon, Nash's keyboardist, is speaking animatedly to Poe, the bassist for the band, about god knows what. In true Monica fashion, she sits at a table with her laptop out. Matt sits next to her, silently observing the mix of personalities displayed in Nash's sitting room.

"Riley!" Nora gasps, dodging an ottoman in her attempt to rush to Riley. As soon as she makes it to her, she's wrapping her tightly in a hug. "Oh my god, I missed you so much. It's been way too long."

"You're the one who's barely come home since you got back together with your famous boyfriend," Riley points out.

The comment makes Nash snicker. "Damn right she hasn't. We were apart almost a year, I'd never let her leave my sight if it were fully up to me."

"You'd never let her leave the bedroom," Aiden corrects.

Nora's cheeks turn pink. "Oh, ignore him, Nora," I joke. "Remember that one time in Colorado we all could hear—"

Nora claps her hands together. "Well, *anyway*." She manages to give Nash, Aiden, and I a dirty look with one fell-swoop of her eyes. "I'm going to go back to assaulting my best friend with attention."

"Do it. Give me all the attention, I live for it." Riley hooks her arm in Nora's, the two of them walking to one of the couches. Lennon joins them. They begin whispering about something, carrying on like they'd never been away from each other.

Walking over to Nash's bar cart, I pour myself a drink. Once I've got a few sips of courage in, I make my way to Nash and Aiden.

"Sebastian, tell Nash it makes perfect sense for me to go

on tour with him," Aiden pleads. His fingers wrap tightly around a drink. Nash however, sips on only water.

When he first returned, we made sure all the liquor was removed from the house, but he stopped that very quickly. His logic was that in his line of work, he was going to be around copious amounts of alcohol. He needed to learn to be around it without feeling the urge to empty a bottle. Now, he barely seems to notice when someone around him drinks. It's incredible how much he's healed.

"Well, take your time thinking it over," Aiden says, annoyed, snapping me back into the conversation.

I throw my arms up in surrender. "I'm not getting involved in this." Curiously, I look at Nash, a little confused. "Why can't Aiden go on tour with you?"

"Yeah big bro, why can't I go on tour with you? You're taking Lennon!" He points in her direction, but she's too busy talking to Riley to notice.

"Lennon gets to go because she doesn't cause trouble and she keeps her mouth shut," Nash quips, taking a drink of his water.

"I can keep my mouth shut," Aiden argues.

Monica lets out a snort in amusement from across the room. She doesn't bother looking up at us, but it's obvious she's laughing at Aiden.

"Got something to say?" Aiden asks, glaring at her.

Shaking her head, she stares at the screen in front of her. "To you? Never."

"That's what I thought."

Monica looks at Matt. "Did you hear something?"

Matt acts as if he doesn't hear either one of them. He looks down at his ice water as if it's the most fascinating thing in the world.

Nash groans, rubbing the bridge of his nose. "For fuck's sake, will you two ever get along?"

"Bad time to try and convince you to let Aiden come

along on the tour?" I gesture between Aiden and Monica. "I'd love a front row ticket to the shit show of them having to constantly be near one another."

I'm rewarded with a glare from all three parties involved: Nash, Aiden and Monica.

"Stop egging them on," Nash begs.

"I'm going to go on tour with you," Aiden persists.

"Prove to me you won't annoy me and it's a *maybe,*" Nash sys.

"A maybe is just a yes that needs to marinate." A large smile graces his face.

Monica gives him a disgusted look, one he returns with a wink.

One of the cooking staff comes out with a tray full of food. Another worker follows closely behind them with a tray of their own and I watch as they set down an arrangement of oysters.

"We got your favorite!" Nora tells Riley, looking at her excited. "Had them flown in from the Northeast and everything."

"She was very picky about where we got them from," Nash adds.

The long dining table behind us is now filled from end to end with oysters on the half shell—a food Riley has already complained to me about not being able to have while pregnant. I try not to laugh at the irony.

Her eyes are wide as she walks arm in arm with Nora and Lennon to the table.

"You're sitting by me," Nora tells her, pointing to a specific chair.

I have to awkwardly run to the table to beat Lennon from taking the spot next to Riley. Lennon gives me an inquisitive look, then smiles. She makes me nervous. She's always quiet, as if she can hear my thoughts. It makes me uneasy.

Nash has already taken the other side of Nora, so Lennon

takes the open seat next to Poe. Whatever he says to her catches her attention, because she looks at him with the biggest smile.

Focusing my attention back on Riley, she stares down at the oysters in front of her as Nora explains the different kinds. Everyone else has already begun to eat the food in front of them.

"Go ahead and grab some," Nora urges.

Riley looks at me hesitantly. It's looking like we may have to spill the beans a little earlier than anticipated.

"I'm not super hungry," Riley says through a fake smile.

Nora frowns. "When are you ever *not* hungry?

It's clear that Nora is disappointed by the look on her face.

"Okay so we're actually having to do this," Riley says under her breath. She wipes her hands on the tops of her thighs, looking at the people around the table anxiously.

"Do what?" Nash asks curiously. He uses a tiny fork to scoop some of his oyster into his mouth.

My hand finds Riley's underneath the table, giving her a reassuring squeeze.

"Well," I begin, clearing my throat. "Riley and I have something to share with you."

Even though there's countless people sitting around the table, I can only look at Nash. His opinion is the only one I care about.

"Riley and you?" he questions.

"Yeah," I drawl. "You see…we're together."

"*Together?*" Nora exclaims. She turns her body to face Riley's. "Like together, together?"

Riley nods. "Like together, together," she confirms.

"I thought you just hooked up?" Nora continues, looking at me for a moment before setting her sights back on Riley to give her the third degree.

"We did," I answer. "And then we continued to…"

Nash is silent as he observes Riley and me. I'm waiting for him to make some kind of comment, but he doesn't.

"Can't say I'm too shocked," Aiden pipes up, talking with his mouth full of food.

Matt stares at me blankly. I know I'm in for a long conversation with him later tonight.

"Oh, just wai—"

"I'm pregnant," Riley blurts out. She says the words so loudly I'm sure every single person in the house heard her.

A fork clatters against a plate, the only sound in the now silent room.

Nora looks at Riley horrified. "You're *what?*"

"Pregnant," Riley answers confidently. "Like… my eggo is preggo. I'm with child. There's a bun in the oven."

Nora puts her hand in the air. "Okay, I get it. But you," her eyes find me, "and Sebastian…are having a baby?"

"Yes we are," I answer, proudly putting my arm around Riley.

"I'm over three months pregnant," Riley continues.

Nora's eyes glaze over. "You've been keeping this secret from me?" She looks at Riley's stomach hidden underneath the table. Her hand goes to touch Riley's expanding waist. "There's a baby in there?"

Riley giggles slightly. "There is. I have pictures I can show you and everything."

"I can't believe this," Nora murmurs.

"Ok, now I'm surprised." Aiden says.

"Well, this makes things interesting," Monica bites out.

People continue to ask questions and congratulate us, but I'm only partially listening as I focus on Nash. He sits like a statue, the look on his face unreadable. Everyone else must catch on that he hasn't said anything, because it starts to get quiet around us as we all look toward him.

"We're excited for them, aren't we babe?" Nora says sweetly, slightly leaning into Nash.

Nash's eyes find mine. "Can we talk?"

The legs of his chair scrape across the floor as he gets up, not giving me time to answer.

"Can't you talk here?" Riley says confidently. Her hand now clasps mine even tighter, as if she's trying to keep me in my seat.

"We'll just be a minute." Nash walks away from the table, heading toward the office he barely spends any time in. I have no choice but to follow him.

As I follow him into the room, all my fears about getting involved with Riley come back in full force. Except now, if given the choice between my job with Nash or my relationship with Riley—I'd choose Riley.

SEBASTIAN

It's eerily quiet in Nash's office. We can barely hear the voices from the gathering down the hallway. The quiet is replaced with the sound of Nash's shoes hitting the hardwood floor as he walks toward the large window overlooking his backyard.

His back is to me when he speaks. "Fuck, I'm going to miss you, Bash."

My feet falter from his words. "Miss me?" I ask, scratching at my chin, confused.

Turning around, his face looks solemn. His lips are pulled tight, and just by his posture I can tell he's upset. "Surely you've thought about this. You can't be spending every minute with me anymore. You've got a kid on the way. This job isn't for someone with a family."

"We can figure it out," I argue.

Truth be told, I have thought about it. I've been avoiding this conversation for that very reason. This job requires me to spend the majority of my time away from LA—protecting Nash. But that lifestyle doesn't really allow for being a good father and partner—which are both my top priorities now.

Nash turns around, letting out a large sigh. "I'm so fucking happy for you, Sebastian."

Stepping closer to him, I lean a hip on his desk. "Thanks, Boss."

"Sebastian Compton is going to be daddy. Who the hell thought that would be a good idea?" he jokes.

I flip him off. "Go to hell," I joke right back.

"I'm just fucking with you, Bash. I have no doubt that you'll be a great father, a hell of a lot better than the shitty ones the two of us were given."

I nod. I've never gone into a ton of detail with Nash, but he knows enough. "They make that pretty damn easy," I say honestly.

Nash leaves the window, nearing me and squeezing my shoulder. "You'll do great. Look at it this way, you'll get to test drive the whole being a dad thing and you'll be able to give me some pointers when Nora and I have kids one day."

"Yeah?" I ask in surprise. "You're that serious?"

He looks at me like that was the dumbest question possible. "I'm going to marry that girl one day and have *all* the babies with her. We just might take the more traditional approach there, unlike you and Riley."

"Speaking of..." I begin, nervously fiddling with the record player by his desk. "Did I mention Riley and I are now dating?"

Nash laughs. "You may have mentioned that when you were announcing that the two of you are having a kid..."

I bite back a smile. "Okay good, just wanted to make that part clear."

"How in the hell did that happen?" he asks. He takes a step back, his shoulders now resting against the window as he gives me his full attention.

"We had sex."

He rolls his eyes. "Wow. Here I was thinking it was an immaculate conception. I want to know how you and Riley happened, you shithead."

I breathe out through my nose. "It's kind of a long story."

"You're not getting out of telling it, Bash. I'll get comfortable."

Nash listens intently as I quickly recount the complicated, yet beautiful mess of a story that is Riley and I.

Once I'm done, he lets my words marinate. I don't fill the silence, instead letting him mull my words over before he gives a response.

"Wow. I really had no idea any of this was going on."

"Apparently we were good at keeping it a secret."

Nash thoughtfully looks out the window. "I'd like to say I wouldn't have cared, that I would've wanted what was best for you. But I'm glad you didn't tell me. I needed to be rid of all things Nora for a while."

"You made a comment that one night at the gala, and I thought you knew."

"It's possible I did. I don't remember much from that night. I don't remember much between the time everything fell apart with Nora and a few weeks into rehab."

"Are you happy you went?" I blurt. Nash and I haven't had that much time to talk just the two of us. He's been caught up in Nora since he got out, and I've been running to Riley's place the second I'm off the clock. It hasn't left much time for us to have a private conversation.

He nods, seeming sure of himself. "Absolutely. I needed that. I needed to be taught ways to cope with all of my shit. It was one of the best things that's ever happened to me. The Nash before rehab was," he sighs sadly, "a total mess. But now, I'm incredibly fucking happy, Sebastian. Way happier than I ever imagined myself being."

I nod in agreement. "Same. I never envisioned this life for me. Didn't really care to give it much thought. But now, with Riley—she's changed everything."

"So, you love her?" Nash asks.

"Is it that obvious?"

He chuckles. "Actually no, surprisingly. I write about love for a living, you'd think I'd have picked up on the vibes from the two of you."

"What can I say, we're good at hiding it."

"Well you don't have to anymore. I'm happy for the two of you. And I'm sure Nora is ecstatic. But we will have to talk later about you taking on a different role."

"Do we really, though?"

He looks at me, his eyes narrowing. "You're just going to leave your family for the entirety of a tour? I can't and won't do that."

The comment shuts me up. My mouth opens and shuts a few times. "We could take the baby."

He quirks an eyebrow. "With a newborn? C'mon, Sebastian. You've lived that life. You know that would never work."

I let out a frustrated sigh. "You can't get rid of me this easily, Boss."

He peels himself from the window. "Oh, I don't plan to. We'll find something else for you to do that lets you be a bit more…in one place."

I nod, muttering my thanks. This conversation went better than I was expecting.

"Think we should get out there before they come looking for us?"

"I think that's a solid idea," I answer.

I'm about to turn and walk out the door when his arm wraps around me. Giving me a hug, he says, "So happy for you man. Can't wait to meet this little spawn of yours."

He pulls away quickly, smiling over his shoulder before opening the door.

Riley stumbles, falling over the threshold as the door opens. She straightens herself, fixing her hair. Her eyes look to Nora out of the corner of her eye before she plasters a smile on her face. "Fancy seeing the two of you here," she announces.

Nash and I share a knowing look. He grabs a guilty looking Nora by the waist. "Were you eavesdropping?"

Nora looks at Riley, panic outstretched on her face as

Riley looks cool as a cucumber—definitely the less guilty-looking party of the two of them.

"We were just looking for some socks," Nora spits out.

Riley looks at her puzzled. "*Socks?*"

Nora throws her hands in the air, flustered. "I don't know what to say!"

Riley lets out a dramatic sigh. "Something better than *socks*."

"Busted," I chime, pulling Riley into my side. Her hair is soft against my lips as I lay a kiss on the top of her head.

"You guys left in a wave of mystery. I couldn't *not* hear every detail," Riley explains.

Nash walks over and takes Riley from my grasp, pulling her into a hug. "I'm not shocked by your nosiness at all." He pauses, holding her in a friendly embrace before saying, "I'm happy for the two of you. I can't wait to be the fun uncle."

Nora gives him a look. "If you guys have a little girl she's going to have quite the time having Bash as a dad and Nash as an uncle."

"What's that supposed to mean?" I ask.

Riley turns around, giving me a knowing look. "It means the two of you are so overprotective. She won't stand a chance at dating."

"How do we know it's a girl?" I retort.

"Oh, I don't. Actually, I'd put money on the fact that we're having a boy."

The four of us walk back to the living room in a group. Nash and Nora take the lead, as Riley and I follow closely behind them.

Nora glances over her shoulder. "When do we get to stop guessing and know for sure?"

Lennon hears this from her spot at the table. Her large eyes light up. "Aw, I would love a little girl to spoil," she says softly.

Riley and I share a look as we take our spots at the table

once again. It feels good to have the news of the baby and our relationship out in the open.

"Well, we're actually not going to find out the gender..." Riley says carefully.

A majority of the guests look at us in shock but it's Nash who speaks up first.

"You're not going to tell us if it's a boy or a girl?" he asks, confused. Waiters step in, setting down a fancy salad in front of everyone at the table. They must have cleared the appetizers while Nash and I were speaking.

I adjust my position in my chair. "We decided that so much of our relationship has been a surprise, that we might as well keep the trend going."

"I'm not one for surprises," Monica adds. Her hands smooth over the napkin in her lap.

"Could have fooled me," Aiden quips.

There's a collective sigh at the table. The mood in the air goes from excitement to awkwardness quickly.

Monica stares him down. I don't think a single person at the table even breathes, waiting to see what her reaction will be.

She's calm and collected, two qualities of Monica that terrify me. It seems like the calmer she is the more she's losing her shit inside. When she finally speaks, it's through gritted teeth.

"You don't know the whole story, Aiden. And for the last time, I don't owe you it."

She points to Nash angrily. "I apologized to Nash. We talked about it. And he *forgave* me. To be frank, I don't need the forgiveness—or understanding—from anybody else at this table but Nash. So, if you could stop wasting your breath trying to insult me, that would be delightful."

Monica stands up, carefully putting her napkin on top of her plate. "If you don't mind, I'm going to excuse myself. I don't want my presence to take away from the joy around the news of the baby." Her heels echo off the floor as she rounds the table, stopping at Riley and me before continuing to the door. "Congratulations, Sebastian and Riley."

"Monica, you don't have to go," Nash says.

"Yeah, Nash, I do," she responds calmly before exiting the room.

Aiden looks over at me, not an ounce of remorse on his face. "Think it was something I said?"

Five Months Later

NORMALLY I'M ALL FOR BEING THE CENTER OF ATTENTION. Being the only girl in my family, I basically thrived on being the object of everyone's attention. But right now, I want to shrink into this fancy wingback chair I'm sitting in.

Nora hands me another elaborately wrapped gift. I can't help but return her wide grin. I don't know how she does it, my cheeks are burning from having to smile so much.

A few months ago Nora had pleaded with me to throw my baby shower. I'd agreed, knowing my mom lives too far away to busy herself with having to plan something for me. Although, mom did want to be involved, just from afar. She and Nora have been planning for months so I'm left with an over the top baby shower that was planned by the two of them. When Nash found out that Nora was going to help throw me a baby shower, he felt left out and demanded that we have a co-ed one for this little baby growing inside me.

At first, it sounded like a great plan. Now, as I stare out into a crowd of people I don't recognize…I'm not so sure. The small get together Nora had first promised snowballed into a star-studded event.

Yes, I said star-studded.

There are celebrities here that I've only dreamt about meeting. I've written articles on them and drooled over their fashion choices and now these same celebrities are sipping mimosas at *my* baby shower.

I glare at Sebastian from across the room as he chats with Nash and Aiden, acting as if opening gifts in front of a large group of people isn't the most awkward thing in the world.

I think I'd rather push a baby out of me in front of all these people instead of open another gift from them. That may be a bit dramatic, but if I have to plaster on one more fake smile and thank someone for a baby item I have no idea how to use, I might scream.

It's not like I'm ungrateful. I'm sure all of these things will come in handy when the baby comes. Right now, I'm too focused on the fact we haven't even made it through half of the giant stack of gifts. My cheeks feel like they're about to fall off from smiling. I'm running out of ways to say thank you for these gifts without sounding ungrateful and this baby is bouncing on top of my bladder.

"Are you going to open it, honey?" My mom asks sweetly from my side. Nash and Nora paid to have her flown down for the week and it was honestly the best gift I could've received. Having to tell my mom over FaceTime that she was getting a grandchild was so hard. I wanted to be able to tell her in person, but it didn't work out that way. I felt her excitement through the phone, and ever since the day I told my parents about my pregnancy, she's checked in with me to see how I'm feeling. This week we've done our fair share of shopping, gossiping and spending girl time together. It's been the best.

She stares at the gift Nora laid in my lap. It's wrapped in delicate white paper with small black and white polka dots all over. Whatever is in the box, it's heavy. It feels like a brick on my lap.

"Oh, that's mine!" a voice says from across the room.

I look up to find one of Hollywood's top models staring at me with a soft smile.

How is this my life right now?

I return her smile, my fingers pulling at the gold bow when an unexpected guest walks through the doors.

Holden, with a mystery woman on his arm. My eyes snap over to Sebastian, finding him still too deep in conversation with Aiden and Nash to notice our new visitor. I'd invited Holden to the shower on my last day of work. I'd loved my time at Modern Millennium, kind of, but with the baby on the way, I figured it was time for me to try something new. I wanted to do some freelance writing. I didn't want to plan events, I want to write.

When I'd put in my two weeks' notice, Holden seemed upset. He'd told me that I didn't have to do it, and that we could keep it professional at work. I'd assured him I wasn't quitting because of what happened between us. To be honest, Holden was more of a gentleman about the whole situation than I could've ever imagined him to be. After I essentially ditched him for Sebastian, he handled it with the utmost class.

That's what made quitting even harder. But with the baby's upcoming arrival, I know that my hands would be full. And when I had the time to work, I wanted to be doing something to chase my dream career, not worrying about tablecloths at an event or planning business meetings.

When I'd handed him the expensive, heavy cardstock invitation I didn't imagine he'd ever come. Yet here he is, still being a good guy and showing up.

Nora must see him too, because she quietly tells those around us that I need a quick break. She squeezes my shoulders in reassurance before whispering in my ear. "Did you invite him?"

"Yes," I whisper back, watching Sebastian carefully. I never told Sebastian that I'd invited Holden. I didn't think it'd matter. I didn't imagine Holden would ever show up. "But I didn't think he'd come."

"Oh man," Nora says slowly. "Well, he came."

I shoot a dirty look in her direction. "Thanks for that, Captain Obvious."

My mom puts her hand on my back, leaning in close to Nora and I. "Is something going on here, girls?"

"Nothing to see here," I mutter nonchalantly. Or what I *hope* comes off as nonchalant. My heart hammers in my chest, waiting for Sebastian to notice our newest guest.

It appears I won't have to panic too long, because mid-conversation Sebastian looks up, his gaze landing on Holden. His shoulders stiffen, and it's clear he no longer pays any attention to what Nash is saying.

He stands up, the muscles in his back pulled tight underneath his button up shirt.

I beeline for Holden and his date as quickly as my legs will take me. Sebastian and I make it to them at the same time.

"What do you think you're doing here?" Sebastian says, his voice strained.

My hand finds Sebastian's elbow, a silent plea to *not* make a scene. "I invited him," I say through a forced smile. People around us are starting to stare. Ziggy, bless his soul, causes a distraction by standing up and offering to refill guest's mimosas.

Holden ignores him completely. He takes a step around Sebastian, and lays his hand on my back. Leaning in, he places a chaste kiss on my cheek. It's short-lived. Sebastian pushes Holden's chest while sliding his body between us.

"Don't touch her," he demands. His voice is low and strained.

"It's fine, Sebastian," I say under my breath. "Like I said, I invited him."

Sebastian looks at me. "Why would you do that?"

Stepping into him, I pull his arm over my shoulder. I lean into his chest, trying to reassure him. Before I can answer, Holden beats me to it.

"I didn't come to cause any drama," he says carefully. "I

just wanted to say congratulations and drop off a gift." He looks at the pretty girl standing at his side. She looks younger than me. Her long red hair is curled into perfect waves, the shiny locks waving all the way down her back. She smiles timidly back at him.

"I'm Riley," I say, extending my hand to her.

She takes it and gently shakes my hand. "I'm Maisie. It's nice to meet you," she responds sweetly.

Holden takes a step closer to Sebastian. He holds his hand out in front of him. "Congratulations, Sebastian. I'm happy Riley's happy. I mean it."

Sebastian scrunches his eyebrows together. I can't tell what direction this will go in. Sebastian could go one of two ways. His possessiveness could continue and he could lose his shit on Holden, or he could realize that Holden never really had a chance. I chose Sebastian and that should be enough.

Shocking me, he takes Holden's hand. "Of course she's happy. She's with me."

Holden snickers. "I don't doubt it."

Sebastian's knuckles are white as he grasps Holden's hand. He must be holding it tightly, because even though he chose the mature route, he's still got to get his point across.

Nash and Nora both swoop in. Nora looks between Maisie and Holden before hooking a thumb over her shoulder. "Well, we spent a small fortune on food and treats so help yourself."

Holden nods, putting his hand on Maisie's waist and ushering her away. I watch the two of them carefully, wondering who she is and what's happening between the two of them.

A hand snakes around my waist. Sebastian pulls my back against his front. His breath is hot against the back of my neck. "I don't like that he's here, trouble. But since he is, I'm going to make it very clear that you are *mine*."

Blood rushes to my cheeks. Our little confrontation clearly caught the attention of many of our guests judging by the amount of eyes on us—I duck my head in an attempt to avoid their stares.

"Nobody but yours," I respond. My mother watches us, making the warmth spreading throughout my body even more awkward.

He presses a soft kiss at the nape of my neck while his hand runs over my growing belly. "We'll talk more about that little secret of yours tonight."

Stepping away, he smiles widely at me as he backs up. He doesn't break eye contact until he joins a group of guys that includes Nash, Aiden and Ziggy.

My mom uses the opportunity to scurry over to me. "Riley, all of these wonderful people are ready for you to finish opening their gifts."

I look sadly at the large amount of gifts I still need to open. I try not to groan as my mom escorts me back to the chair that is decorated saying *Mom to Be*. I don't feel like opening more gifts and smiling until my face feels as if it's going to crack—actually, I'd venture to say it's one of the very last things I feel like doing.

Sitting down, I look at Sebastian in jealousy. Why does the mom have to be the one to suffer through the embarrassment of opening gifts in front of everyone? I'd way rather be huddled in a group of my friends shooting the shit.

Not wanting to seem ungrateful, I sit back down and continue the *exciting* task of opening gifts from people I don't even know.

I CAN BARELY SEE OVER THE PILE OF BOXES IN MY HANDS. THE box at the top teeters from left to right.

"Be careful!" Riley shouts from behind me. If there weren't boxes piled in front of my face I'd be giving her a dirty look.

"You can't be serious," I deadpan, feeling around with my foot, trying to find where the curb is so I don't eat shit.

"What?" she says. "You're holding the best of the best of baby items. We can't have anything break!"

"How much can one baby even need?" I mutter under my breath, slowly making my way to the door of my place.

"Apparently a *lot*," she returns. Her voice now comes from in front of me.

"Can't we return some of this? I don't know if all of this is even going to fit in our apartment."

She gasps. "Sebastian, we were given baby items that are worth more than what I made in a week. We aren't getting rid of anything, we're going to be using all of this."

I sigh, waiting for her to tell me the door is unlocked.

"Come in," she says shortly after.

I drop the stack of boxes as soon as I step through the door. Taking a deep breath, I look at the pile, dreading the many more trips I need to make to bring everything from the shower in.

I should've known that Nash and Nora would go overboard with a baby shower for us. I appreciate the thoughtfulness of the party. They went above and beyond to make sure we know how much our baby is loved already. The guest list was much larger than I'd expected, though.

I'd have been fine with our closest friends and Riley's family coming together to celebrate the baby. Instead, we had an event with a massive guest list, Riley's ex showing up, and now enough gifts to care for ten babies, not just our one.

"Okay let's grab the next batch," Riley says, clapping her hands together.

"Do I not get any kind of a break?" I say in mock exhaustion.

She shrugs. "I want to get all of it out of my car before Matt brings another load over."

I groan, making my way to the couch. Falling into the cushions, I take a deep breath. "The fact that we need to have things brought over to us in *loads* is probably a huge indicator that we have way too much shit."

"Probably. But I can't tell that to Nora, it would break her heart."

"Well then Nora can be the one to bring them inside."

She laughs, closing the front door. Her footsteps are soft on the floor as she pads in my direction. Plopping down next to me, she lets out a long sigh. "Today I learned I hate opening gifts in front of people."

A laugh escapes my lips. "I couldn't tell."

"You were too busy having the time of your life with your guys to notice my pain."

Turning my body to face her, I run my hand down her cheek. "Yeah, well, then I became too busy making sure Holden didn't get any ideas."

She rolls her eyes. "That ship has sailed, Sebastian. It's in a totally different ocean." She rubs a hand over her stomach. "Nobody wants me with this big thing."

I nudge her hand away, grasping her belly with both my hands. "I'm not so convinced."

"He was only there to say congratulations. He knows there's no chance for anyone but you at this point. Plus, it looked like he's moved on."

I slide her dress up until I'm met with her naked stomach. "That doesn't mean I have to enjoy that he was there. I'll never like the guy. He had the balls to touch what's mine."

She sucks in a breath when my fingers play with the edge of her underwear. "I think touching is a stretch," she says.

"I don't give a damn. At one point he thought he had a chance. Now I'm going to remind *you* why he never really did."

I slide her underwear down her legs and throw them off to the side. The tip of my finger runs down her center, eliciting a moan from her lips.

"Sebastian, we have to finish bringing the gifts up."

Shaking my head, I scoot off the couch. My knees meet the rug as I square my body with her center. "They can wait. Right now I need this. I need *you*."

My tongue runs over her. If she had any more reasons why we shouldn't be doing this they all disappear the moment my mouth connects with her. The entirety of the baby shower I'd wondered how I could sneak off with her to get a moment alone with her to do just this. I'd been patient, not interrupting her as she was spoiled with attention.

But now it's time for her to bask in *my* attention. And my attention is a lot more fun.

Moans leave her throat as I bring her closer and closer to the edge. Before she gets the chance to come, I pull away.

Hair falls around her face as she looks at me angrily. "Why did you stop?"

Laying a peck to her exposed stomach, I relish the feeling of my lips against her skin. "That's for not telling me that you invited Holden."

Putting each of my hands on the sides of her hips, I push myself off the floor. I bring my face in front of hers, running my finger across her lips. "You look cute when you're angry."

Unexpectedly, she reaches up, grabbing the bulge in my pants. "I'll look a lot cuter when you let me finish."

I smile, not able to resist kissing her for another moment. When our lips collide I know I won't make her wait long for an orgasm, no matter how much I hated seeing Holden show up.

She's quick at unbuttoning my pants. They're one of my nice pairs of slacks, ones that I only wear when Nash or Monica tell me I have to dress up. Not wasting time, she slides her hand underneath my briefs and pumps up and down along my dick.

Breaking away from her mouth, I lift her dress the rest of the way off her. As much as I want to stay and admire her laying underneath me in just her bra, I make quick work at unclasping her bra as well.

She begins to try to unbutton my shirt, but I stop her, quickly pulling it up and over my head instead. Standing up, my pants and briefs hit the floor shortly after. I take a moment to admire her sprawled out on the couch, watching me through hooded eyes.

"Turn around," I instruct.

She pauses, acting like she's not going to do as she's told. Eventually, she turns around. Her hands grasp the back of the couch while her ass stays in the air. The position reminds me of the first time we had sex in that cabin.

My hand runs along her spine, feeling the soft skin of her back. Her spine arches, her silent way of telling me she's ready for me.

I push into her, seating deeply inside.

"This is way better than bringing in presents I have no idea what to do with," she says.

Picking up pace I say, "It better be. All I could think about from the moment we left that shower was how I was going to get that dress off of you."

"You didn't have to think very hard," she says. She pushes the top half of her body off the couch, bringing her back to my chest. This position allows me to kiss up and down her neck while I plunge into her from behind.

"Right there," she moans. By the tone of her voice I know she's close. I slow down, dragging out the feeling of her wrapped around me for as long as possible. The further she gets in her pregnancy, the more desperate I am for her at all times. There's something incredibly sexy about her carrying my child.

"Sebastian," she breathes, her body beginning to go limp in my arms.

"Come apart for me, trouble," I say, picking up speed to reach my own orgasm.

She comes, her moans loudly bouncing off the walls. She's reeling back from her own orgasm when I find mine.

The two of us fall into the couch as we each catch our breath. We lay in silence, soaking up a calm moment after our exciting day. Pulling her into my chest, I revel in the feeling of her naked skin against mine.

"I'm starving," Riley finally says, looking up at me with a mischievous smile.

"Are you ever *not* hungry?" I joke, twisting her blonde hair around my finger.

She shrugs. "I'm growing a human. I get a hall pass on the *aren't you always hungry* comments."

"Oh, do you?"

"Yep! Now feed me," she demands, dramatically crossing her arms over her chest.

I kiss the top of her head. "I feel like all I'm good for recently is fetching you food."

"Aw don't say that. I can also count on you for great sex." She aims a playful wink in my direction.

I sigh dramatically, walking into my bedroom to find something to wear.

Something tells me that even after we have this baby, I'll be doing whatever she asks of me. Even though I would never admit it to anyone but her, she's got me wrapped around her finger.

Hopefully we have a little boy or there will be two women in this house I can't say no to.

RILEY

A TINY FOOT KICKS ME IN THE RIBCAGE FOR THE MILLIONTH time today. The move takes my breath away, forcing me to double over and stop moving.

"Ouch," I whine as I bend over and apply pressure to my stomach, trying to move the baby into a more comfortable spot inside of me.

A large hand gently massages my back. "Is the little guy kicking you again?" Sebastian questions.

Nodding, I try to take a deep breath. The baby has rearranged my organs so much that it's hard to get enough air in anymore.

Our baby isn't so little anymore. We're a few weeks away from my due date and I'm more than ready to get this thing out of me. Apparently the baby is taking after its father, measuring large at every appointment.

"We don't know it's a boy," I point out. I'm to the point where even a task as simple as walking is difficult. We make our way to the house the two of us just moved into, Sebastian walking as I more or less waddle.

Nora and I decided not to renew the lease on our apartment. It didn't make sense to pay for a space that sat vacant most of the time. Nash doesn't let her out of his sight often, and I'm always with Sebastian. It made sense for Sebastian and me to move in with one another. Instead of staying at his place, we found a place of our own. Moving while nine months pregnant wasn't the best idea possible, but it was worth it to have the space a house has to offer. The house is small, and way overpriced, but it's ours.

I blame the hormones for the constant stream of tears I cried saying goodbye to the tiny place we called home for so many years. It was where we shared so many laughs and plenty of cries. It was the place where Sebastian and I got to know one another. The corner of my room where we built a fort and he told me about his life will forever be special to me. I found out I was pregnant with this kicking-machine inside me at that same apartment. It's special, and hard to say goodbye, but necessary. I'm saying goodbye to my old life and making a new one with Sebastian and our child.

"For fuck sake, not again." Sebastian says as we get closer to his door. The angry tone of his voice takes me by surprise. I find him staring intently at the man standing in front of our door.

Once the stranger turns around to face us, there's no mistaking who this could be. He looks like an older, washed-up version of Sebastian. The only difference is where Sebastian's hair is dark, this man's is fully grey.

"Sebastian," the man exclaims. He runs a hand through his scraggly beard.

Sebastian removes his hand from my back, walking quickly to beat me to the man at our door.

"You shouldn't be here," Sebastian bites out.

He's almost a head taller than his dad. The scowl on Sebastian's face makes it clear to his dad that this isn't a happy reunion.

After Sebastian and I stopped fighting our feelings and committed to making this work, he'd told me about how his dad had been trying to get ahold of him, even going as far as showing up at his place.

Sebastian hadn't been thrilled about him showing up then, and I'm assuming he shares that same sentiment now.

His dad ignores him, too busy staring at me. Too busy staring at my hard-to-miss bowling ball of a stomach.

"Is that a baby?" he mumbles.

"No, it's a stomach," Sebastian deadpans. "What the fuck are you doing here? How did you find this new place, too?"

Finally he stops looking at my stomach in amazement. His gaze finds his son's.

"I wanted to talk to you, son."

Sebastian lets out a manic laugh. "I thought I'd made it clear last time, I'm not your son. Not in the ways that matter. Go the fuck away."

The two of them argue back and forth as I take in the man that shaped Sebastian into the man he is today. When I look at him, there's a visceral amount of rage bubbling inside me. I think of all the things Sebastian has confessed to me in the time we've been together, all at the hands of the man standing in front of me.

The man that was supposed to love and protect his son from anything.

But it's still Sebastian's dad, and I think he'd regret not hearing why his dad has showed up again.

"Want to come in?" I ask, watching Sebastian carefully. If he seems like he absolutely doesn't want to speak to his father, I'll revoke my invitation. But deep down, I wonder if Sebastian needs to talk some of this through with his dad. If it would help him process his own new upcoming role of being a father himself.

Sebastian looks at me in horror. His eyes are wide. I'm about to find a way to backpedal when he nods his head slightly. Looking to his dad he says, "You've got five minutes to explain what the fuck you're doing here."

His dad nods his head enthusiastically. "I'll take it."

Sebastian's shoulder hits his dad's as he goes to unlock the front door. I stand off to the side, letting the two of them walk into the house before following closely behind.

His dad walks into the small foyer, his eyes assessing the space.

"This is a nice place," he states. "A step up from the places you grew up in."

"You mean the crack houses you *chose* for us to live in?"

His dad takes a deep breath in, sticking his hand in his pocket. He turns around, looking at me. "I'm Scott," he says, a defeated tone to his voice.

I stare at the hand in front of me, letting it hang in the air for a few moments before I take it. His hand feels like leather as it wraps around mine. "I'm Riley."

"Pleasure to meet you, Riley."

"You're running low on minutes," Sebastian says, catching our attention.

Scott nods, pulling what looks to be a bible out of his pocket. It's worn and weathered, as if it's seen a lot. He clutches it to his side tightly.

"Can we sit?" he asks, gesturing to the couches in the living room.

Sebastian gives one curt nod as his answer. The three of us awkwardly make our way to the couch. For a minute, you can hear a pin drop. It's so quiet.

"I've been clean for two years, son," he begins. "I found a nice woman who helped lead me to God. I wanted to see you again, to apologize for…"

"For the trauma you put me through?" Sebastian interrupts.

"Yes. For all of it. I was an addict, I wasn't in any place to take care of a kid."

"You're sure as hell right about that."

"But now…my son is going to have a baby."

I smile tightly. "We're due in a couple of weeks," I admit,

trying to break the tension and give Sebastian time to process what's happening.

"When was the wedding?" Scott asks.

"We're not married," I answer truthfully.

"Not yet. Not that it matters," Sebastian adds.

"Son, don't you think that baby deserves a mother and father who are married in the eyes of God?"

My jaw falls open at the same moment Sebastian springs to his feet. He laughs hysterically, running a hand over his mouth.

"Oh that's good, real good coming from the man who got a kick out of watching women hang all over his teenage son."

"It's because of my mistakes that I say this."

"I can't fucking deal with you. Your five minutes is up." Sebastian leaves the living room in a blaze of fury. He paces around the kitchen angrily, still able to keep an eye on us from his spot.

Leaning forward, I stare at the man who did so much damage to the man that I love.

"Now listen here, Scott," I say quietly enough that Sebastian can't hear. "I'm more than aware of how much of a piece of shit dad you were to the man I'm deeply in love with. It's a miracle that he grew up to be the upstanding guy that he is today, no thanks to you."

Scott opens his mouth to speak, but I cut him off by holding my hand up and continuing to talk. "I'm not finished. Personally, after this whole confrontation I'm thinking Sebastian should tell you to fuck off forever. But that's his decision, not mine. If you want *any* kind of relationship with your son, you're going to tell him how excited you are for this baby. You're going to do whatever the fuck it takes to get back into his good graces and you're going to stop spewing this holy judging bullshit. Because no matter if Sebastian and I are married or not, this baby will have a way better life than the one you gave your son. You were a shitty father. This is your chance to be a better grandfather."

Sebastian comes back into the room before I can elaborate any further. I put on a fake smile, sitting back in my seat a bit.

Scott looks like he's seen a damn ghost. His skin has a pale sheen to it, and he grasps onto his bible as if it'll hold all the answers for him.

"It's time for you to go," Sebastian demands. He stands behind me, staring down at his father. His arms are crossed over his chest, his posture stiff.

Scott focuses on me, nodding. "I don't want to overstay my welcome."

He stands up, cautiously reaching out to grab Sebastian by the shoulder. "I'm happy for you, son. I know you're going to be a great father to that kid." Reaching into his pocket, he gives him a business card.

"I do handiwork here and there. This is my card with my number. I'd love to be able to speak with you again, to maybe eventually meet my grandkid. You give me a call when you're ready."

Sebastian doesn't give any indications that he's going to take the business card. Reaching out, I pluck it from Scott's fingers, putting it in my pocket just in case.

"Goodbye, Scott," I tell him, escorting him to the door.

Shutting the door, I turn around to face Sebastian. My back hits the cold metal. I take a deep breath. "Well that was unexpected."

Sebastian stares at me. He looks angry. His breathing is shallow, and the muscle in his clenched jaw ticks quickly.

"What the hell was that?" he seethes, his tone angrier than I was anticipating.

I cross my arms over my chest defensively. "Are you mad at me?"

"You were nice to my pathetic excuse of a father!"

"I think *nice* is pushing it."

He lets out a sordid laugh. "I don't think it is. You invited the fucker in."

I nod, not arguing with the fact. "I let him in for you, Sebastian. I was only trying to help you."

"Help *me?* You could help me by saying no to him."

"I thought maybe now that you're going to have a baby that you might want to repair the relationship…or at least have the option to."

"Well you thought wrong, Riley. You're supposed to be on my side."

I tear my body from the door, closing the distance until I'm standing directly in front of him. Reaching out, I stroke his cheek. "I'm always on your side, Sebastian. I'm sorry." I grab the business card from my pocket. Holding out between us, I tear at it until it's in shreds at our feet.

Looking at him, I stare into those familiar eyes. "It's you and me, Sebastian. I'm always on your side. It makes no difference to me if your dad is in your life again. I read the room wrong. I figured you may…"

I'm relieved when he wraps his arms around me, doing his best to pull me into him despite my large stomach. "You're right, trouble. I needed to tell him how I felt. I needed him to understand what he's done to me. Seeing him when we're so close to having our own child—it just flooded me with emotions. With rage. Knowing how much I already love this baby, and how excited I am to be a dad, I saw him and wondered how the hell he could do what he did. How he could be that kind of father to his own flesh and blood. I don't want anything to do with him, trouble. And I hope you're okay with that."

Pulling away, I look up at him, emphasizing my next words. "I don't need you to forgive your dad, Sebastian. I really don't. What he did to you was *unforgivable*. I can't fault you for wanting nothing to do with him. It isn't really my business, the trauma wasn't inflicted on me. It was inflicted on you."

"I just see him and everything goes red. I'm taken back to that place."

I caress his cheek. "Leave that place. Come back to me. I'm sorry for inviting him in. We'll never talk to him again. Okay?"

He nods before laying a soft kiss to my forehead. "I'm sorry for taking my frustration out on you, I love you."

"Oh my god," I say, looking down at my feet. Feeling warmth in a spot I shouldn't be feeling.

"You're not going to say it back? Riley don't—"

I don't give him the time to finish his sentence, stepping away I look down at my feet. Wetness begins to trickle down my leg.

"Sebastian, I think my water just broke."

His eyes almost bulge out of his head. He jumps backwards, staring at the small stream of wetness rolling down my leg. "Are you sure you didn't just pee?" he asks, staring at the water in horror.

I laugh nervously. "I don't know! It won't stop." It continues to run down my legs. "I don't *think* this is pee..."

He kicks into overdrive, backing up in a rush. "Holy fuck, trouble! Your water broke. Did we pack our hospital bags?"

I try not to grimace. "Well...I was going to do that soon."

I power waddle to our bedroom, following him there. He pulls a suitcase from the closet, throwing it onto the bed.

I grab a towel from our bathroom, trying to clean myself up a bit while Sebastian begins to throw everything he finds into the suitcase.

"Why'd you pack the alarm clock?" I ask, bending over when I begin to feel cramping.

I try to breathe through the pain as he stares at the suitcase. "What if we need to know the time the baby comes?"

My eyes roll to the back of my head. "We don't need a damn alarm clock, Sebastian! They'll have a clock there."

He nods. "Okay, yeah, you're probably right."

My teeth clench from the pain. "Probably?"

"I don't know what the fuck to pack, trouble! I've never had a kid before." Flustered, he tips the suitcase over, sending the contents crashing to the bed.

"Oh my god, don't start over again," I grimace.

He puts his hands on his hips, looking at me. "I don't know what to pack. I didn't prepare…"

Cutting him off I say, "We need clothes for us and for the baby. And phone chargers. Just grab things you would take on a trip."

"Okay so *not* the alarm clock," he quips, turning to pull his phone charger from the wall socket. "We have so much shit from the shower I don't know what we need in the hospital and what we don't need."

"Just guess," I respond.

Leaving him to it, I walk to our makeshift nursery. Eventually we want to find a bigger house, but this was all we could find on short notice. It's perfect for us for now.

Pulling drawers open, I grab a few outfits for the baby, not knowing what size they'll even be in. I should've done more research on the difference between newborn sizing and three-month sizing. My solution is to stuff multiple outfits in both sizes in the bag, some of them are bound to fit.

I grab all the baby things I think we'll need. My mind has suddenly gone blank on everything the birthing classes told us to bring. I'm regretting putting off packing the bags, but surely I've grabbed what we'll need.

Grabbing the baby bag, I head back into our room and find Sebastian attempting to zip up the suitcase. He leans on top of it, applying his weight to try and squeeze the two sides together. Finally, there's a loud *zip*, and the bag is officially closed.

Pulling it off the bed, he looks at me with the biggest smile on his face.

"Let's go have this baby, trouble!"

RILEY

ZOE ELEANOR COMPTON CAME INTO THE WORLD IN A RUSH—she was born dramatic. By the time we'd made it to the hospital, I was dilated to a six and barely had time to get an epidural.

Things progressed quickly, and before we knew it, our sweet little surprise was brought into the world.

She came out with a full head of jet-black hair, and looks almost identical to her dad. All I can see right now is that tuft of hair swaddled in a pink blanket in Sebastian's arms. He stares down at her in amazement, her tiny little hand wrapping around just one of his fingers.

"Hi baby girl," he whispers. She makes a grunting sound, one dramatic enough for Sebastian to look up at me in alarm.

"What does she want?" he whispers, going back to staring at her.

I adjust myself in the hospital bed, shrugging. "Your guess is as good as mine. The first time I held a baby was two hours ago when they set her in my arms."

"I just didn't expect to love her so much already."

I watch the two of them, happiness blooming in my heart. I knew seeing Sebastian become a father would make me fall in love with him all over again, but I was unprepared for how much love I have for him now. He was my rock throughout her birth. The look on his face when he got to hold her for the first time will forever be etched into my memory.

A soft knock echoes on the door, catching our attention. Nora stands in the doorway, a large bouquet of balloons hiding two bodies behind her.

She walks into the room, her eyes zoning in on the baby in Sebastian's arms.

"It's a girl?" she marvels, barely looking back at the two men behind her.

Matt pops out from the mass amount of balloons, reaching to shut the door. Once shut, Nash's head pops out from the middle of them. "Congratulations!" he cheers, pushing a balloon away from his face.

Sebastian gently places Zoe in Nora's arms. Nora looks over at me through misty eyes. "My best friend had a baby girl!"

I nod. "You wouldn't know I'm her mom, she looks identical to Sebastian."

"Yeah, but way cuter," Nash jokes, stepping in front of Sebastian and pulling him into a hug.

"How did you get in here?" Sebastian asks, looking between Matt and Nash.

Matt gives Nash a look. "I advised him it wouldn't be the best idea. That the two of you wouldn't want a swarm of people coming to the hospital once they knew he was here."

"So I came up with a plan," Nash says, smiling wide. He points to the balloons, walking to stand next to Nora as she holds Zoe.

"Well, at first I tried to get him to wear a disguise," Matt explains.

Sebastian smiles. "Yeah? And I'm sure that went terribly."

Nash rubs the back of Zoe's tiny hand with the pad of his finger and she latches onto him. "I've told you, I hate disguises."

Matt and Sebastian both roll their eyes.

"Plus," Nash adds, "I came up with a brilliant idea to hide behind the balloons."

Nora laughs softly, snuggling a bundle Zoe to her chest. "Somehow, I think it worked."

Matt shakes Sebastian's hand. "Congratulations, Sebastian. I'm so happy for you."

Sebastian crosses the room, taking Matt under one arm and Nash under the other. "I'm so happy you're both here."

"Wouldn't miss this for the world," Nash responds.

"Had to make sure you were being responsible with this whole dad thing," Matt continues.

Sebastian pulls Matt in closer. It's clear by the tight smile on Matt's face that he's slightly uncomfortable with contact. "*Me?* Irresponsible? I have no idea what you're talking about."

The three of them laugh. Sebastian pulls his arms back. "So can we all agree that I have the cutest kid in the world?"

Nora stands up cautiously, carrying Zoe the short distance to my bed. Scooting over, I make room for her in the small space. She slowly sits down, making sure the now sleeping Zoe doesn't stir.

Nora looks over to me in wonder. "You made this," she whispers.

Zoe's small little lips pucker together in her sleep. She looks like a tiny little burrito in the swaddle blanket the hospital provided. She's got the same high cheekbones that Sebastian has, as well as his signature dark locks.

Reaching over, I lightly run my finger over Zoe's little face. "I still can't believe she came out of me."

Nora chuckles. "So how *was* pushing a human out of you?"

"The wildest experience of my life," Sebastian interjects.

I look up at him. "We don't need to go into all of the details."

"Yeah I don't need to know the specifics," Nash adds.

Matt nods in agreement. He steps carefully toward the

bed, looking down at the sleeping Zoe. He's silent as he observes her, but a slight smile does grace his face.

Nash rounds the bed, stopping to stand at the spot next to Nora. She looks up at him. "Do you want to hold her?"

He freezes for a moment, looking unsure.

"You have to hold my baby, Boss," Sebastian says.

Nash shakes his head. "I'm okay just looking for right now. She looks…extremely breakable."

"You'll do great," Nora coaxes. "She's wrapped so tightly in the blanket it's fine."

Nash holds his hands up. "I'm okay, really. I can see how cute she is from here."

Sebastian mocks hurt. "Wow, the man I've protected for years doesn't want to hold my baby? I see how it is."

Nash groans, looking down at Zoe nervously. "The tour may be a lot less interesting now that you're not there to constantly pester me." He goes to sit down, gesturing for Nora to hand him Zoe.

"Oh, don't worry, you'll get enough of me when you're home."

"I don't doubt that," Nash adds, looking completely terrified when Zoe is placed fully in his arms. He freezes, not moving a muscle as he stiffly holds her.

Sebastian did end up taking a step back from being a bodyguard for Nash. It took weeks for him and Matt to find a replacement they thought was suitable to take his place. We're fortunate Sebastian and Nash have formed such a close friendship over the years, because Sebastian is now the head of security for Nash's estate here in LA. This job alleviates some responsibilities from Matt, but also gives Sebastian the opportunity to manage people while also having time for our family.

"I'm sure my brother and Monica's constant bickering will keep the tour more than interesting," Nash adds. He finally gets the nerve to move slightly. He leans back in the chair, allowing himself to get comfortable.

Sebastian smiles. "I knew Aiden would convince you he could go."

Nash doesn't respond, he's too busy marveling over Zoe.

Twenty minutes later, you'd never have known he was terrified to hold her. She's awake and ready to eat, but Nash doesn't want to give her up just yet.

"Can she wait just five more minutes?" he jokes, smiling down at her. She stares at him, fascinated with the faces he's making at her.

Sebastian has joined me in the hospital bed, his toned arm wrapped around me tightly.

We watch as Nora scolds Nash, telling him he has to hand the baby over. He argues back, saying she just wants to steal Zoe from him. Matt, true to his personality, looks out the window silently.

Finally, Nash begrudgingly hands Zoe over to me before saying goodbye and ducking into the crowd of balloons they brought in.

The room falls quiet as Sebastian and I stare down at Zoe as she eats. She happily drinks milk, not realizing that moments ago one of the most famous men in the world was wrapped around her tiny finger.

"Have I told you I love you, trouble?"

I look up at him, smiling. "I wouldn't mind you telling me again."

He presses a firm kiss to my forehead, his lips warm and comforting. "I love you with everything that I am. You're my home. The family I always hoped for but never believed I would get. You, Zoe, our friends, all of it. I'm the luckiest guy in the world."

"I love you too, Sebastian," I respond, going in for a kiss.

I never would've imagined we'd end up here. There were so many times that I wanted to give up on the man sitting next to me. It would've been easier if I'd continued to ignore my feelings for him. It would have been safer to date someone else

—and I tried. But he never stopped surprising me. Even when I doubted him, he didn't falter in his love for me. I'm so in love with him, it's crazy. The two of us made a lot of mistakes, but those mistakes are what brought us to this moment.

To this perfect little girl.

To our perfect family.

To our perfect love story.

My heart begins beating erratically when I hear footsteps echoing down our staircase. Giggles erupt from Zoe as she and Riley come into view.

Riley sets down a screeching Zoe. The moment her little feet hit the ground, she's running for me.

"Daddy!" She cheers.

Crouching to the ground, I wrap my daughter in my arms. For being two years old, she's already extremely talkative. Can't say I'm surprised, considering both her parents love to hear themselves talk.

"Hi Zo-Zo," I say, planting a kiss on her round cheek.

"For me?" she asks, an adorable smile on her face. Her eyes roam over the array of food laid out on the kitchen island.

I pick up her favorite plate with her food already prepared on it. There's french toast piled high with ice cream, chocolate syrup and sprinkles.

"What's all this?" Riley asks, coming into the kitchen and noticing all of the food.

I take Zoe to her high chair, placing the plate in front of her. She wastes no time trying to shove the entire piece of bread into her mouth.

Turning around, I come to stop in front of Riley. She's got a robe on, and I know from experience that this early in the morning, there's not much on underneath it. "Breakfast," I tell her, leaning in to give her a kiss.

"Did I forget an anniversary? Or birthday?" she jokes, dipping her hand into a glob of whipped cream.

"Not exactly," I answer, butterflies erupting in my stomach.

Zoe pays us no mind as she continues to choke down her food. There's ice cream and chocolate syrup all over her face and in her hair.

Riley props a hip against the island, swiping another glob of whipped cream into her mouth. Caging her in, I rest my palms on either side of her hips.

"No seriously, did I forget something?" she questions.

I smile, grabbing either side of her face. "Can you do something for me, trouble?"

"Can you tell me if I missed an important date?" she retorts.

"Close your eyes," I instruct.

She cocks her head to the side. I don't say anything, waiting for her to follow directions. Finally she concedes, closing her eyes dramatically.

"Now keep them closed." My thumb brushes her cheek softly. I remember the first time I did such an innocent thing. She'd been sleeping the morning after we first met and hooked up. At the time, I'd believed there was no way I would ever get to call her mine, but deep down, part of me had wondered *what if*. As she slept, I brushed her cheek and for a short moment, thought about what it'd be like to stay in bed with her. To actually watch her wake up. What it would be like to be the guy that stayed.

And now, it's something I get to do every morning. Something I will never take for granted.

"Now I want you to imagine this kitchen."

She smiles. "Can't I just open my eyes and *see* this kitchen?"

"No, trouble, we're imagining here. Imagine you're standing right in the spot that you are. Your feet are bare against the cold hardwood. Our daughter happily inhales triple the amount of sugar she should eat in one sitting. Are you imagining it?" I ask.

She nods, keeping her eyes closed tightly.

"Now, imagine that I move my hands from your face. You miss my warmth, but you know I'll always come back for more," I pause, working up the courage.

"And then I want you to imagine me dropping to one knee, as I hold up a ring and ask you to love me forever."

Her eyes pop open, finding me bent on one knee in front of her. Her eyes gloss over immediately.

"Sebastian…" she prods, her hands covering her mouth.

"Imagine the life we've built, what we can continue to build together forever. You, me, our little girl and the soccer team of children we will have because nothing is sexier than seeing you pregnant."

She chokes on a laugh, looking at me as tears spill out her eyes.

"I want to spend the rest of my life with you Riley Adams. I want to go full-speed ahead with everything that we do, including marrying you. I'd marry you today if you'd let me."

Pulling a velvet ring box out of my pocket, I hold it out in front of her and open it. She stares at the ring in the box in amazement.

She reaches to grab it out of the box before I have the chance to do it myself.

"Woah!" I say, watching her slide it onto her finger greedily.

She admires the ring on her finger. "Of course I'll marry you, Sebastian! Took you long enough," she jokes.

Standing up from the ground, I pull the love of my life into my arms.

My love.

My home.

My family.

"I've also booked us a trip to Tahiti next month to celebrate. I hope you don't mind."

She looks up from the ring on her finger, tears in her eyes. "You remembered."

I kiss the top of her head. "Of course I remembered."

"I love you so much," she says against my chest.

"Not as much as I love you," I respond. It's the truth. I didn't know a love like this even existed. I definitely didn't think I'd ever experience a love this deep. Yet here I am, so madly in love with this woman that I can't imagine my life without her.

"Maybe I'll convince you to marry me there," I say under my breath.

She laughs. "Maybe you will."

I hold her against me, committing this to memory forever. We've worked so hard to be in the place we are now, and I can't wait for the moment that she takes my last name. There's been a push and pull between us from the very beginning. At times, one of us pushed or pulled too harshly, resulting in almost losing one another in the process. Despite it all, I'm proud of Riley and I. We put in the work, committed to one another—even when things weren't perfect.

Riley and I don't have the most conventional of love stories. Hell, we rearranged the typical trajectory of a relationship multiple times. Still, I wouldn't change a thing about how our love story played out. Every single rearranged milestone brought us directly to this moment.

I get to marry the woman of my dreams.

We're going to promise each other forever.

Riley and I are proof that even the most beautiful, craziest relationships can be founded on temptation.

THE END

ACKNOWLEDGMENTS

There are so many people who put their heart and soul into Sebastian and Riley's story. For them I will be eternally grateful. Being an indie author isn't always easy, but I'm fortunate to have the best team of people behind me who make all my wildest dreams come true.

To my husband, ten years later and I'm as deeply in love with you as ever. Thank you for putting in the long days and nights to help bring this story to life. Your fierce devotion in helping me make my dreams come true will be something I'll always be thankful for. This book is what it is because of you. I love you so much.

To my mom. I'm sorry it took me so long to tell you that I was writing books. Surprise! You will forever be my hero and my best friend. I love you.

To my baby boy for making me want to be and do better. I hope we have about twenty years until you realize mom writes books about sex.

Ashlee, you're the person I can go to for anything and the best friend I have. All of my books are what they are because of you. You bring my characters to life through covers, teasers, trailers, and all of the other things you do for me. I wouldn't be able to function as author, or as a person, without a friend like you. I love you.

Tori, how do I even begin to thank you? You dropped everything to help make Sebastian and Riley's story perfect.

Thank you for believing in their story and for believing in me. You're amazing and I'm forever grateful for you!

Stevie! I feel like the first thing I have to say is thank you for putting up with my antics. I know I'm not the easiest or most organized client but somehow you still stick it out with me. Thank you for all that you do so I can focus on writing. I'm a better human because of you. Love you long time.

To my betas. You got the hot mess of Sebastian and Riley in their rawest form and somehow you still loved them. Thank you for helping me become a better author and giving it to me straight so I can produce the best story possible. I'm forever appreciative of you and I hope you stick with me forever.

To the bloggers, bookstagrammers, booktokers, and people in this community that share my books, I'm so incredibly thankful for you. I've connected with so many amazing people since I started this author adventure. I'm so appreciative of the fact that you take the time to talk about my words on your platform. I notice every single one of your posts, videos, pictures, etc., and it means the world to me. You're the lifeblood of this community. Thank you for everything you do.

To all the ladies with Give Me Books. Thank you for supporting me through the release of Founded on Temptation!

I have the privilege of having a growing group of people I can run to on Facebook for anything—Kat Singleton's Sweethearts. The members there are always there for me and I'm so fortunate to have you in my corner. I owe you so much gratitude for being there on the hard days and on the good days. Y'all are my people.

Lastly, to the readers. If you've made it this far, I wish I could envelop you in the biggest hug ever. I want to say THANK YOU for taking the time to read my words. I wouldn't be able to follow my dream and release books if there weren't people like you to read them. There is a numerous amount of amazing, badass, breathtaking books out in the world. The fact you chose mine from all of the options out there is incredible! Thank you! I hope you continue to tune in to the many more books I have planned.

ABOUT THE AUTHOR

Kat Singleton is an author who developed a passion for reading and writing at a young age. When writing stories, she strives to write an authentically raw love story for her characters. She feels that no book is complete without some angst and emotional turmoil before the characters can live out their happily ever after. She lives in Kansas with her husband, her baby boy and her two doodles. In her spare time, you can find her surviving off iced coffee and sneaking in a few pages of her current read. If you're a fan of angsty, emotional, contemporary romances then you'll love a Kat Singleton book.

ALSO BY KAT SINGLETON

THE AFTERSHOCK SERIES

Vol. 1: *The Consequence of Loving Me*

www.books2read.com/TCOLM

Vol. 2: *The Road to Finding Us*

www.books2read.com/TRTFU

THE MIXTAPE SERIES

Founded on Goodbye

www.books2read.com/fog

Founded on Deception: Coming soon!

www.books2read.com/fodc

LINKS

THE MIXTAPE SERIES

***Founded on Temptation* Pinterest:**

https://bit.ly/FOTpinterest

***Founded on Temptation* Playlist:**

https://bit.ly/FOTplaylist

Preorder *Founded on Deception*:

www.books2read.com/fodc

Email:

authorkatsingleton@gmail.com

Website:

authorkatsingleton.com

Facebook Reader Group:

bit.ly/katsingletonSWEETHEARTS

Free Download of

The Waves of Wanting You:

dl.bookfunnel.com/7buobclx4i

Facebook:

facebook.com/authorkatsingleton

Instagram:

instagram.com/authorkatsingleton

Goodreads:

goodreads.com/author/show/19920088.Kat_Singleton

Tiktok:

www.tiktok.com/@authorkatsingleton

If you enjoyed *Founded on Temptation*, please consider leaving a review on the reading platform of your choice and Goodreads.

Printed in Great Britain
by Amazon